Sexual tension hung in the air around them.

Thick and hungry.

The lights had gore.
might be making h
But all he could th
him.

She stilled, and he stared down at the shadows wreathing her face, trying and failing to penetrate the dark to see her eyes.

She made a sound of distress.

"Are you okay?" he asked. He knew she was afraid of the dark, ever since the crash when she was young.

"No." A pause. "I want to kiss you, but I think it would be a mistake."

His entire being stilled, holding its breath. All of a sudden, he wanted nothing more in the world than for her to kiss him. Even if she was right that it would be a terrible mistake.

They weren't meant to be. He sucked at relationships, and she was too damned vulnerable to protect herself from him and his baggage.

"Don't kiss me if you're afraid of the dark," he said. "That's all you'll find inside me."

* * *

Be sure to check out the next books
in this exciting new miniseries, Code: Warrior SEALs:
Meet these fierce warriors, who take on the most
dangerous secret missions around the world!

* * *

If you're on Twitter, tell us what you think of
Harlequin Romantic Suspense!
#harlequinromsuspense

Dear Reader,

It was with great pleasure that I finally got to return to New Orleans this past year for the first time since Hurricane Katrina devastated that lovely city. I was thrilled to see that the Grand Lady of the South has come back strong and that she's as fun and fabulous as ever. And what better way to celebrate the recovery of New Orleans than to write a book set there? My only problem in writing this story was choosing where in the parish to set the book!

Fortunately, my heroine (who announced to me early on that she goes by the improbable nickname Hank) and her navy SEAL hero, Ashe, are both N'awlins natives and knew just where to go to best unfold their story. It turns out that a blend of steamy romance, dark suspense, towering love and simmering danger is pretty darned close to the perfect tale to tell when those hot summer nights come calling in the Big Easy.

So, pour yourself a mint julep, turn on the ceiling fan slow and lazy, put on a little Preservation Hall jazz, and get ready to go undercover with a SEAL in a hot story of love and danger that I'm excited to share with you!

Happy reading,

Cindy

UNDERCOVER
WITH A SEAL

Cindy Dees

HARLEQUIN® ROMANTIC SUSPENSE

Recycling programs
for this product may
not exist in your area.

ISBN-13: 978-0-373-27927-2

Undercover with a SEAL

Printed in U.S.A.

www.Harlequin.com

New York Times and *USA TODAY* bestselling author **Cindy Dees** started flying airplanes while sitting in her dad's lap at the age of three and got a pilot's license before she got a driver's license. At age fifteen, she dropped out of high school and left the horse farm in Michigan, where she grew up, to attend the University of Michigan. After earning a degree in Russian and East European studies, she joined the US Air Force and became the youngest female pilot in its history. She flew supersonic jets, VIP airlift and the C-5 Galaxy, the world's largest airplane. During her military career, she traveled to forty countries on five continents, was detained by the KGB and East German secret police, got shot at, flew in the first Gulf War and amassed a lifetime's worth of war stories.

Her hobbies include medieval reenacting, professional Middle Eastern dancing and Japanese gardening.

This RITA® Award–winning author's first book was published in 2002 and since then she has published more than twenty-five bestselling and award-winning novels. She loves to hear from readers and can be contacted at cindydees.com.

Books by Cindy Dees

Harlequin Romantic Suspense

Soldier's Last Stand
The Spy's Secret Family
Captain's Call of Duty
Soldier's Rescue Mission
Her Hero After Dark
Breathless Encounter
Flash of Death
Deadly Sight
A Billionaire's Redemption
High-Stakes Bachelor

Code: Warrior SEALs

Undercover with a SEAL

Harlequin HQN

Close Pursuit
Hot Intent

Visit Cindy's Author Profile page at Harlequin.com for more titles!

Chapter 1

Asher Konig looked around Bourbon Street in the heart of New Orleans as something akin to shock crept into his gut. What was this place? Granted, he hadn't been home in years, but he felt like he'd landed on an alien planet.

The buildings were mostly the same—painted bright colors and adorned by elaborate wrought-iron balconies. The sweet smell of beignets still wrestled with the sour smell of vomit. People and music still poured out of bars into the street. But somehow, it was *not* the same. The vibe was all wrong.

Damn. He'd heard things had changed since Hurricane Katrina, but he hadn't guessed how much.

It wasn't just that so many storefronts and restaurants had new names. Or that the music forming a cacophony in the background was more generic pop now and less jazz or twangy zydeco. Or even that the throngs of people had changed. Even at a glance there were more out-of-towners, fewer locals, less authenticity. Less unapologetic seediness.

The French Quarter had been transformed into a sanitized tourist version of itself.

The whole casual, *laissez les bons temps rouler* culture was missing. Oh, the tourists were living their cartoon version of it, drinking and laughing and flashing bare breasts for beads. But if he looked closer, he saw hawkers urgently coaxing tourists and their wallets inside their establishments, vendors shoving schlocky souvenirs in people's faces. It was all hustle, hustle, hustle.

Hell, maybe he was the one who'd changed. A decade on the SEAL teams did that to a guy.

Not that he had actually wanted to come home after all this time. But his boss, Commander Cole Perriman, had sent him here with orders to "Eff-ing relax and don't come back until you do." Translation: get your head together and stop taking stupid, suicidal risks, or else you're off the teams.

Secretly panicked by the unspoken ultimatum, he'd agreed to take this rare vacation in the hope that it actually would help him get his head together. He'd always been all about the job. *He was the job.* Also, his old man had died nearly six months ago, and he had yet to put his father's final affairs in order. It was time to get that unpleasant task out of the way.

It had been pure luck that he'd been downrange and *way* deep undercover, unable to get home after his father had his last and fatal heart attack. He'd been relieved not to have to face the people who would have genuinely mourned his old man's passing. Thank God Mom went first. She would never have survived burying her husband.

It wasn't as if Asher would have had anything decent to say to the bastard in farewell. *Thanks for sucking as a parent. Thanks for never noticing anything I tried to get your attention and approval. Thanks for being incapable of love.* Yup, it was just as well that he hadn't been able to make it home.

But he was home now. Such as it was.

How in the hell was he supposed to relax? Perriman had ordered him to do it as if he actually knew how to wind down. As if he wasn't always walking on the razor's edge, always a warrior, always ready to act or react. Even now, wading through the noisy, raucous French Quarter on a Friday night, he scrutinized every person he passed for hostile body language, for darting or furtive looks, for unusual bulges under jackets, anything to indicate a threat.

Frankly, being among this many people was making him *more* tense, not less. Crowds this dense were the perfect target for a suicide bomber—

Wait. United States soil. Lawful, secure, peaceful soil. No terrorists lurking about as a rule. Jeez, he was wired tight. He shook his upper body in an attempt to release the tension across his neck and shoulders. Yeah. Like that worked. He was the goddamn job.

Frustrated, he yanked out his cell phone and texted Commander Perriman, More uptight than ever. I hope you're happy.

He'd known Frosty Perriman for his entire SEAL career. The guy had been one of his BUD/S instructors and had handpicked him to be in a super classified unit Frosty had been in charge of putting together and training. They specialized in rescuing kidnapped American civilians. The rescues themselves hadn't been the tricky bit. The hard part had been staying out of the damned news and keeping the existence of their group secret.

But the task force had run afoul of a congressional investigation a few months back when a journalist they'd been assigned to rescue had been killed before they could get to the guy. Never mind that their team hadn't been given enough intel to actually find the guy, and that they had scoured the mountains in the middle of nowhere for weeks, trying to track down the journalist and his captors. In the end, it had been a colossal CIA failure, but the SEAL team had taken the heat for it and was disbanded.

Of course, it probably had more to do with the current Congress not liking the SEALs doing anything secret and off the books. Meddling politicians. They wanted to poke their fingers into everything. It wasn't like the bastards did anything useful. They just wanted front row seats at the show. To feel like they were part of the Cool Kids' Club. And when the navy wouldn't let them randomly interfere, they threw a Congress-sized tantrum.

Bunch of freaking amateurs.

Someone jostled Asher from behind and he whipped around, hands at the ready to take names and break necks. The accosters turned out to be some sort of bachelor party. Plastic cups of beer sloshed, and someone slurred an apology as he bathed his own T-shirt with a generous portion of beer. Shaking his head, Asher stood down and moved on. *Relaxing, dammit.* He was supposed to be relaxing—not killing drunk kids. The same drunk kids he'd sworn an oath to protect and defend, along with the Constitution that gave them a sacred right to act like idiots.

Desperate to get away from the bright lights and sheer noisy wrongness of the place, he ducked down a side street toward a neighborhood that no sane tourist should have ventured into. But then, he was neither entirely sane nor a regular tourist. When the streets had turned into dark, dank alleys and the men lounging in doorways eyed him with as much hostility and suspicion as he eyed them, Asher breathed a sigh of relief. This was more his speed.

"Hey, big guy," a raspy female voice crooned from just ahead. "Wanna free drink? First one's on the house."

He eyed the hard-looking woman slouching beneath a hanging sign for some joint called the Who Do Voodoo. "Strippers or just booze?" he asked.

"We got girls," the woman drawled.

"And they're actually female under the hood?"

The woman grinned, revealing gaps on each side of her yellowed teeth. "No impersonators here, handsome. They're one block down on the other side of the street. C'mon in. You look like you could use a drink."

How exactly did that look? A shot of whiskey did sound good, though. Maybe several shots. In fast succession. Enough to wipe the whole stupid idea of relaxing out of his gullet for a while.

The music was loud, pounding against his skull when he walked into what turned out to be a pole-dancing club, complete with a raised stage and topless women gyrating without much enthusiasm. Jesus, they looked like children up there on stage. Or maybe he was just getting old.

Asher spotted a table in the corner well away from the stereo speakers and slipped into a seat with his back to the wall. He scanned the room and frowned. Trouble was brewing. Two men were glaring at each other from opposite sides of the catwalk that extended out into the audience. A stripper shook her booty between the two of them, for all the world looking like she was egging them on. Being a tease was what she was paid to do, but jeez. She was provoking the guys like crazy. Drunks and half-naked women never did mix well.

Sure enough, the fight broke out, and he watched impassively as a huge bouncer dived in to break up the fray. But what Asher didn't expect was a good chunk of the audience diving into the fight, too. When knives came out in multiple fists, he rolled his eyes.

Dammit, he didn't want to have to be a hero tonight. He

was on vacation. But it wasn't like he could sit here and watch those jackasses carve each other up and possibly injure innocent bystanders. Not to mention that drawing weapons meant the cops would be called, and he really didn't need to spend all damned night giving statements to the police.

He sighed and stood up. Grabbing the collar of the nearest idiot with a knife, he disarmed the guy with a twist of the man's wrist so fast the guy didn't know what had happened.

Asher spun to face another drunk. A hard, quick fist to the chin and the guy went down. He wasn't unconscious, but he was stunned enough not to rejoin the fight right away. Asher stepped over him and disarmed two more men before the remaining drunks figured out a wrecking ball had swung into the fight, and they all staggered back from one another.

His shock-and-awe approach gave the bouncer time to get ahead of the knife wielders on his side of the stage and toss them out of the club, with a kick in the pants for emphasis on the way out the front door.

Shaking his head, Asher returned to his seat to watch the waitresses scurry around righting tables and hauling out broken chairs.

A slender arm appeared over his shoulder, and a glass of neat whiskey plunked down on the table in front of him. Startled, he reflexively grabbed the female wrist and gave its owner a yank. A young woman landed in his lap with a surprised *oomph*.

"Hey!" she protested. Eyes so blue they hurt to look at blinked up at him. Other sensations bombarded him all at once. A resilient tush pressing down rather suggestively on his man parts. A spectacular view of cleavage. Not huge breasts, but perfectly shaped. A nice handful. Slender limbs going every which way in his arms. Silky, straight blond hair wisping across a face that would be pretty— really pretty—without all that heavy makeup caked on.

But all of that paled before the bizarre sense of…connection…he felt with this woman as they stared at one another. Like they'd met before. Maybe in a past life. Not that he believed in any of that woo-woo stuff for a second.

"It's not wise to sneak up on a guy like that," he muttered. "Especially not after he's just disarmed a bunch of dudes with switchblades."

She stared up at him for a moment more and then, inexplicably, relaxed in his arms. Like she trusted him or something. As if she knew instinctively that he was one of the good guys. *What the hell?*

"You handled yourself well in the fight," she murmured.

"Are you Russian, too?" he asked. Everyone else in this joint so far seemed to be. He'd apparently stumbled into the local Slavic hangout.

"Russian by heritage, born and bred in New Orleans, though," she answered in an entirely convincing New Orleans drawl, her sapphire gaze flickering furtively toward the bar. Fear radiated off her.

His arms tightened instinctively around her sweet, now tense, body. A shocking urge came over him to carry her out of here, to take her someplace quiet and alone to…to do what? He didn't take advantage of women. And he'd never been fond of hook-up sex. It always left him feeling cheap and more alone than ever. Was he so desperate for a human connection that the first chick to fall into his lap seemed like a gift from God? Hell, maybe Frosty had been right to force this shore leave on him, after all.

He frowned down at the girl now cowering in his arms. "Are you illegal?"

Her attention snapped back to him. Their gazes clashed

but still managed to meld together as heat flared between them. Talk about instant chemistry.

She sounded a little out of breath as she mumbled, "I have to go. Let me up or else the owner will charge you for a lap dance."

He cast about for something—anything—to keep her in his arms a little longer. "What's your name?"

"Hank."

He blinked, echoing, "Hank?" His arms loosened in surprise, and she leaped to her feet.

"Short for Hankova. You want another whiskey?"

"Sure...*Hank*. Make it a double." Anything to get her to come back to him. To look at him again and thaw some of the ice encasing his heart.

He watched her hustle away from him toward the bar. Her legs were a mile long in black fishnet, and those seams running down the back of each leg, ending in little bows on the backs of her ankles, were the sexiest things he'd seen in a long time. He slugged the first whiskey without tasting it, let alone feeling the bite of it going down his throat.

Asher heard a commotion at the front door and tensed— no doubt one or both of the drunks from before were trying to get back in—but the bouncer handled it and kept the troublemakers out. He released the tension from his body but wouldn't go so far as to say he actually relaxed.

His phone vibrated, signaling an incoming text, and he fished it out without ever taking his eyes off Hank. She moved around quickly and discreetly among the other patrons like she didn't want to be seen. Not that he blamed her. Roaming hands seemed to be epidemic around this place.

His jaw tightened a little more each time some bastard grabbed her ass and gave it a squeeze. When she made her way back to the bar to place an order and got a second's respite from the groping, he spared a glance down at his phone.

The text was from Perriman. Don't come back until you've relaxed, Hollywood. That's an order.

Hollywood. His nickname on the team and a reference to his movie-star good looks. As he recalled, Perriman had been the first of his instructors to start calling him that back when he'd been a snot-nosed kid with a chip on his shoulder, hell-bent on showing his father that he was a bigger, badder dude than the old man had ever been.

He silently cursed his boss in all of the many languages he spoke. Idly, Asher noted a patron ducking through a door at the back of the club. The passage was guarded by a beefy guy wearing a dress shirt and tie. The lap dance lounge must have been back there. Although as several more guys strolled into the back over the next few minutes and none returned to the bar, he began to suspect the patrons were going upstairs instead. Which meant this place was a front for a whorehouse.

Was Hank a working girl?

The idea didn't even faze him, as it turned out. He had to find a way to get to know her better. Seduce her. Have a passionate affair—paid or otherwise.

Except, he was on only a couple weeks' leave. Just passing through. For all he knew, she was looking for a long-term relationship. Permanence. Commitment. He had no right to pursue her randomly. His gut clenched in frustration at the thought of letting her slip away.

Speak of the devil. She was sauntering back toward him with a bottle of pretty decent whiskey and a shot glass balanced on her tray. She set both down in front of him and gave him a fleeting, secret little smile that only he could see.

"What do I owe you?"

She smiled again, a little bigger this time. Her whole being lit up when she smiled like that. Jeez, he couldn't remember the last time a woman had knocked him this off balance. She murmured, "It's on the house for helping break up the fight."

"Wow. Generous. Who's the owner so I can say thanks?"

Her eyes went furtive again, and she suddenly glanced toward the door beside the bar.

His senses went on high alert. "Are you safe here, Hank?" he asked.

A pregnant pause. Her doe-eyed gaze flickered to him and then skittered away again. "Yes. Of course."

Not safe. And there went his protective instincts, firing on all cylinders. "What time do you get off work tonight? I'll walk you home."

Massive alarm fired off in her big, scared eyes. "No!" she blurted.

"It's nothing like that," he explained quickly. "I'm just offering to see you home safely. I swear I won't come on to you or anything. But after that fight, those drunks will hang around outside looking for trouble." It was a lie, but he really did want only to protect her from the threat scaring her inside the bar. And she obviously wouldn't let him walk her home without an excuse.

"I can take care of myself," she said.

He frowned, studying her face closely. Lord, she was mesmerizing. He greedily memorized every nuance of her face. Then he asked bluntly, "Do you ever work upstairs?"

Chapter 2

Hank stared down at the big, intimidating man seated before her and answered forcefully, "No!" She ought to be offended by his far too personal question, but she got the distinct impression he wasn't asking because he wanted to buy an hour's use of her body.

Not that she would necessarily say no to him if he offered. He was handsome with a capital *H*. Fashion magazine hot. He had that whole chiseled features thing going. Dark hair. Dark tan. And Lord, his light eyes looked right through her. She couldn't tell in this light if they were gray or blue. A hint of pain clung to him, masked by his deep reserve. She never could resist a man with a dark past.

Not just his big, athletic body, but his entire being, was perfectly still as he watched everything that went on around him. She got the feeling that his all-encompassing stare could turn predatory in a second. But so far, whenever he'd turned it on her, his eyes had lit up with something reminiscent of a volcanic eruption—hot and molten.

If only she could tell him the truth. That her brother was lost somewhere inside the criminal organization that ran this place. That she was trying to infiltrate the Russian mob far enough to find him and save him from whatever he'd gotten mixed up in. Or at least to find out what had happened to him. That he was her big brother, and he'd practically raised her after the car accident.

She turned her attention back to the man lurking in the shadows. She was a total sucker for brooding, dangerous men, and he was both in spades. She couldn't get over how well his dark hair was set off by those light gunmetal eyes of his. And the way he'd handled himself in the bar fight left no doubt how deadly he really was. He'd waded through seasoned brawlers and armed mob muscle like they were school children.

She spoke earnestly under her breath. "You seem like a decent guy. This isn't the kind of place you should hang out in. Go have a nice life and don't worry about me." *Find yourself a supermodel and have insanely great sex...*

He poured himself a healthy shot of whiskey from the open bottle she'd put in front of him. "Not how I roll." *How then, did he roll?* God, she'd love to find out firsthand. Of course, any idiot could see he was severely out of her league. Men like him just didn't want anything to do with cheap waitresses in sleazy joints like this.

"I'm not everyone...Hank. Hankova is a feminine patronymic. What's your actual first name?"

She frowned. He knew how patronymics worked? Practically no American had ever heard of the universal Slavic custom of taking the father's first name, adding an ending, and making it the child's middle name. "It's Evgeniya. My first name, that is."

He winced sympathetically, for which she might just have loved him a little, and then smiled ruefully. "I see now why you prefer Hank. It's going to take a little getting used to, though."

He planned to stick around long enough to adjust to her weird name? Whoa. Cue the stunned happy dance. She smiled shyly. "My mother called me Eve."

"Eve. That's nice."

Nice? Well, crap. There went any chance of him ever seeing her as a sexy femme fatale. The kind of woman he would consider having a torrid affair with. "I always thought it made me sound like an old lady."

"Well, then, Hank it is. But you're still nice."

Frantic to dispel the nice image that went hand-in-hand with "girl next door" and "my best friend's off-limits little sister," she took a step closer to the table. Then she leaned down, planted her palm on the table beside the whiskey bottle and gave him a generous look down her shirt.

Reaching for her toughest, most threatening tone of voice, the one she used to back off drunks who simply would *not* take no for an answer, she purred, "I'm a lot of things, mister, but nice isn't one of them."

Lifting a brow, he leaned back in his seat and pinned her with an intent look. Well, that wasn't exactly the response she'd been hoping for at all! She'd wanted heat. Interest. Acknowledgment that she was torrid-affair material. Instead, it felt like he was stripping her bare with that laser stare of his, analyzing her psyche with computer-like precision.

She had to fight not to squirm under his probing gaze as the layers of her deception fell away. Drat and double drat. He'd seen right through her ruse.

At long last, analysis apparently complete, a wry smile curled up one corner of his mouth and he looked away from her, his gaze casually scanning the club. She sagged in relief and released the breath she hadn't realized she was holding. *Intense guy*.

He murmured mildly, "Put your claws away, kitten. I'm no threat to you."

Hah. He had no idea. She did not need any distractions. Nor did she need some high-profile guy coming in and making waves around her—the kind of waves that would attract undue attention in her direction. Her whole plan revolved around being invisible. Innocuous. Quietly sliding so deep inside the Russian mob outfit running this place that she could unearth the truth and maybe get some closure. Figure out whether Max was alive or dead—

"Take this," the man seated before her murmured. He passed her a business card.

Disappointment coursed through her. Really? He was giving her his phone number to get a date? One word was written on the back. *Asher*. And a phone number.

"Is that your first name or last?" she asked.

"First. And my mother called me Ashe."

She couldn't picture this hard-edged man ever having had a mother. Glancing back down at the card, she frowned. What was that area code? It wasn't local. She turned the card over. It was for some sort of sporting goods and ammunition warehouse in Baton Rouge. "You sell tents and guns, Asher?" she asked drily.

His voice was low, sexy as he murmured, "You can call me Ashe, too."

Cripes. Her toes curled in her high-heeled platform shoes as the masculine confidence in that low rumble vibrated through her belly.

He was speaking again. "…only thing I had to write on. That's my cell phone number on the back. You ever get into any trouble you can't handle, call me. Okay?"

She looked up from the scrawled number quickly. "You're some kind of hired muscle?"

The corner of his mouth curled up again. "Something like that. Keep it, eh? No strings attached if you call the number. Just a helping hand. You're a good kid, and you're clearly in over your head."

Oh, God. That was so nice of him. Something hot and sharp caught in her throat, choking her a little. She'd nearly forgotten what it was like to have a decent human being give a damn about her. An urge to take him up on his offer and confide everything to someone—anyone—nearly overcame her. Heck, the temptation just to have a simple, honest conversation was almost more than she could resist.

But then her spine stiffened. Her work here was not done. She had to maintain her cover. Her life, and possibly her brother's, depended on it. She was in too deep to back out now. A list of names, deals, dates and crimes she'd already procured was etched in her mind. There would be no leaving this quest until she succeeded…or died.

Belatedly, she smiled cynically at Asher—Ashe—and spoke with utter sincerity. "Believe me. I'm not a kid. Not anymore."

"Take care of yourself, Evgeniya Hankova." He pronounced her name exactly right, palatalized vowels and all, as if he was a native speaker of Russian.

Her gaze snapped to his. Surely he wasn't one of them! Had this been a test? Ohmigod. Had she said something to give away her real motives for being here? Frantically she reviewed their brief conversation while her face froze into a mask of a smile. She backed away from his table quickly, turned, and fled to the storeroom behind the bar to catch her breath.

Vitaly, the owner and manager of the whole establishment, poked his head into the filthy little room far too soon. "I need you out front. Candy's done with her set, and everyone wants drinks."

Great. Candy was one of the sexiest pole dancers in the entire club. She was also all of fifteen years old. The patrons would be horny and grabby after her performance. Steeling herself to ignore the lewd comments and inappropriately groping hands, she nodded at her boss and stepped back out into the bar.

He was gone.

She knew it without even having to glance over at the table in the corner. Ashe's absence was a cold chill against her skin where there should have been warmth. She smiled down blankly at the mobster who'd just proposed vulgar sex with her in Russian she wasn't supposed to understand. *Take the drink order. Move on to the next table.* Keep moving. Just keep moving...

God. For a minute there, she remembered what life had been like before everything went to hell. A nice, normal guy treating her with a modicum of respect and concern. Was it possible to be homesick for America while standing on American soil? Apparently, yes, because she felt tears welling up in the backs of her eyes.

Stop it. No feelings. No fear. She was a stone. She would have her answers, and then nothing else mattered.

The bar closed at 2:00 a.m., but Hank and the other waitresses were expected to stick around to clean up after that. The Voodoo was particularly trashed tonight because of the fight. The one Ashe had broken up with such ease. She yanked her thoughts away from the enigmatic American who had wandered so far from where he should have been and ended up in this little corner of hell. He was not for her. That whole normalcy thing was not for her, not anymore. She bent down to pick up the remains of a broken chair.

The good news was she was not one of the trafficked, drug-addicted girls upstairs. She was still free to walk out of here and never come back if she chose to. At least for now.

She could turn the crew in charge of this place in to the police. But a) she wasn't entirely certain the police weren't being paid to ignore the goings-on at the Who Do Voodoo, and b) then she would never find Max. Besides, she was convinced this place was a small fish in the overall crime ring running it.

Her goal was to work her way up to the big sharks before she called the authorities. She had names and pictures of a few of the girls that she'd snuck on her cell phone over the past few months. Those would go to the police as soon as she concluded her own investigation.

She even had pictures of a few men who came into the bar and disappeared quickly into the back any time they showed up. Vitaly was always surly when they left, and his complaints about how much money his bosses took out of the till always happened right after those silent strangers paid a visit.

The bar was finally restored to a semblance of its usual squalor, and Vitaly growled at the waitresses to go on home. She took off her apron, hung it in the storeroom and slung her purse over her shoulder. Wearily she headed outside with the other girls. They traded good-nights and went their various ways. As for her, she trudged deeper into the bowels of the Warehouse District's worst section.

The darkness at this time of night was thick and impenetrable, shrouding her in heavy menace. Ever since the car accident, she'd been terrified of being alone in the dark. She walked fast and tried to project a badassery she was far from feeling as she hurried home. If she could call it a home. Her apartment was, at best, a dive. But it had a bed, a sofa, a tiny kitchen and a tinier bathroom. And she could afford it on her meager pay.

She'd graduated from college the previous June with a degree in art history and restoration, just before Max went AWOL. She could probably land a decent job given her family connections in the art business, and there was the cash she'd inherited when her father had died. It had covered the cost of her college with enough left over to start her own art restoration business if she wanted. Instead, she was living in a slum as part of her cover and waiting tables in a cesspool while she searched for her brother.

Her humble abode was on the second floor of a hundred-year-old building situated over an Oriental rug showroom. The rug merchant downstairs had stashed a girlfriend in the apartment until his wife caught him and forced him to ditch the mistress and rent the place out. Hank suspected the only reason she was allowed to be here was because the wife didn't realize that Hank the Renter was a girl. A young, single, reasonably good-looking one at that. The rug merchant had made a few overtures to her to take up with him where the former tenant had left off, but she'd turned him down firmly and nailed the door shut that led from her living room downstairs to the old lecher's office.

She turned into a puddle-strewn alley running alongside the rug store and started up the rickety wood stairs that led to her place. A sound behind her made her whip around, hand plunging into her purse to grip her can of pepper spray.

A man-sized shadow rushed toward her from the alley entrance, and she froze. What to do? How to react? Hank's heart lurched in her throat. She had to do *something*, but what? The back of the alley was a dead end. Nobody would hear her scream, and even if someone did hear her, no one in this neighborhood would call the police. Oh, God. She was in huge trouble.

But as quickly as that thought rushed through her brain and panic crashed through her body, a second, taller shadow raced out of the darkness from behind the first one. The fight—if she could call it that—was quick and brutal. Shadow Number Two chopped her would-be assailant in the back of the head with a vicious backhand blow that dropped Shadow Number One like a brick.

The violent second shadow took off running straight at her. Crap. The set of the big man's shoulders was grim. Determined. She didn't need to see his face to know she was his next target.

She turned and raced up the stairs, half-sobbing in terror. She stumbled, grabbed the rail and hauled herself upright. Splinters from the aged and cracked wood railing stabbed her palm, but she ignored them. She was going to die if she didn't get inside and behind a locked door *now*.

Footsteps closed in too damned fast from behind. Oh, God. A half dozen steps to go. The stairs shook as the shadow's weight crashed onto them. She fled across the tiny landing. *Keys. Dammit. Where were her keys?*

She fumbled desperately in her purse as her attacker took the steps behind her in great leaps that devoured the long staircase all too fast.

There. Her fingers found the jumble of keys. She snatched them out of her purse and found the familiar shape of her door key. Oh, God. He was almost on her. She whirled, threw her purse at him with all her strength and turned to unlock the door.

Not fast enough.

Big, strong hands grabbed her upper arms. Yanked her around.

Pepper spray. She still had the pepper spray in her left

hand. She lifted the small canister and mashed down the button.

"Oww. Bloody hell!" her attacker grunted.

He ducked away from the worst of the spray, barreled into her, and propelled both her and himself against her door. His weight knocked the breath out of her for a moment, during which he released her with one hand, just long enough to turn the doorknob. Which, of course, she'd managed to unlock right before he jumped her.

She opened her mouth to scream, but her attacker shoved her inside and slammed the door shut behind them before she could let it rip.

"Jeez, Hank. It's me. *Ashe*."

Her scream cut off just as it got started. "Ashe? What the heck?" She flipped on the light switch and stared at him in disbelief.

"Christ. Where's a sink? I gotta rinse that pepper spray out of my eyes." His eyes were, indeed, watering copiously, and he took a half-blind step toward her kitchenette.

"Are you going to attack me?" she asked suspiciously, backing away from him.

"Hell, no. I just took out the bastard who was about to jump you."

Her jaw dropped. "Who was he?"

"No idea. Sink?"

"Oh. Over here." Taking him by the arm, she guided him to her kitchen sink and turned on the spigot. It coughed then began to emit a sluggish stream of smelly New Orleans tap water.

He splashed great handfuls of it over his face again and again, rinsing away the pepper spray from around his eyes. His back muscles flexed under his taut T-shirt as he bent over the sink. Yowza. The guy was *ripped*. She hovered nearby, feeling helpless and guilty that she was the cause of his hissing breaths of pain and watering eyes. Eventually he stood upright. He was easily six foot two. And freaking built like an Olympic athlete.

She opened her mouth to speak, but he held up a hand to forestall her. "Stay here." She watched as he cautiously opened her front door. Stepped out onto the landing. Looked around. Came back inside and announced, "He's gone." She sagged in relief and realized abruptly that her knees felt weak.

Meanwhile, Ashe pulled out his cell phone and dialed a number.

She eavesdropped shamelessly as he asked, "Is Bastien LeBlanc by any chance on duty tonight...? Perfect. Could you ask him to cruise by Malouf's Oriental Rug Shop in the Warehouse District when he gets a chance? There was a minor scuffle in the alley beside the store, and a black-and-white drive-by would help ensure that no more trouble flares up. Tell him Asher Konig will owe him one...thanks."

"What was that all about?" she demanded. "Who's Bastien LeBlanc?"

"NOPD patrol officer. And an old friend. He'll cruise by and make sure your would-be assailant doesn't stick around for seconds."

Wow. It must be nice to have one's very own cop on call to do favors. If only she had the same. Maybe then she would know where her brother was by now. "You should have told me who you were instead of chasing me up the stairs," she said accusingly.

"I didn't know if I had knocked the bastard out fully or not," he retorted. "Unlike on television, people can pop up pretty fast after getting walloped in the head. I needed to get you behind cover and in a defensible position before I bothered with niceties."

"Oh." A pause. "Sorry I nailed you with my pepper spray."

"Don't apologize to me. You didn't realize who I was."

Did he have to be so nice about it? Now she felt even guiltier than before. "Let me get you a towel. You're soaked."

She retreated to her bathroom, grabbed the cleaner of her two towels off the rack and hurried back to the main room. Sheesh. What was wrong with her? Was she afraid he was going to bolt from her place before she got a chance to flirt with him or something?

Oh, my. As she stepped into the living room, she was just in time to see him grab the back of his T-shirt and haul the wet garment over his head.

Oh, *my.* Acres of bulging pecs and rippling abs came into sight as he straightened. Top-tier male models had *nothing* on this guy's physique.

"Wow," she breathed. "You're pretty without a shirt."

He glanced up and smiled wryly. "Thanks. And thanks for the towel." He lifted it gently out of her nerveless fingers and began toweling off his muscular acreage...while she stood there and basically drooled at him.

"You okay...?"

Wait. *What?* He'd asked her something. She replayed the garbled syllables and blurted belatedly, "Yeah, sure. I'm fine."

"Let me see your hand."

Huh?

Before she could figure out what he was talking about, he'd moved swiftly to her side and lifted her hand in his, palm up. Oh, hey. Look. There were three angry red scratches running the length of her hand and culminating in big gouges.

"Tweezers," he bit out.

"Medicine cabinet."

He turned and strode swiftly into the bathroom. Oh, God. A half dozen skimpy thongs and lacy bras were draped over the shower rod, drying. Too late to stop him.

Sure enough, he was smirking a little as he emerged from her postage-stamp-sized bathroom. But then he picked up her hand and started digging around.

"Youch!" She tried to yank her hand away but might as well have had it lodged in a block of concrete for all it moved.

"Splinters," he muttered. "Stay still."

Obediently she stopped squirming and leaned closer to watch as he deftly extracted several splinters from her hand. He was actually really good at it. His fingers were steady and swift. Exquisitely gentle. Then suddenly, he glanced up at her and asked, "You holding up okay?"

"Uh-huh."

"One more to go. You're being very brave."

This from a man who'd cracked heads twice in the same evening without breaking a sweat. The last splinter surrendered to him, and he rubbed the pad of his thumb across her palm, soothing it tenderly.

"I think the patient is going to live," he murmured.

"Thank you. For everything."

He looked up from her hand, and their gazes met—or rather, tangled together in a sexually charged dance of intense awareness of one another. Of hot, undeniable attraction, of hunger and need...

Yowza. The man sure knew how to, well, *look* at a woman.

Some sort of bright light flashed outside her window. "That would be Bastien," Ashe said. "He's shining his spotlight down the alley."

"Wow. That was fast."

"We're good friends. Used to work together. He knows I wouldn't bother him unless it was important."

He took a careful step back from her and glided over beside the window like James Bond, peering furtively past the blinds at an oblique angle that spoke of cloaks and daggers. What was up with that? Her other window onto the street got the same treatment.

A text came in on his phone, and as soon as he read it, the tense set of his shoulders relaxed. "Bastien says the alley's clear. He drove around the block a couple times, too. Your attacker has left the area."

She was more relieved than she liked to admit. Thank God Ashe had been there to save her. And that he knew a cop who would come scope out the area so quickly and thoroughly.

Ashe moved away from the windows and settled on the lurid red velveteen sofa, part of the furnishings that came with the dive.

She had never thought of her apartment as particularly small, but he filled the space with his large frame and even larger presence. His silver-blue gaze honed in on her again, but this time it was filled with questions. Speculation. Determination to find answers. And more of that disconcerting heat.

"What's a nice girl like you doing in a nasty joint like that?"

How did he manage to fill such a straightforward question with so much loaded innuendo? Her heart fluttered—actually fluttered—in response. Belatedly she mumbled, "You mean the bar?"

A frown pleated his dark brow. "You and I both know the Who Do Voodoo is a lot more than a bar."

Caution stilled her entire being. She knew it because she'd been working there for months. But how did *he* know after only a few hours spent sipping booze in the corner? Who was this guy? Surely he didn't work for Vitaly's bosses. "Are you a cop?" she blurted.

"No." His answer was prompt and without hesitation.

"FBI or something?"

"Nope."

"Why do you care if I work at the Voodoo, then?" she asked. "It's a steady paycheck."

"It's not worth the money. That place is trouble."

"I'll work where I want," she snapped. "It's my life."

He leaned back, stretching an arm along the back of her sofa. Deeply tanned, it was wreathed from wrist to shoulder in corded muscle and bulging veins that spoke of ridiculous strength. And she was alone in her isolated apartment with this total stranger who could overpower her without even exerting himself. She really ought to be scared silly of him. But she couldn't work up anything but a sense of complete trust in this man. Clearly, she'd lost her mind.

"So what's the deal with the club?" he asked.

"What do you mean?"

"I'd bet my next paycheck there's a whorehouse upstairs. Given how young the dancers looked, I'm guessing it's a sex trafficking outfit. You may be too scared to call the FBI, but I'm not." He tilted up on one hip to fish his cell phone out of a back pocket of his jeans.

"You can't call them!" she exclaimed.

He froze. Eased back down to the sofa slowly, phone still in pocket. "Why not?" Something dark and dangerous vibrated in his voice. It wasn't menace exactly, but it was a reminder to tread lightly around this man.

"You'll ruin everything!"

"I'm afraid you're going to have to be more specific than that. What 'everything' do you mean, exactly?"

She huffed. She didn't want to tell him anything, let alone involve him in her secret investigation. But if the FBI raided the bar and shut it down, her only lead to Max would be lost.

After weeks of frantic searching and the police seeming to ignore her, she couldn't take the constant panic anymore and had walked into the Voodoo bar to demand answers. It was the last place her brother had been seen going into the day he disappeared. And given that it wasn't the kind of joint he would normally have been caught dead in, logic suggested the place had something to do with his disappearance.

When she'd barged into the club, Vitaly had mistaken her for someone applying for the waitress job advertised in the window. He'd offered her the position on the spot, and in a combination of instinct and impulse, she'd taken it.

For the past two months, she'd been watching and listening and learning. But the mob bosses who employed Vitaly were extremely cautious. They rarely showed their faces, and they never did anything to hint at illegal activity—not counting the whorehouse upstairs.

She occasionally served drinks in the back lounge where the lap dances happened, but she'd never waited on the mob bosses where she could get a chance to eavesdrop on their conversation.

She had also never set foot above the ground floor of the bar and didn't intend to, either. In all honesty, she was scared to death of getting sucked into the inescapable downward spiral that was the sex trafficking industry.

"You haven't given me a good reason not to call the feds…yet," Ashe said, jarring her from her thoughts. "And I happen to believe trafficking in underage girls is about the worst form of exploitation there is. I have zero sympathy for anyone engaged in it."

"Neither do I," she muttered.

"Well, then?"

He hadn't moved a muscle, but a promise rolled off him to have answers out of her tonight, come hell or high water. She studied him closely. He'd shown genuine concern for her in the club and had even subjected himself to bodily harm to save her from that thug. Plus, he seemed prepared to listen to her. So heck…maybe she *should* take him up on his offer. Because thus far, she'd had zero success on her own finding out anything about Max.

Decision made, she released a long, slow breath that made her entire being feel as if it had deflated. It seemed as if she'd been holding that breath for months. Had she really been living under so much tension and stress? As good as it felt to trust him at least a little, she wasn't prepared to give up all her secrets to this man she barely knew. So she chose her words carefully. "Someone I know used to hang out at the Voodoo, and then we lost touch. I'm trying to figure out what happened."

"A girl?" he asked quickly.

Oh, God. He thought she knew one of the trafficked girls from Eastern Europe who were virtual prisoners upstairs without identification documents or knowledge of the English language or American laws. Not to mention many of the girls were drug addicts who were paid for sex with heroin or crack.

"No, no. Nothing like that. A *guy.* I'm hoping I'll run across someone who knew him and may know something about why he was there and where he went."

"Ahh." Ashe's expression shuttered abruptly, and he leaned forward to reach for his wet shirt.

Good grief. He thought Max was her boyfriend. Cripes. He must think she was a weirdo stalker chick working at the Voodoo to chase down some poor guy who'd fled from her and intentionally left no contact information.

She winced as she bit the inside of her lip to stop herself from correcting Ashe's mistaken impression. It was for the best. As hot as he might be, she had no time in her life for a dalliance that might distract her from finding her big brother.

Her gut howled at her that Max was in trouble and until that internal scream was silenced, she was off the market for men.

Ashe shrugged into his damp T-shirt. "How long do you need to find your...*friend*...before I call the feds?"

"I don't know. I've been there two months and haven't caught a lead yet."

"And you're sure he's still alive?"

Her spine stiffened in denial at the notion of Max being dead. It was what the cops thought. All this time with not a hint of him, no credit card hits, no banking transactions, no sightings...

"I *know* he's alive," she declared.

"How?" Ashe asked the question evenly enough. As if he was willing to hear her reasoning.

She sighed heavily. "I feel it in my gut, okay? I know that sounds lame, but I would *know* if he were dead. And I'm telling you he's not."

He stared at her for a second and then nodded briefly. Really? He believed her? No scoffing comments about how stupid it was to rely on a gut instinct? On how the facts said she was wrong? Wow.

He spoke gruffly. "Two weeks. I'll help you look for your boyfriend during that time, but that's all you get. It'll take the law that long to gather evidence, get the warrants and set up a raid. Innocent girls are suffering every day there."

Oh, God. She'd never thought of it in those terms. In her panic to find Max, she'd had the power to save those girls and hadn't. She was a horrible human being! In that context, giving her two weeks was frankly damned generous.

"Don't have the cops wait on my account," she said grimly. "When they're ready, they should shut the place down. I'll tell you this, though. The Voodoo is the tip of a much bigger iceberg."

Ashe gave her a sharp look. "What do you mean by that? What iceberg?"

Chapter 3

He leaned forward, watching every nuance of Hank's body language intently. *Now* they were getting somewhere. What the hell wasn't she telling him, though? He sensed lies in her words as sure as he was sitting here.

She answered, "Vitaly, the owner of the Voodoo, has bosses. Russian mob bosses. I haven't seen many of them around the joint, but his place is definitely a front for them."

"What kind of front?"

"I imagine they launder money through the place, although I haven't seen Vitaly's ledgers. He keeps all of those on his cell phone, and that thing never leaves his hands or his pocket." She blew out a breath. "Believe me, I've tried to get a look at it. But I've never seen him lay his phone down once."

"Anything else?"

She snorted. "He's a moneymaker for his bosses. Vitaly gripes all the time about the measly cut of the Voodoo's income that he gets. The rest is going up his chain of command."

Ashe frowned. "The mob, be it traditional Cosa Nostra or the Russians, usually takes only a small cut of the profits as protection money."

"Not at the Voodoo. Someone is taking the bulk of the income and giving Vitaly only a tiny piece of the pie to run the club."

"Tell me about Vitaly."

"His last name is Parenko. He's tough. Smart. Mean. Organized. He actually runs a pretty tight ship."

"Any mob ink on him?" he asked.

"He has a tattoo on his left arm, up high. It's a globe with four compass points coming out of it. There are two flags above the globe and a submarine across it."

Ashe's jaw flexed. "Are the Cyrillic letters em-cheh-peh-veh on it anywhere?"

Frowning, she thought about his question. "Yes. There's a little banner under the globe with those letters on it. And some numbers."

"Russian Navy symbol. And he has no other Russian mob tattoos?"

"Not the traditional ones that cover the whole torso. Now and then someone spills a drink on him, and I've seen him change his shirt a couple of times." She hesitated, her brow furrowing. "He's got only one other tat. It's on his left shoulder blade and is small. It's a shield with a star over it and a sword going down through the star."

"Jesus," Ashe breathed. That was the symbol for the KGB, the Soviet Union's equivalent of a combination FBI and CIA before it had been summarily disbanded in the mid-1990s and replaced with the FSB, the Federal Security Service of Russia. The abrupt disbanding of the KGB had stranded thousands of trained special operatives without jobs, incomes or pensions. Not surprisingly, many of them had turned their unusual skill sets to crime. In under a decade, the Russian mob had become one of the most feared criminal organizations on earth.

"How old is Vitaly?" Ashe asked.

"Midforties. But he's in really good shape for his age."

The guy was old enough to have been a young KGB agent in the early 1990s. "Does he ever do anything that strikes you as...paranoid?"

Hank rolled her eyes. "All the time. He does background checks on everyone who works there. Rumor is that he has all of his employees followed randomly—oh, God. What if that guy you jumped is working for him? I'll lose my job for sure—"

He cut her off quickly. "The guy I took out was moving toward you aggressively. A simple tail wouldn't have shown himself or moved that forcefully toward his subject."

She nodded slowly, but doubt still clouded her gaze.

He continued his interrogation. "Any other paranoid behaviors?"

"Well, there's the time I came into the bar in the afternoon before it was open because I forgot to pick up my paycheck the night before. Vitaly was going over the walls with some sort of electronic device. When I asked him what he was doing, he told me he was looking for bugs. But I thought he meant cockroaches."

"Have you seen other men around the bar with mob ink?" Russian mob tattoos were a complex art form with traditional symbologies to indicate which gang a man belonged to, his mob rank and even how many kills he had. The ink tended to cover most or all of a man's arms and torso and was hard to miss.

She shrugged. "Sure."

"What about the men who take so much of Vitaly's money?"

"Can't tell. They tend to wear suits."

Was her missing boyfriend one of them? She obviously knew what Russian mob ink looked like because she hadn't asked for any clarification when he referred to it. If her ex was a mobster and caught wind of her stalking him like this, she'd be killed for being such a nuisance. Had that been the purpose of the guy he'd chased off in the alley?

"Look, Hank. You are in more danger than you know. You need to back off looking for this friend of yours and stop working at the Voodoo."

"Not a chance."

Dammit. Her reply was emphatic. She wasn't about to be talked out of looking for her boyfriend. "Did it ever occur to you that this *friend* of yours doesn't want to be found? That if he wanted you to know where he was, he would have let you know?"

Tears welled up in her eyes, and in spite of knowing that he was right, Ashe felt like a heel. God, he hated it when women cried. Especially when he made them do it. Which wasn't often. In his line of work, he rarely had time to interact with women at all, let alone get to know one well enough to break her heart.

She swallowed hard. "It's not like that. We weren't dating. But I know...I *know*...something is wrong. Call it woman's intuition if you like. I *feel* it."

She didn't have to convince him of the accuracy of her intuition. His life depended on listening to his all the time. More times than he could count, a gut feeling had saved his hide in the field.

Whoa. Rewind. She and this guy weren't dating? For a moment, triumph leaped in his gut. Then who was this man she was so torn up over?

She was lying. She loved this mystery man heart and soul.

Dammit. He glanced down at her hands and noticed that she was wringing them continuously as she paced. Her slender fingers were red, she was pulling at them so hard. Oh, yeah. Head over heels for the missing dude. Disappointment rolled over him. He'd really thought for a minute there that they had some kind of connection.

"Come here, Hank. Sit down and talk to me."

She looked up at him, stress distorting her lovely features so much that his stomach twisted in sympathy. She moved around the scarred coffee table and sank onto the other sofa cushion. He reached out and captured her hands in his, stilling their restless activity.

"Tell me about your friend."

For a minute, he didn't think she was going to answer. But then she let out another one of those great, relieved sighs of hers and started to talk.

"His name is Max. He's an art and antiques broker. Acquires—well, *acquired*—pieces for private clients and for an auction house here in New Orleans. He got a commission to find something for someone, and soon after, he disappeared. No one's seen or heard from him since."

"What was he commissioned to find, and who commissioned him?"

"The auction house has no idea," she replied. "You see, he's an independent broker, and the commission didn't come through the house. For the last week before he disappeared, he went into the Who Do Voodoo on a daily basis. As if he'd gotten a job there—which makes no sense at all. The day he disappeared, the name of the club was written down in his appointment book, too."

"Who was the last person to see him?"

"I found the taxi driver who dropped him off there that

night. He says he didn't see Max meet or speak to anyone. He just went inside the club."

"What does Max look like?" he asked.

"Six feet tall. Athletic. Brown hair. Blue eyes. I have a picture of him if you want to see it."

"That would be great."

She jumped up and went into the bedroom. He heard a drawer squeak open and closed, and then she was coming back toward him. Transfixed, he watched her slow, sensuous return. Her body was slender, and she moved like a dancer. She was still wearing those sexy stockings with their hot little bows, but she'd kicked off the high heels and was padding around in her stocking feet, which was almost sexier. Her feet were elegantly shaped, and her toenails were painted a sassy shade of red beneath the black fishnet. Jeez, it had been way too long since he'd had a woman if some girl's feet were a turn-on.

"Here's a picture of Max."

No wonder she was stalking the guy. He exuded breezy, classy charm, and it was just a damned picture. Ashe memorized Max's face carefully while he snapped a picture of the photo with his cell phone. He took a moment to encrypt the picture so a casual search of his phone wouldn't show the image. If he was dealing with former KGB types, he couldn't afford to leave any trace of his real purpose lying around to be found.

Because he was, of course, going to help this girl find her lost lover or whoever the guy was to her. She was completely unequipped to deal with mobsters, let alone mobsters of this ilk. And he was a sucker for damsels in distress.

He placed a call to his SEAL team's ops center. It was a 24/7/365 outfit equipped to do just about anything a SEAL team could think up by way of support, from pulling in real-time intel, to tapping satellite feeds, to getting oddball-caliber ammo delivered to hellholes halfway around the globe on a moment's notice. Illegally. And without being detected.

A familiar female voice answered the phone. Awesome. Jennie Finch was one of the best ops specialists in the outfit. "Hey, Jen. I need you to run a name. Vitaly Parenko, which is likely an alias. Former KGB type. Russian Navy submariner. Living in New Orleans now. In his midforties."

"I thought you were supposed to be on vacation, Hollywood."

Ashe sighed in response. God knew Jen had helped him and his guys out enough times to rate using his team nickname. He often asked for her specifically to run point in ops on his missions because she was smart as hell, had a knack for anticipating what he was going to need and had it waiting for him by the time he asked for it.

"Are you running an op I didn't hear about?" she demanded, a shade indignantly.

"Something like that."

"Why didn't Perriman brief it to us here in ops?"

He grimaced. "Perriman doesn't know about it yet. I want to get my ducks in a row before I brief him."

"Oooh, you're gonna be in big *truh*-ble when he finds out you're working during your shore leave."

"Don't rat me out, okay?"

"If you'll promise that I get to watch the fireworks when he finds out, I'll keep my mouth shut."

"Deal," he said.

"Okay. Vitaly Parenko doesn't exist before the year 2005."

She must've had her computer searching for data while

they bantered back and forth. "What does that mean, he doesn't exist?" he asked.

"Your guess that the name is an alias is correct. You got a picture I can work off?"

"Not yet. But I'll get you one. Speaking of pictures, I need you to see what you can find out on another guy. Name's Max. Lemme send you the image now."

While he pulled the phone away from his ear to send the image to Jennie, he glanced up at Hank. "What's Max's last name?"

"Kuznetsov."

He put the phone back to his ear. "Last name Kuznetsov. Went missing around—"

Hank supplied, "June tenth of this year."

"—June tenth." Almost three months ago. The trail had to be getting damned cold by now. He relayed the other information Hank had shared with him to Jennie and ended with, "And I need you to check out a strip joint called the Who Do Voodoo in New Orleans. Parenko nominally owns the place, but someone else is pulling out most of the cash it makes. And be quiet about it. I don't want to tip off the Russian mob that I'm poking around."

"Would I do it any other way?" Jennie challenged him.

"Nah. You're the best."

"Get me a picture of this Parenko guy if you can."

"Roger that. Gimme till tomorrow night."

"Okay. I'll work on this other stuff in the meantime."

Ashe disconnected the call to find Hank glaring at him. "Who was that? You didn't just drag the authorities into this, did you?"

"Nah. That's just Jennie. She researches stuff for me from time to time."

Hank's expression fell. Yeah, he knew the feeling. He'd felt a spark of interest for her, too, until he'd found out she was willing to risk her life to track down some ex-boyfriend she was still carrying a torch for.

It was for the best that she thought Jennie was some sort of romantic interest of his. If nothing else, it made him look a little less pathetic for having been interested in her when she was still in love with this Max guy. Too bad her heart was given elsewhere. He sensed that the two of them could've been good together. *Really good.*

He asked in resignation, "You gonna be okay tonight, or do you need me to crash on your couch?"

A combination of heat and alarm raced across her lovely, mobile features. She really was a pretty girl beneath the cheap, gaudy makeup. The kind of genuine pretty that would age with grace and grow more elegant with time. Her skin was smooth and soft and fair. It matched her light-haired, blue-eyed Nordic looks…

And she was not for him.

He rose to his feet and moved swiftly to her windows, checking the locks before he headed to the door. "Lock this after me. I'll stand outside until I hear the dead bolt thrown home."

She nodded, and if he wasn't mistaken, a note of fear pinged in her gaze. She wanted him to stay but wasn't going to ask it of him. He didn't know whether to label her brave or just stubborn. Probably a little of both.

Knowing Bastien LeBlanc, the guy would spend the rest of the night hanging out in this neighborhood, keeping an eye on it. Hank would be plenty safe tonight. Bastien had been on the teams with Ashe for years and was a hell of a soldier, not to mention a loyal friend. Since Ashe had asked for help, Bastien would lend a hand and more.

"Be careful, Hank. You're in way deeper than you know. Please reconsider and don't go back to that place."

"Thanks for your help earlier and for your concern. But I know what I'm doing."

No. She didn't. But it was an argument he wouldn't win with her. He was going to have to go around her and just hope she forgave him for it.

Chapter 4

Hank stood at the bar, yawning. The combination of jumping at every sound outside and jangling nerves left-over from her intense encounter with Asher Konig had added up to a basically sleepless night for her.

The bartender was just filling her tray with beers when she felt *his* presence. It raced across her skin and sank into her awareness like hot sunshine before she could register dismay that he was back. What the hell was Ashe trying to do? He was going to mess up everything!

It was a busy Saturday night. Football season had started and Vitaly had installed a bunch of flat-screen TVs a few weeks back. The customers could toss back a brew, watch football, and get a lap dance from an under-age girl. What more could a guy want? It also meant Vitaly would be watching the bar closely. He wouldn't fail to no-tice that the patron who'd shown an interest in her last night had returned tonight. Crap, crap, crap. She had to ignore Ashe and hope he caught the hint and ignored her back.

She studiously avoided even looking at him until it dawned on her that she might be avoiding him so much that her body language would draw Vitaly's attention, anyway. Damn. She hated trying to outthink her diabolically smart boss. What to do?

Her dilemma was interrupted as she passed close to the doorway into the lap dance lounge.

"Psst," someone hissed.

Startled, she glanced at the door. The usual bouncer wasn't there. He'd probably gone to the bathroom for a minute.

"Psst."

She stepped close to the door. A girl stood there, dressed in a pair of skimpy satin boxer shorts and an even skimpier tank top that her large breasts all but spilled out of in multiple directions. The girl's mascara was almost clown-like on ridiculously long false eyelashes, and a generous helping of mascara was running down her cheeks.

"Have you been crying?" Hank asked in alarm. "Are you all right?"

The girl patted her cheeks absently as if they had no feeling in them. "Oh. That. Huh. Can't feel my face…" Her voice trailed off. Then she asked abruptly, "Have you seen the blue man?"

Hank frowned. "What blue man?"

"In the bowler hat. He's all blue and his suit is melting. And his tie was purple, but it turned green…"

Wow. This girl was high as a kite on something. Hank ducked inside the lap dance lounge, backing the girl up, out of sight of the main bar. She leaned close to whisper, "Do you need me to get you out of here?"

"Out?" The girl stared blankly. "What? No. You got more juice? Need my juice."

The girl looked plenty juiced up already. "What's your name?" Hank asked.

"Sveta. You likey? Call me Jane. Or Grrmblahhum-bugama…" Sveta dissolved into laughter. Assuming that was her name. Hank whipped out her cell phone and took a quick photo of the girl.

"Do you want to take a walk with me, Sveta? Maybe outside? To clear your head?" *And call an ambulance and the cops?*

"Wanna go to my room. Sleep." And all of a sudden, the girl drooped like she was on the verge of passing out.

"Umm, okay. Let me help you." Hank wedged her shoulder under the taller girl's armpit as Sveta sagged.

She'd taken maybe a half dozen awkward steps beside the staggering girl, guiding her toward the back of the lap dance lounge and the emergency exit to an alley, when a sharp male voice bit out from behind them, "What are you doing down here, Sveta? You know that's against the rules."

Crap. Vitaly.

The girl whimpered and shrank against Hank's side. "She was on her way out into the bar in search of a drink," Hank explained lamely.

Vitaly moved swiftly to Sveta's other side, pulling the girl toward the stairs that led upward into the bowels of whatever went on up there. "I'll take her from here, Hank."

"I can help you get her upstairs."

"No!" She started at the harshness of Vitaly's tone. "You are never to go up there. I don't want you getting near any of what goes on up there. You understand?" He stared at her intently over the nearly unconscious hooker's head.

"Uhh, sure," Hank stammered.

"You stay away from that place."

She frowned, confused. The guy almost sounded concerned for her. Like he was trying to protect her from upstairs, not urge her into it. He all but lifted Sveta off her shoulder, muttering under his breath in Russian to the hooker, "C'mon. Let's get you some candy. Let's find you a sugar daddy to love you, baby. Does that sound good? Say goodbye to the real world, baby doll…"

He and Sveta disappeared around a corner in the stairs.

"Hey? Whatchoo doing back he'uh?" another male voice demanded from behind her.

The bouncer. Back from the restroom or wherever he'd disappeared to.

"You ain't s'posed to be in he'uh." His Cajun accent was so thick she could barely make out the words.

"Yeah, well, a girl came out looking for some juice. Vitaly just took her back upstairs."

The bouncer pulled a face. "Dang ho. How she git loose?"

Loose? As in the girls were locked in or restrained in some way? Horror skittered down Hank's spine. She managed a reasonably unconcerned shrug and pushed past the bouncer into the main bar. She paused for a moment to catch her breath. God. That poor girl. She'd been stoned out of her mind.

"You okay?" yet another male voice asked from behind her.

Ashe.

Vitaly was upstairs for the moment and the bouncer back at his post. She hurried over to Ashe's table and spoke fast and low. "I just saw one of the girls from upstairs. She was high on something psychedelic. Vitaly's taking her back upstairs. We've got to shut this place down. Now."

"Patience, Hank. Let the cops do it right."

"But they're on it? They're getting everything in place?"

"Yeah." He glanced over her shoulder and bit out,

"Bring me a vodka, neat." Under his breath, he added, "We're on camera. We'll talk later."

Vitaly moved up beside her. "Everything okay here? My girl taking care of you?" He gave her backside a stinging slap that she expected was meant to serve as a warning to keep her mouth shut about what she'd just seen.

"Yes, she's doing fine," Ashe answered easily. He looked over at her, letting his gaze roam boldly up and down her body. Heat burst through her. Even her face grew hot. Great! How in the heck was she supposed to convince Vitaly she had no interest in Ashe if he made her freaking blush?

She headed toward the bar and was alarmed when Vitaly followed, crowding her against the wood and brass counter. He leaned in close and muttered, "Forget what you saw, Hank. You're a good kid, understand? You don't want any part of what goes on up there. The clients would mistake you for someone you're not."

Once again, he sounded genuinely concerned for her. She half turned to look him in the eye. "Thanks for looking out for me, Vitaly. I appreciate it."

He nodded tersely and headed into his office. Son of a gun. Who'd have thunk the SOB would look out for her like that? Or was he just trying to get on her good side to prevent her from telling anyone about Sveta? Man, she sucked at all this undercover stuff. She was by nature a straightforward person, and subterfuge of any kind messed with her head. Although her family hadn't been exactly the most forthcoming bunch to grow up around. Maybe her honesty was a twisted form of youthful rebellion.

Or maybe she was just overthinking Vitaly's motives. Maybe he really did want to protect her. Cripes, this place was making a cynic out of her. But then, she got to see the worst humanity had to offer in this den of iniquity.

The next two weeks couldn't pass fast enough for her. When they talked later, she would ask Ashe to move up the timetable of the FBI raid...or whatever it was he'd arranged with his girlfriend on the phone last night.

She'd been startled by the surge of jealousy that had swept through her when she'd realized that was a woman he'd been flirting with so comfortably on the phone. She'd give anything to have a man like him flirt with her like that. Maybe someday when this nightmare passed.

Assuming she survived it.

The bartender plunked a glass down in front of her and poured a sloppy shot of vodka into it. "For your boyfriend," he announced.

She snapped back, "He's not my boyfriend."

"He's watching you like he is. Guy's warning off every dude in the room with his glare."

Was *that* why no one had been groping or swatting her tonight? Except, of course, Vitaly. Crud. Ashe wasn't helping matters by protecting her. He had to ignore her...or at least just treat her like one of the other girls. He mustn't give any sign that she was anything special to him. Vitaly saw *everything* that went on around here. The man was like a spider sitting in his web.

The other waitresses whispered that Vitaly had secret cameras in the club and spied on them. Hank had even seen him sitting at his desk from time to time, studying his computer screen intently. But any time she'd had an excuse to go into his office, he'd turned off his monitor before she could glimpse whatever had been on it.

Hence her need for caution now. She ignored Ashe's whiskey on the bar and instead delivered a tray of drinks to a table full of regulars. They were Russians, but just customers who came in for the good vodka Vitaly stocked.

"Hey, Hank," Vitaly called from the doorway of his office. "Your boyfriend is waiting for his drink. Go serve him…and be nice to him."

She winced. Drat. He'd seen her skip giving Ashe his drink. She'd hoped another one of the waitresses would want to flirt with the hunk in the corner and take his vodka to him in her place. No such luck.

She nodded in Vitaly's direction without making eye contact with her boss and swerved toward Ashe's table. He took the shot glass directly out of her hand. Their finger-tips brushed, and she gasped as her pulse jumped. Lord, he had a crazy effect on her.

"Can I get you another drink?" she asked him mechanically as he handed the empty shot glass back to her.

"Do you carry Kauffman Vintage Vodka?"

She stared at him in surprise. "You know premium vodkas?"

"I like to think so."

"I don't know if we carry that. I'll ask the bartender."

"If not, I'll take a shot of Russian Standard or the best the house has got."

She headed for the bar and got raised eyebrows from the bartender at the request for Kauffman. He commented, "That stuff runs over two hundred bucks a bottle. Maybe Vitaly has some in his special stock. You'll have to ask him."

Hank poked her head into her boss's office. "The guy from last night is asking for some vodka called Kauffman. The bartender told me to come ask you for it."

"Kauffman, eh? Perhaps I should meet your boyfriend."

"He's not my boyfriend," she retorted in exasperation she didn't have to fake.

"You a lesbian or something?" Vitaly asked.

She bit back a snappy reply and merely mumbled, "Nah. He's just not my boyfriend." Sometimes it was a struggle to keep up her charade of not being the brightest bulb in the box.

Vitaly got up from his desk and moved to a tall locked wooden cabinet in the corner. She moved a little to have a sight line into the cabinet and was stunned to see several big honking weapons standing in the case. They looked like machine guns. Holy cow—

"Here we go." Vitaly pulled out a fat spherical bottle with a big silver cap that reminded her of a parrot's beak. Clear liquid filled the round belly of the bottle. She shifted back to her original position and pasted a look of dull disinterest on her face as he locked the case and turned to face her.

"Bring us two of the good vodka shot glasses in a bowl of ice," he ordered as he herded her out of the office and headed for Ashe's table. Planning on checking out the new patron personally, was he? Sheesh, Vitaly was paranoid.

She dutifully brought the men a deep bowl with two crystal shot glasses nestled in crushed ice. She set the bowl on the table and Vitaly ordered her brusquely, "Go away. My new friend and I want private conversation."

Every now and then, Vitaly's flawless American accent slipped a little and took on a faint Russian tinge like it just had. But that usually happened only when he was furious or under stress. Alarmed, she glanced between the two men. Dammit, there was no way to warn Ashe that Vitaly was on high alert.

She made brief eye contact with Ashe, who merely looked vaguely irritated that she was still hanging around. Frustrated, she retreated to the bar. "What's Kauffman, anyway?" she asked the barkeep, even though she knew full well what it was. Her brother used to drink it from time to time.

"One of the best Russian vodkas on earth. They only

make it in years when the wheat crop is of especially high quality."

She sniffed. "Sounds snooty to me."

"It's not the stuff regular guys order, that's for sure. Who's that dude Vitaly's sitting with?"

"No idea. Just some customer."

"Isn't he the one who broke up the fight last night?"

Crap, crap, crap. Ashe had called attention to himself—and now to her—by coming back tonight. "I dunno. I guess so."

"Looks like he and the boss are hitting it off."

Great. Ashe was horning in on her investigation. She'd kill him if he messed it all up. What could Ashe and Vitaly be talking about so intently anyway?

"He hot for you or something?" The bartender's blunt question quickly derailed her curiosity.

She rolled her eyes at the bartender. "As if I'd date any of the slimeballs who come in here."

The guy guffawed and poured her a plain soda with a twist of lemon, the way she liked it. She sipped at the drink for a few seconds, her back pointedly turned to Ashe and Vitaly and whatever bromance the two of them were having.

She moved around the club, serving patrons and enduring their lewd comments. Just another night in downtown hell. Except that it wasn't. She couldn't shake her hyperawareness of Ashe sitting in the corner with her boss. Her dangerous mobster boss. Their heads were close together, and they laughed uproariously now and then like they were trading war stories.

Vitaly called for a refill of crushed ice, and when she approached the table, she was stunned to hear them conversing in Russian. Ashe was freaking fluent? Bastard. Unreasonable jealousy surged through her that he was getting further with her boss in one lousy hour than she had in months.

It wasn't fair. She was a no-account female, and Vitaly ignored her existence for the most part. But Ashe could stroll in here and order some hoity-toity vodka, and just like that, Vitaly was hanging on his every word.

The level of vodka in the parrot-beak bottle dropped steadily over the next hour, and Vitaly demanded yet another refill on the ice. But this time, when she approached the table, her boss grabbed her rear end under her short skirt and gave it a humiliatingly familiar squeeze through her panties.

It was all she could do not to pull away from his hard fingers digging into her tender flesh. "Evgeniya the Ice Queen," he drawled in Russian. "Needs a man to screw her lights out. I tell her the pay is much better in the lap dance lounge, but always she refuses."

"Maybe a real man hasn't offered to do the job right," Ashe replied drily in the same language.

It was all she could do not to stick her tongue out at him. To date, Vitaly thought she understood only a few words of the simplest Russian, and she needed to keep it that way. She'd been able to eavesdrop on countless conversations between him and his associates because of it.

"You think you're man enough?" Vitaly hooted. "I'll give you a bottle of this vodka on the house if you convince her to do it. Make a lap dancer of her if you can. I'll earn a fortune on her in the lap dance lounge if I can get her back there. Get a load of those legs. And just feel this ass…"

Ashe glanced up at her for just a moment, his eyes mirroring regret for just an instant. But it was enough for her to know he was not enjoying this any more than she was. "Come over here," he drawled in English. "Vitaly says you have a great ass. I want to check it out."

Was he kidding? Apparently not, for he stared at her expectantly. Silently livid at her boss, she stepped away from his invasive grip and moved to Ashe's side, standing so close that her knees rubbed his thigh. "Go ahead, buddy. It's not like you'll ever get more than a handful of this action."

Vitaly hooted with laughter. He sounded more drunk than not, but she never could tell with him. He held vodka like nobody's business.

Ashe's palm cupped the back of her knee, sliding up the back of her thigh with maddening slowness. With light pressure, he pushed her leg until she took a step to the side, turning so her back was to the room. What? He didn't want the other patrons to see him checking out her posterior regions? If the man weren't feeling her up, she might actually think his action was chivalrous. But as it was, his hand headed inexorably toward her rear end.

His fingertips traced the seam of her stockings up under her miniskirt, up to the swell of her backside, paused, and then continued higher until her entire cheek was cupped in his big, warm hand. Her glute muscles clenched involuntarily.

His hand kneaded her gently and he murmured cajolingly, "Relax, baby. I'm not gonna hurt you."

No, but he was embarrassing her to death. It was one thing to have random drunk strangers grab her as she passed by them. But he was no stranger, and this was no random grope. It was a full-scale invasion. His fingers dipped into the tight crevasse between her cheeks, in the same place Vitaly's had, but where her boss's grasp had been rough and impersonal, Ashe's fingers were beguiling. Intent on winning her acceptance. They stroked and probed gently, asking and waiting for her to relax and give him access to her most secret places. Something hot and liquid erupted low in her belly, startling the hell out of her and momentarily distracting her long enough that she did relax her tush.

Ashe's hand dipped deep between her legs immediately, and she tensed up once more. But the damage was done. His hand cupped her lady parts with shocking intimacy, and any move she made would rub said parts against said hand. She froze, staring down at him in shock. It was one thing to go along with Vitaly's misogyny for the sake of gaining the guy's trust. It was another thing entirely to embarrass her in public. Although, truth be told, the worst of her embarrassment stemmed from the fact that she was a little turned on by Ashe's hand cupping her like she already belonged to him.

"Trust me, Vitaly," he declared in Russian. "She's no ice queen. She's all woman. And hot for me."

She didn't stop to think about it. She went with her reflex reaction and slapped Ashe's cheek with all her might.

Vitaly surged halfway to his feet, swearing and apologizing as words tumbled out of his mouth in a garbled jumble. But it was Ashe's reaction that shocked her. He stared up at her in stunned disbelief for a heartbeat and then threw his head back and laughed. Heartily.

"Sit, sit, Vitaly," he chortled in Russian. "I like my women a little wild. It's more fun that way to tame them."

Her gaze narrowed. As if he would ever tame her. Hah!

Vitaly sank back into his chair, but he was looked genuinely angry and glared at her with a grim promise of serious retribution when Ashe left this place. So much for looking out for her best interests. Heck, for all she knew, her boss might drag her upstairs by the hair and let the clients do their worst to her. Her insides turned to jelly and her entire being quailed at the thought of what could happen to her up there. They could shoot her up with heroin until she was hooked, lock her into a room in the brothel...

Who would come looking for her? There was no one to rescue her from the hellhole Vitaly could throw her into. She would be lost. And now that Max was gone, not a living soul would care.

"...don't let women slap me without punishment," Ashe was saying in Russian. He leaned back in his chair, tossed back a shot of the expensive vodka and grinned at Vitaly. "How do you propose I do that, my friend?"

Vitaly scowled. "I'd beat her until she couldn't sit for a week."

Ashe tilted his head to one side and studied her while she defiantly glared back at him. "Nah. She's got fair skin. She would bruise like mad. Someone would call the cops on you."

Vitaly jerked his chin at her. "What would *you* do to punish her?"

A slow smile unfolded on Ashe's face. "You want her to work in the lap dance lounge, yes?"

Aghast, she stared at him. He was not actually going to throw her to the wolves like this, was he? Ashe was supposed to be one of the good guys! Worse, she wasn't supposed to know Russian, so she couldn't respond in any way to this little exchange between the men.

"Yes, of course," Vitaly answered a little too eagerly. Apparently he wasn't so drunk that he'd missed where Ashe was going with his line of reasoning, either. Dammit.

Ashe asked in English, "How about I teach her how to do a decent lap dance?"

It was Vitaly's turn to throw back his head and laugh. "Done."

"No way—" she began.

Vitaly surged to his feet and grabbed a fistful of her

hair at the back of her neck, yanking her head violently and forcing her to endure his fetid breath in her face. Out of the corner of her eye, she saw Ashe tense. "You make my friend happy, or I will take you upstairs and put you to work up there. Understood?"

She tried to nod, but even the smallest movement of her head caused her hair to pull painfully against his fist. He leaned in closer to growl, "Do what this man says or I'll make you pay."

Terror roared through her. It was her worst nightmare. She was going to get sucked into the abyss and never escape Vitaly's clutches. And it was all Ashe's fault, damn him. Why, oh, why did he have to show up here and mess up everything?

Ashe surged out of his chair, his big fist suddenly encompassing Vitaly's at her neck. "Let the lady go." His voice was low and cold and dripped with violence.

Vitaly shoved her at Ashe. "Be a good girl and show the nice man how very sorry you are."

Ashe caught her as she half fell against him. He set her gently back on her feet and loomed close beside her, never releasing her arm just above the elbow. "Come along, naughty little girl." His words might be what Vitaly wanted to hear, but his tone was soothing.

Without further ado, he led her over to the lap dance lounge's entrance. The bouncer opened it, grinning, and Ashe ushered her into what surely was a special corner of hell.

What little lighting there was in the lounge came from red bulbs shrouded in colored scarves that hung from the ceiling and fat black candles dripping in sconces around the walls. Necklaces of bones, snakeskins, animal skulls and braids of herbs decorated the kidney-colored walls. The place reeked of incense and pot and sweat, and maybe a hint of blood. A rooster even clucked quietly in a small cage on a table off to one side of the room. More drippy candles, dried chicken feet and knives lay on the table beside the live chicken. Small curtained alcoves lined the room, and a row of chairs filled its center.

Ashe led her to an alcove with the curtain pulled back and ushered her inside. He yanked the cloth shut behind them. A low armless chair stood against the wall, and he smirked at her before turning her arm loose and plunking down on it.

She whispered furiously, "You don't seriously expect me to do this, do you?"

He murmured back sotto voce, "I seriously expect that there are cameras in here, and that your boss will be watching. I'm not exactly thrilled about the position you've put me in, either. You really shouldn't have slapped me. At least not in front of a misogynistic chauvinist like your boss."

"What did you expect me to do?" she said with a hiss. "Let him manhandle me like that and treat me like a piece of meat he can give to whomever he wants?"

"I expected you to trust me. I'd have seen to it the bastard gets what's coming to him and I'd have gotten you out of there without this little detour."

She swore under her breath. He was, of course, right. It was her own impulsive nature and stupid temper that had put her in this pickle.

"I'll fake it if you will," he muttered.

"Right. Fake it." But fake *what*? As if she had any idea how to do a lap dance. The subject had not been covered in any of her art history classes in college. Scowling, she scooted forward until her knees bumped against his shins.

He smiled. "Go for it, baby."

"You're going to hell for this," she grumbled.

His grin widened, and he leaned back in the chair a little. "Ahh, but what a way to go. I dare you. Give me your best shot."

Oh, a dare, was it? That changed things. Glaring fiercely at him, she threw her leg across his hips and plopped down on his lap. He tensed beneath her as her lady parts passed across the zipper of his jeans.

Crud. Now what? She was undoubtedly supposed to engage in some sort of bump-and-grind routine next. After all, it was called a lap *dance*. But that left a whole lot to the imagination by way of technical details.

Experimentally she tilted her hips forward and then back. Oh, my. That felt rather nice. She tried it again. Her nervous tension eased a little, and this time it felt even better.

"That all you got?" Ashe murmured in obvious amusement.

Concentrating intensely, she tried circling her hips to the left. Ooh, that was interesting. And better, unwilling heat flared in Ashe's eyes. Quite a bit of heat, in fact. If she wasn't mistaken, the region behind his zipper was getting harder. More enthusiastically, she circled back to the right.

"This may not be the right moment to mention it, but most lap dancers do it facing away from the guy. It costs extra to get a full frontal. I expect the girls don't want to get their chests grabbed, nor do they want to be tongued or kissed."

She sprang to her feet, outraged. "You let me writhe all over your lap the wrong way?"

"I didn't say it was wrong. Just more suggestive than usual."

"You are such. A. Jerk."

His voice dropped so low she could barely hear it over the Jamaican music blaring from hidden speakers overhead. "No, baby. It's called protecting your cover. Vitaly's going to be watching us when we leave here. And I'd better have a hard-on and you'd better be embarrassed all to hell when we walk out of here if you want either of us to make it out of this club alive."

Of course he was right. Darn it. "How in the heck do you know so much about this stuff, anyway?" she demanded, chagrined.

The corner of his mouth quirked up. "I'm not exactly a teenaged virgin. Of course, I don't generally have to pay for what I want from women, either."

She glared at him a moment more, then whirled around and backed onto his lap. Her toes barely reached the floor, and she overbalanced slightly. His hands came up to clasp her hips. He didn't do anything crude like pull her down onto his male parts, but he did steady her until she regained her balance.

Ashe shifted beneath her. Abruptly, warm breath caressed her neck. He must have taken pity on her because he murmured, "Most girls squat over the guy and keep their weight on their feet, which is why this chair is so low and has no arms. That way, the girl can pull away if the guy gets fresh with her. Then the girls twerk a little."

"I don't know how to twerk," she wailed under her breath.

"It basically involves relaxing your rear end and shaking it up and down. Don't worry about it. The view I'm getting is fine just the way it is."

Thank *God* she had a skirt on. And stockings. And panties. This was embarrassing enough without her having her rear end hanging out of a skimpy thong.

"My thighs are burning."

"Then sit down on me, silly." He gave a little tug, and her tired legs gave out. She plopped down unceremoniously on his lap. She lurched, but he held her in place with that easy, overwhelming strength of his.

"I cannot believe you're making me do this." Her mouth was saying one thing, but her body was starting to say something else entirely. It wasn't all bad having her hips nestled in his lap. His zipper bulged against parts of her she'd never…rubbed…against anyone before. The intimacy of it was staggering.

She'd had sex, of course. She was twenty-five, after all. But never like this. She'd never been the type blatantly to take control of the sex, or to be…naughty…about it. Okay, so she was a prude. There. She'd said it. Or at least thought it very loudly.

Ashe relaxed beneath her, seemingly completely at ease with having a woman squirming around on his lap. But she felt vulnerable. Terribly exposed. Even though her mini-skirt flared around both of their hips, hiding most of what was going on underneath it.

"Move your hips like this," he instructed, guiding her hips through a slow figure eight. "You can rock like before or do those circles you were doing, too."

"This is hard," she complained.

A low chuckle rumbled behind her. "I believe hard is the point."

She looked over her shoulder to roll her eyes at him.

He grinned. "Just sayin'."

"Behave."

He shrugged. "It's not like either of us has any choice here. If I don't have a grin on my face or a pronounced limp, Vitaly's going to try to hurt you. And since I'm not about to let him do that, all hell will break loose."

"So you're *not* enjoying this?" She didn't know whether to be relieved or disappointed.

"Well, now, I didn't say that," he drawled. "I think if

you put a little enthusiasm into it, maybe pretended I was your boyfriend, you might have a future in the profession."

Imagine him as her boyfriend, huh? That wasn't much of a stretch. The memory of his magnificent naked chest in her apartment last night popped into her head. Nope. Not a stretch at all. Let alone the steamy dreams of him that had disrupted her sleep.

She realized with a start that she was moving more sensuously against him, enjoying the feel of him growing restless beneath her. Tense. Hungry.

He was faking it, of course, which was really sweet of him. Warming up to the ruse a little more, she let her mind wander into a pleasant fantasy of the two of them together.

They would be in a beautiful old room with antique furniture, hardwood floors and white gauze curtains. The big four-poster bed would have fat pillows and white linen sheets. A fan would turn lazily overhead, stirring the sultry air. They would make love slowly. Easily. With aching tenderness that gradually turned into raging, sweaty passion...

"Okay, then," Ashe ground out. "That should be enough to shut up your boss."

She stilled abruptly. Ohmigosh. Her hips had been undulating all over the place. She'd been riding him like a total hussy.

"I'm sorry—" she started.

"Hush," he muttered, cutting her off. "Vitaly will be delighted." A pause, and then he added wryly, "*Too* delighted. Bastard's gonna want to put you to work back here after that performance." He swore quietly as he lifted her off his lap.

She turned to face him, surprised that he hadn't stood up already. But a quick, unwilling glance at his lap revealed the source of his delay. His zipper strained to contain the raging erection behind it. He'd been genuinely turned on by her lap dance? "I didn't suck, then?" she blurted.

A short bark of laughter slipped out of him. "You did not suck."

He gritted his teeth and visibly reached for self-control. Sympathetically she suggested, "Think about your grandmother. Church. An ice-cold shower."

Another laugh, this time a little pained. "I've got this, thanks. Just give me a second."

She turned her back to give him a little privacy to get his body under control. It was more like a minute, but he eventually rose to his feet behind her. He leaned close, his big body radiating heat against her spine. "Don't argue with me when I talk to Vitaly. I have a plan."

Now what on earth did that mean?

Chapter 5

Ashe's head reeled as he escorted Hank out of the back room. What in the hell had just happened between them? Sure, he'd been turned on by her innocent little dance that had reeked of sensuality. But that wasn't what had him reeling. The violence that had bubbled up in his gut at the idea of Vitaly witnessing her performance was what had him thrown.

When it had occurred to him that the bastard would no doubt be watching Hank's dance, a real urge to toss her off his lap, find the Russian and choke him to death had roared through him. His entire life was about discipline. Self-control. No emotion got the best of him. Ever.

Sure enough, Vitaly emerged from his office as Ashe and Hank stepped out of the lap dance lounge. And the guy was grinning from ear to ear.

Ashe's grip on Hank's arm tightened until she sucked in a sharp breath. "Sorry," he mumbled, loosening his grasp.

"Told you she would have a talent for being a slut," Vitaly boomed in Russian.

The man's choice of a language only a few people currently in the club would understand saved his life in that moment. Ashe ground a couple of his back molars into dust, though, before responding in rapid Russian, "If we're going to do business, I want the girl."

"What does that mean?" Vitaly challenged him, startled.

"You own the girls around here, right?"

"Well, yes. Of course," the Russian blustered.

"I want exclusive use of this one for the duration of our business dealings."

Hank tensed under Ashe's hand. Did she understand enough Russian to know what he just demanded of Vitaly? Clever little minx, to have played dumb around her boss.

Vitaly glanced back and forth between him and Hank for a few seconds. "I need to speak with her. Alone."

"Sure thing." But before he passed her arm to Vitaly, Ashe said to her in English, "If you want more of what you just tasted, agree to the offer he's about to make you. I promise you won't regret it."

Vitaly grinned and took her arm, dragging her unceremoniously into the back office. Ashe didn't like it when the door closed behind the pair, and he checked the time grimly. Sixty seconds. That was all the Russian got with her before Ashe broke down the door.

At second fifty-two, the door opened. "She's yours. And she understands that if she pisses you off, she answers to me."

Ashe drawled back in Russian, "I can keep my own women in line, thanks. If she pisses me off, I'll take care of it myself."

A knowing grin spread across Vitaly's features.

Ass. He got off on roughing up helpless, weaker women,

huh? Ashe made a mental note to make the guy pay for that someday.

"C'mon, kitten. You've got a dance to finish for me."

"Where are we going?" she asked in an appropriately quavering tone.

"My place. Get your purse."

She nodded and disappeared into the storeroom, emerging in just a few seconds. Although his natural tendency was to put an arm around her and use his body to shield her from the drunks, he refrained and merely strode toward the exit, leaving her to trail along behind him.

But the second they hit the street, he turned and placed a protective hand in the small of her back. Her slender frame trembled beneath his palm. "This way," he murmured gently.

He guided her quickly away from the club and the prying eyes of Vitaly's potential flunkies. If the guy was as paranoid as Ashe suspected he was, there could be a sniper hidden somewhere on this street. The shooter was probably upstairs over the club, but given what he already knew of Vitaly's caution, it was entirely possible the hypothetical sniper had a hideout somewhere else along the street.

Early in their drinking spree tonight, a text had come from Jennie alerting Ashe that his fake identity had been probed online. The timing of it corresponded exactly with when Vitaly had excused himself briefly to go into his office to check on "club business."

"Where are we actually going?" Hank asked, panting a little to keep up with him as he hustled along the dark street.

"Save your breath and keep moving."

"What's going on?"

Civilians. Couldn't take an order to save their lives. Always asking questions and wanting to know why. He replied without moving his lips. "Possible gunman out here." He added sharply when she drew breath again, "Don't ask questions. Just walk faster."

"If you want me to walk faster, I'll need to take off these shoes."

He glanced down at her stupidly high platform heels and mentally shook his head in disgust. Not that he didn't appreciate how they shaped her calves or made her legs seem even longer and sexier than they already were. But women should be allowed to wear comfortable shoes that they could freaking run in if they had to.

The two of them ducked around a corner and out of sight of the Who Do Voodoo, and he slowed his pace a little.

Where *was* he going to take her? He couldn't take her back to her place. At least not until they'd talked in a secure location and he'd explained the risks she faced in going back to her apartment. He would bet his next paycheck the place would be bugged shortly. Vitaly would want to know everything he could about Ashe before they actually did any business.

He could take her to the home he'd grown up in, which was now his. But he hadn't been back there since his father died, and he wasn't interested in dealing with all of that baggage in the middle of an op.

For surely this had just become an op. Vitaly had leaped all over the hint he'd thrown out that he was an arms dealer. It had been a test to find out how Vitaly would react to a suggestion of illegal activity. Instead, the guy had jumped on it like a starving dog on a bone. Was Vitaly trying to prove himself by bringing in a big fish to impress his bosses?

Ashe needed someplace safe and neutral to talk with Hank. To find out exactly what she knew of her former lover's activities before his disappearance and to learn ev-

erything she knew about Vitaly's organization. *A hotel.*
And he knew exactly the one.

There were no cabs in this part of town, let alone at this
time of night. It was well past midnight. They were going
to have to walk to the French Quarter if they wanted to
catch a ride anywhere.

A light mist started to fall, and he shrugged out of his
jacket and draped it over Hank's shoulders.

"You don't have to do that," she protested.

"Actually, I do. My mother would haunt me from the
grave if I didn't."

"Scary woman, your mother?"

"A saint. She put up with my old man for nearly forty
years before he drove her to an early grave."

"I'm sorry for your loss."

He shrugged. He appreciated the sentiment, but no
words would ever lessen the pain of losing his mother.

"What's your father like?"

He detected a wistful note in her voice. Didn't grow up
with her father, huh? Turning his attention to her question, he answered reluctantly, "Dyed-in-the-wool sonofabitch. A marine. Volunteered for every tour in Vietnam
they would let him serve until they finally forced him to
come home. He was pissed off for years afterward that he
couldn't keep killing commies."

Of course, that was only the tip of the iceberg regarding his father. The man had been incapable of expressing
love. Hell, Ashe was fairly sure the man wasn't capable of
feeling a "sissy" emotion like love. Walt Konig had been
an OCD perfectionist and harried his mother constantly
to keep the house neater, cleaner. Shipshape. He'd had a
short temper. Suffered from flashbacks and nightmares.
Had been a harsh disciplinarian. All in all, a deeply unpleasant human being.

Ashe knew in his head that the man had suffered from serious post-traumatic stress. But the little boy who still peeked out of his gut from time to time hadn't much cared for the reasons why he'd never been good enough for his dad.

Maybe without Walt for a parent, he wouldn't have pushed himself so hard. Maybe he wouldn't have become a SEAL. Maybe he wouldn't have pulled crazy, suicidal stunts to be a hero all the damned time. The same stunts that had his boss sending him on extended leave and telling him to power down before he got his team killed.

With a start, he realized they'd stepped out into the carnival atmosphere of Bourbon Street. The mist had stopped temporarily, and the street was full of people. This late on a Saturday night, the party was in full swing. Folks danced and drank and shouted with laughter as couples hung all over each other. Guys on balconies overlooking the street exhorted passing women to flash their breasts in return for plastic bead necklaces.

He sighed. The tourists seemed to think Mardi Gras was a year-round event down here. Or maybe it was, nowadays.

He led Hank to the nearest high-end restaurant and tipped the maître d' a twenty to call them a cab. In a few minutes, he'd handed Hank into the relative quiet of a taxi and named a small, upscale hotel in the Metairie district as their destination.

They pulled up in front of the elegant mansion, and he caught Hank's wince as she tugged at her miniskirt. "They're going to think I'm a hooker you've brought back to your room. Will they even let me in there?"

Ashe grinned. "My aunt owns the place. They'll let you in."

"Your father's sister?"

"No," he replied a tad sharply. "My mother's sister, Eloise. Nice lady."

"Not fond of your father, are you?"

"Past tense. He died a few months ago." Not too long before her boyfriend had disappeared. Apparently, the two of them were leading somewhat parallel lives.

"I'm sorry."

"Don't be." He tipped the cabbie and handed her out of the car. She paused to take in the hotel's classical semicircle portico, Grecian columns and lush landscaping. He glanced at the tableau briefly, long accustomed to its old-world grace. His father had always hated the place. Called it snooty and prissy.

As for him, he'd snuck over here as often as he could without getting caught to hang out in the kitchen or in Aunt Eloise's office.

"C'mon," he muttered.

Hank's steps dragged reluctantly until she saw the lobby was deserted. The Hotel Fontenac's usual clientele would be long abed by now.

"Asher!" the night manager exclaimed. "It has been too long! Madame Eloise has gone home for the evening. You'll stay until tomorrow and see her, yes? She'll have your head if you don't."

Ashe grinned at the gray-haired man who'd been a fixture at the hotel for as long as he could remember. "Hi, Mr. Tibbs."

"Good heavens. Call me Gregory. You're all grown up, now."

Ashe shook his head. "Time flies, huh?"

"It surely does. What can I do for you and your lovely friend tonight? A room perhaps?"

"That would be great. We've just gotten to town and could use a shower and a clean bed."

"We definitely have both of those here." Gregory passed him a room key that was an actual key. No modern plastic cards for the Fontenac, thank you very much.

Ashe leaned across the counter to murmur, "If anyone but Auntie El asks, I'm not here."

"Understood," Gregory answered smoothly. But then he asked in a conspiratorial whisper, "Are you still doing that fancy secret stuff for the military?"

Hank jolted beside him as he gave the man a noncommittal shrug. *Dammit*. He scooped up the key and herded her toward the elevator. She was tense, stiff, all of a sudden. The filigree metal cage closed behind them, and the lift jerked into motion.

She asked tightly, "What did he mean, *secret stuff for the military*? What secret stuff?"

He pitched his voice low. "Patience. We'll talk in the room."

"You bet your sweet bippy we will."

He arched an amused eyebrow at her. "My sweet bippy? Do I want to know what that is?"

She sniffed. "Pop culture reference from the early '70s and revived recently. You must have been overseas doing fancy secret stuff and missed it."

Well, at least he knew now that she wasn't a Special Forces groupie chick. That was something, at least. If she ever decided she liked him, it wouldn't be for his job or for the thrill of bedding a trained killer.

He led them into what he knew to be one of the hotel's best suites. It was good to be family. And by giving them this two-bedroom suite, Gregory had neatly sidestepped the question of one bed or two for them.

"Bedroom for you over there with your own bathroom. I'll take the room by the door, and I've got my own shower, too. I'll call downstairs and see if Gregory can scare up a snack for us. I don't know about you, but I'm famished."

"After all that vodka you drank?"

He snorted. "That's why I need food. To soak up some of it."

"I'm going to take a shower and wash the stink of the club off me," she announced. "And then you and I need to talk."

Indeed. He jumped in his shower, as well, and emerged in time to let Gregory in the door pushing a catering cart full of cold sandwiches and fruit. He pronounced the man a miracle worker and ushered him out.

"Who was that?" Hank asked from the doorway of her bedroom.

He looked up and did a double take. She was swathed in one of the Fontenac's fluffy terry-cloth robes, her towel-dried hair a golden halo around her face. Without makeup, she looked entirely different. Gone was the hard edge of a woman pushing thirty and working in a rough joint. She looked about sixteen years old, her skin fresh and dewy. God, she looked young.

"How old are you?" he blurted.

"Twenty-five." She added a little defensively, "I'm not a college student anymore. Granted, I did just graduate. But it took me a couple of extra years to get out of college because I had to help my brother take care of my mom until she died, and I could go to school only part-time."

He sort of followed all of that. "What was wrong with your mother?"

"She was paralyzed from the neck down in a car accident when I was thirteen." Shame entered her voice as she finished with, "I wasn't badly hurt in the crash."

"I'm sorry for your loss and her suffering."

A shrug of a slender shoulder under the fluffy robe. "Life sucks."

"That's a pessimistic outlook for someone as young as you."

She looked up at him. "How old are you, then?"

"Thirty-two."

"Wow. You're almost ready for the old folks' home."

He snorted. In his line of work, she wasn't far wrong. Special ops was a young man's game. The low-level hum of underlying panic in his gut over what he would do with the rest of his life notched up a bit.

"What's this?" she asked, taking a step toward the covered table.

He whisked off the white linen napkins covering the plates and held a chair for her while she sat down. "A picnic."

"In my world, this qualifies as a bona fide feast," she declared.

"In mine, too. We eat some weird shi—" he corrected himself, "—stuff in the field."

She picked up a chicken salad sandwich. "What's the weirdest thing you've ever eaten?"

He picked up a tuna sandwich and considered. "Monkey brain. And it was as gross as it sounds."

"Eeyew," she exclaimed, laughing. "I think we'd better change the subject before I lose my appetite."

He leaped on the opening. "Have you ever seen your boss have meetings with anyone while you've been working at the Who Do Voodoo?"

"Of course. He has meetings all the time."

"Ever see him with any men who looked like his bosses? Maybe older men, or men he treated with special deference?"

"Now and then."

"Did you find out their names, or can you describe them?"

"I don't know any names. But I got a picture of one of them once."

He put down his sandwich abruptly. "May I see it?"

"It's a bad photo, and it's very dark. I took it with my cell phone in the bar."

"No problem." Jennie could perform magic on anything with pixels. He could barely make out the features of a balding, middle-aged man seated in the dark corner of the club. But he forwarded the digital picture to his headquarters quickly with an urgent request for identification.

"Why are you so interested in Vitaly?" Hank queried.

"You want to find your boyfriend, right?"

She grimaced a little. "He's not actually my boyfriend. He's my brother."

Ashe blinked. Brother? There was no lover? Well, *that* put a whole new spin on things. So...she wasn't as off-limits as he'd thought. And he wasn't a total douche bag for being turned on by her lap dance. Hmm, and they were alone in a hotel room together. Late at night. With her wearing a bathrobe, and him shirtless. He cleared his throat, suddenly more aware of her as an attractive, sexy female than he cared to be.

"I guess this is where I admit that Jennie isn't my girlfriend, either, huh?"

The same progression of surprise, relief and then chagrin passed through Hank's gaze before she murmured, "Who is she?"

"My ops and logistics support specialist."

"Meaning what?"

"She does basically anything my team needs while we're out in the field," he explained in a matter-of-fact tone. "She gathers intel for us and arranges deliveries and pickups of supplies, reserves hotel rooms, hires informants—you name it."

"So this is an actual mission you're on? For which government agency? And what—or who—is the target?"

"Technically, I'm on leave. But let's just say your boss triggered my internal alarm system. I asked Jennie to poke around and find out what she can about him."

She quirked a delicate brow. "Why does Vitaly alarm you?"

"He's a smart, competent guy who would make a hell of a dangerous criminal. The club itself raises some questions in my mind…it's obviously much more than meets the eye."

Hank deflated in what looked like disappointment. Ashe asked quickly, "What's wrong?"

"I keep hoping my brother didn't get involved in anything illegal or dangerous at the Voodoo, but everything you're saying confirms my worst fears. He's gotten himself mixed up in something real bad, hasn't he?"

An urge to comfort her, to go to her and wrap his arms around her, nearly overcame him. He forcibly stopped himself from moving toward her, however. He had no intention of taking advantage of her vulnerability to seduce her.

It wasn't that he wouldn't willingly jump into the sack with her and have a great time. But that wasn't what he was here to do. He needed to focus on the job at hand. On helping the damsel in distress, not humping her. He repeated his old mantra to himself grimly: *he was the job.* Dammit.

He asked abruptly, "Do you have any idea what Vitaly is up to—"

The lights flickered once and then went out, plunging the suite into darkness.

A gasp from Hank located her position in his mental picture of the room. He responded to the frightened acceleration of her breathing by murmuring, "Stay where you are. The lights will come back on in a few seconds."

Except they didn't.

"Is it him? Has he come for us?" she whispered.

Battle alert roared through him. "Do you have reason to believe Vitaly would cut the power and burst into your room to harm or kill you?"

"No. But he's the suspicious type. And your arrival in the club and interest in me will have drawn Vitaly's attention to me. What if he figured out that I'm Max's little sister?"

Ashe swore silently. She was a civilian with neither the knowledge nor resources to create a false legend that would hold up to Vitaly's scrutiny. He asked quickly, "Does Vitaly know your real last name?"

"He knows my real first name, but I told him my last name is Smith and that everyone calls me Hank." She'd told him Max's last name was Kuznetsov—he caught the play on words and nodded. "*Kuznets*. Russian for *blacksmith*. You call yourself Smith. Got it."

"I use a local check-cashing service. They cash my paychecks for me in spite of the name discrepancy. After all, how many women out there are named Hank? It's a running joke with me and the manager that my employer keeps getting my name wrong on my checks."

It was a small misdirection, but possibly enough to throw off Vitaly in the short run. "Don't move. I'm going over to the phone to call the front desk."

He maneuvered around the catering table with their meal on it and headed unerringly toward the rotary phone sitting on the end of the bar. He pushed the operator button.

"Hey Gregory, it's Asher. You okay down there?"

A sound of exasperation in his ear. "Yes. The power's out up and down the whole street. Ever since Katrina, we have a blackout whenever it rains. It may be a few hours before the power company restores it. Would you like me to bring up some candles?"

"Nah. We're good. Call me if you need help with any of the guests."

"Thankfully, most of them are asleep. The worst of it will be making sure the morning's wake-up calls come off without a hitch."

"You can handle it," Ashe replied encouragingly. He hung up the phone and turned to face the darker shadow within the other shadows that was Hank. "The whole street lost power. This wasn't targeted at us. It's all good."

"Umm, okay."

He frowned. That was a faint tremor of some kind in her voice. "What's wrong?"

"Nothing."

He might not know much about women, but he did know one thing. When a woman sounded upset and then told you nothing was wrong, something was definitely wrong.

He moved swiftly toward her, and she cringed as he drew close. He stopped an arm's length in front of her, perplexed. "Tell me what's wrong so I can fix it," he demanded.

"I...nothing."

"Translation: something *is* wrong. Spill."

A sigh. A pause. Then, in a small voice, she confessed, "I'm afraid of the dark. Ever since the car crash, I hate being alone in the dark."

He stepped forward and swept her into a hug. She stiffened for a moment, and then her arms crept around his waist. Her hands were cold against his back, and he recalled with a start that he was shirtless. At least she had on that thick bathrobe for modesty's sake.

Gradually she relaxed against him. Even through the

fluffy robe, she was slender in his arms. She felt fragile and breakable. But maybe that impression came from the faint trembling still making her shudder.

"I've got you, kitten. No one's going to hurt you."

"Who are you?" she mumbled against his chest.

"I'm military." She knew that much already from Gregory. "I work on a Special Forces team." Which she could also assume from Gregory's "secret stuff" remark. He hoped she didn't know enough about the armed forces to ask for any more details than that. In an effort to distract her, he asked, "What do you think Max was doing in the Voodoo?"

"I don't know. I can't imagine him going into a place like that on his own."

He pursed his lips above her head. Her perfect big brother didn't have male urges or look at half-naked women, huh? Color Hank naive.

She continued, "I figure it had something to do with his job. But I can't imagine what."

"You said he's an art and antiques dealer, right? Have you ever seen Vitaly show an interest in that sort of stuff?"

She snorted against his chest. "He wouldn't know a piece of art if it reached out and bit him."

"Is it possible that Max went there just to have a drink and…take in the scenery?"

Another snort. "Max is no monk. But sleazy strip joints with underage lap dancers are not his style."

Correction: Hank wasn't as naive as he'd thought. "You said he found art pieces and antiques for people. Is it possible that Vitaly or someone who frequents the Voodoo hired Max to find something?" As soon as he expressed the idea aloud, it felt right to him.

Hank sighed. "I've talked to all the regulars and brought

up the subject of art or antiques at one time or another. Nobody ever showed an interest in the subject."

Asher frowned. What if Max had been commissioned to find something that wasn't art? The same investigative techniques that an art dealer used might apply.

"What kind of education and training does your brother have?"

"He has an art history degree from Tulane University and an MBA. And my dad was an art finder. Taught him the ropes from the time he was a kid. He and my dad stayed close after my parents divorced."

"And you and your father? Did you stay close?" he asked.

"Not so much."

Ashe's arms tightened a little more around her. He knew how painful it was to feel unloved by a parent. This was the first time she'd mentioned her father. Hmm...maybe she had daddy issues, too. "Tell me about your dad."

Hank tensed against him. "My parents divorced when I was six. He got me every other Wednesday night for dinner and one weekend a month, assuming he was home that weekend. Which didn't happen often." She took a breath, let it out slowly. "Bottom line...I didn't know him well nor were we close. He died a few years after the accident."

"How?"

"No idea. Mom just got a notification from the Social Security Administration that because I was a minor, I would get a payment every month until I turned eighteen because my father had passed away."

Whoa. "And no one knows the cause of death?"

"I imagine someone knows. But nobody in my family knows."

She'd lost her father, then her mother, and then Max in

quick succession. Her obsession with finding her brother made a little more sense now.

Something rattled against the window, and Hank lurched against him. "Oh, God. What's that?" she whispered.

"That's a tree branch knocking against the window glass." He clutched her even closer. "I told you. I've got you. You're safe."

"We have to get out of here," she muttered frantically. "We're trapped. If someone barges in the door or through the window, we're sitting ducks."

"Oh, I don't know about that," he replied in a soft, reassuring voice. "It's pretty dark in here. And an intruder won't know the layout of the furniture like I do. There are plenty of spots we could go for cover, like behind the bar or in either bedroom. And those are solid oak doors to the bedrooms. A bad guy would have a hell of a time busting one of them down."

Hank was not calmed by his observations. She really was afraid and still trembled in his arms. Now probably was not the moment to lecture her on how unproductive fear was as an emotion nor to attempt to teach her techniques for managing and harnessing fear. Such training was standard ops in his line of work. While he occasionally registered momentary apprehension about a situation, fear was not something he allowed to creep into his psyche.

"What would make you feel safer?" he asked her.

"Could we go somewhere else?"

"Do you want to hide in a closet?" he suggested. He'd meant it as a joke, but he really was at a loss as to how to comfort a frightened civilian female.

"No," she answered quickly. "That would be too much like being in the car after the crash, waiting for help to come."

Oh, jeez. "How long did it take for someone to get you out of the car?" he asked gently.

"It took hours for someone to see us, and another two hours for fire trucks to come and rip the doors off to get me and my mom out. She quit moaning after about the first hour. I spent the rest of that time thinking my mom was dead…"

He gathered her even closer to him. God, that had to have been horrible. If he wasn't mistaken, something wet was touching his chest. She was crying? Aww, hell. He bent down, scooped her off her feet and carried her into his bedroom. He kicked the door shut and then sat down on his bed with her in his lap. He adjusted the big pile of pillows so he could recline against the headboard with her cradled in his arms.

"You've had a rough go of things, haven't you, Hank?"

Her shoulders shook harder.

"Go ahead. Let it all out. I won't melt." He'd learned over the years with his men that sometimes a good venting of all the pent-up emotions inside a person was therapeutic. Of course, with his guys, it usually happened over a bottle of whiskey and maybe a good old-fashioned bar fight.

But to his surprise, Hank seemed to fight off the crying jag. "I can't," she mumbled. "I have to be strong until I find Max."

It took some real toughness to reel back in the powerful emotions he'd just glimpsed. His admiration for her grew even more.

"What I need is distraction. Talk to me about your work, Ashe."

Oh, no. Not going there. His work was classified. And for some reason, he didn't want her to see his job when she looked at him. He wanted her to see *him.* Which went against all his training. In his line of work, the last thing an operator wanted was to be seen and noticed. Invisibility was his best friend. He commented wryly, "I do secret stuff for the military."

"Can you be more specific than that?"

"Nope," he replied lightly. "Anyway, I'm more interested in talking about your time at the Voodoo. What's it like working there?"

She was silent a long time before she finally answered, "It's appalling. The women there are treated like pieces of meat. It's degrading and soul-sucking. And I'm not even up on the catwalk or working in the back. Or, God forbid, upstairs."

"My lap dance notwithstanding?" he couldn't resist commenting.

"I was cornered into that by my own stupid temper. And for the record, that is the only lap dance I have ever performed."

"I'm honored."

She swatted his arm, and he laughed, low and deep in his chest.

All of a sudden, sexual tension hung in the darkness around them, thick and hungry. Hank burrowed closer against his side, and he stared down at the shadows wreathing her face, trying and failing to penetrate the dark to see her eyes.

She made a small sound of distress.

"Are you okay?" he asked immediately.

"No." A pause. "I want to kiss you, but I think it would be a mistake."

His entire being stilled, holding its breath. All of a sudden, he wanted nothing more in the entire world than for her to kiss him. Even if she was right that it would be a terrible mistake.

They weren't meant to be. He was the kind of man who

sucked at relationships, and she was too damned vulnerable to protect herself from him and his baggage.

"Don't kiss me if you're afraid of the dark, Hank. That's all you'll find inside me."

Chapter 6

Hank stared up at Ashe but was unable to make out his features. His warning resonated as truth in her head, but something visceral deep inside her didn't care in the least. She wanted this man.

The wanting was so foreign to her she hardly knew how to react to it. It had been one thing to casually date guys in college. She wasn't looking for an MRS degree, and the guys she'd slept with weren't looking to settle down, either. The sex had been easy. Fun. Not the slightest bit serious.

But this man would be different. For one thing, he was not some college frat boy who had no idea who he was or what he wanted out of life—or from the women he slept with. For another thing, an aura of danger clung to this man like a second skin. He didn't strike her as the type to do anything casually or just for fun.

He wasn't kidding. Darkness *did* cling to him. It draped around him like clothing. He breathed it in and out. Darkness was a part of him.

And still, she wanted to kiss him.

Was she trying to hide from her fears, or was she just pathetically lonely and trying to make a human connection with someone—anyone? Heck, maybe she was just horny. He was extremely hot, after all.

"Talk to me, Hank. I can't read you right now."

She huffed. "I'm overthinking the situation. I always do this."

"How's that?"

"I hear what you're saying. I appreciate you being decent enough to warn me off…and I get that I should steer clear of you and your inner darkness. But I still want to kiss you. Why am I feeling that way if, intellectually, I know that it's a bad idea?"

"You're not kidding. You *do* overthink things," he muttered. His body shifted quickly beneath her arm and her ear, and his mouth closed on hers without warning.

And he had not been wrong. Darkness closed in around her, enveloping her in corded muscles and a big, hard body as firm, warm lips claimed hers. Lust roared through her, but not just any lust. This was the real deal. Adult desire for passion and sweat and debauchery overtook her. She embraced the darkness within him. Threw herself into it. And was scared to death. But still she did it.

He kissed her like the night, stealing past her defenses, inspiring genuine terror as he showed her how she'd never really been kissed before. Not until now. This man was unlike any she'd ever known before. She was in over her head with him, totally unprepared to deal with a man like him. But still she kissed him.

He claimed her whole body, drawing her up against his large frame, his legs tangling with hers, his hands roaming across her back and plunging into her hair. His teeth nipped her ear, his lips outlined her jaw, his tongue traced her lips. And then he took her entire mouth with his, kissing her voraciously. She should have pulled away from him. Gotten up and left his bed that very minute. And still she stayed with him.

She surged against him, stunned at the fervent reaction he drew from her. Her wanting from before exploded into more. Into greed and gluttony and obsession. Something dark, indeed, clawed low in her belly, seeking release.

And then hot, strong fingers were on her skin as the bathrobe sagged away from her shoulders. His hands moved gently, but possessively, across her back. One hand swept around her ribs to cup her breast, and she cried out softly as his thumb rubbed across the sensitive peak.

"Tell me to stop now, kitten, or this is going to get out of hand."

"Don't stop," she gasped.

He swore under his breath. "I was afraid you'd say that."

"I want this. I want you, Ashe. I want the darkness."

"I'm not going to be good for you. I'll hurt you. Wreck your heart. Ruin you for any other man."

And still, Hank gave herself to him. She arched up into him in blatant invitation. She didn't just dive into the black lake of his soul. She did a running cannonball into it, crashing into him with a mighty splash, consequences be damned. She'd had enough of shying away from living. Of never taking chances. Of hiding from everything and everyone.

He seemed to sense her decision because his mouth lifted away from her skin and he stared down at her quizzically in the dark.

He wasn't going to pull away from her, was he? Fear that he would be the one to step away from this madness gripped her. She wrapped her arms around his neck and hung on for dear life. "Don't leave me, Ashe. Stay with me. Make love to me."

"Aww, hell. This is a crappy idea."

But his head lowered to hers once more and he kissed her again, more thoroughly this time. As if, now that the decision was made, he could slow down and take his time claiming her. His hands roamed her body more boldly now. He seemed interested in knowing where she was most sensitive, what made her inhale with surprise or exhale in pleasure.

He pushed her gently onto her back and finished unwrapping her from the bathrobe, laying it open on the bed. And then he explored her, head to foot, with his mouth and hands. He found ticklish spots she didn't even know she had and stirred her erogenous zones in ways she'd never dreamed possible.

The man stood for no evasion or shyness from her, but in return, he seemed to gustily enjoy every inch of her far-from-perfect body. Bless him. Gradually, she relaxed and even found herself impatient to explore his body the same way.

When she finally pushed at his shoulders, he gave way in spite of his vastly superior strength and let her explore him in return.

"What's this scar?" she murmured as her lips found a puckered circle on his shoulder.

"Gunshot. Long time ago. Africa." He sounded tense. Was she really turning him on enough that he was having to restrain himself that tightly? Cool.

She kissed her way across his washboard abs to his side. Just below his waist she encountered another scar, this time a thin line. She spoke against his warm skin. "Let me guess. You were stabbed here."

"No." He chuckled. "I had my appendix out when I was a kid."

She had trouble imagining this lethal panther of a man ever having been a child. Her fingers drifted across his lower belly, and the muscles there tightened violently. A faint groan rumbled through him.

She was too chicken to go for the obvious next target of exploration. Instead she trailed her fingertips down his muscular thigh to a long scar on the side of his knee that was self-explanatory and lower to his calves and feet.

"I used to massage my mother's feet to help her circulation," she murmured. "She couldn't feel it, though." She dug her thumbs into the arch of his foot and rubbed from heel to toe the way the physical therapist had shown her.

Another groan from Ashe.

"Did that hurt?" she asked quickly.

"God, no." She leaned down to suck his toes while she rubbed his arch again.

That game didn't last very long, though. Ashe surged upright and dragged her up his body, effectively ending her explorations. He laid her on her back and pinned her hands to the mattress with his, their fingers firmly interlocked.

"Last chance," he gritted out.

To do what? Back out of this insanity? Not a chance. She undulated against his body in crystal clear invitation. And he, not the slightest bit slow on the uptake, got the message. But just to be sure, she murmured, "I want you, Ashe."

"All right, then," he murmured. That almost sounded like relief in his voice. He was really holding himself back that hard on her account?

"Now would be nice."

He laughed under his breath and then went still, as if he were pausing to savor the moment.

Warmth flowed through her, and she lifted her head off the pillow to kiss him. She didn't know how else to give him permission to let go of all that tightly reined self-control.

He eased her knees apart with his and brushed her tangled hair off her face with one hand. "God, you're beautiful."

She didn't know if he could see it, but she smiled up at him. Her eyes were adjusting to the darkness enough for her to make out the grim set of his jaw and the incendiary desire blazing in his eyes.

And then his body demanded her full attention as he pressed slowly and inexorably into her. It had been a long time since she'd had sex, and her internal muscles clenched him tightly. Finally, seated to the hilt within her, he paused, staring down at her. What was he waiting for?

"Are you okay?" she asked anxiously.

A short laugh was his answer. "Honey, I haven't been this okay in a long time."

Huh. She'd assumed that he would be as cavalier about sex as he was about risking his life. But apparently, physical intimacy wasn't something he took for granted.

"Are *you* okay?" he asked.

"Completely." She smiled up at him shyly.

He began to move slowly, reverently even, within her. It felt incredible. She met each of his deliberate thrusts with one of her own, impatient for more. He maintained the maddeningly slow rhythm until she was all but sobbing with need into the crook of his neck and shoulder. Her body shuddered with pleasure every time he withdrew and then filled her to bursting again.

Her body grew damp with perspiration born of hunger, while his body grew slick with what she assumed was his excessive restraint. Desperate for him to let go, she clenched and unclenched her internal muscles and wrapped both arms and legs around him, drawing him deeper into her.

"Will you quit torturing me?" she finally complained.

"And here I was, thinking *you* were torturing *me*. I'd love to do this forever. I can't get enough of you."

"If I promise you can do this again anytime you want, will you stop trying to hold back?" she asked.

He laughed grimly. "Aww, kitten. You shouldn't have said that."

"I promise already!"

His chest shook with silent laughter, but the smile faded from his face as she stared up at him. The darkness overtook him once more and he pulled it close around himself, clothing himself in the night. He withdrew almost all the way from her and then drove forward into her with enough power to make her sob for real. Her entire body convulsed in ecstasy around the delicious invasion.

"Again," she gasped.

He obliged, wringing a soul-deep moan from her.

And then it was all about the sex. Slapping flesh and heavy breathing and sweat-slippery skin on skin. She gripped his flexed biceps braced on either side of her head, relishing his strength as he surged into her and she arched up against him. They were two waves crashing against one another, obliterating each other in the process. Over and over they collided, smashing each other to smithereens.

It was wild and uncontained, a raging storm breaking on the rocky coast of desire. She'd never experienced anything remotely like it. Sex swept her out of herself and threw her into a place of pure sensation, of exhilaration, of escape from the prison of her doubts and fears.

Something electric and galvanizing clawed at her insides, growing like a ravenous beast in her belly and consuming her from the inside out. The sensation was unfamiliar to her, but greed for more of it drove her onward, deeper into the darkness of their shared passion.

The sensation built until she thought she was going to explode. She paused for a second, shocked by what was happening to her. And then her whole body detonated in pleasure so intense that she arched against Ashe as taut as a drawn bow. A cry escaped her throat as the awful, delicious tension released all at once. The arrow flew, and her entire being resonated with the vibration of its flight. She shuddered uncontrollably against the bulwark of Ashe's unmovable body.

"What was that?" she gasped.

"Umm, an orgasm?" he mused.

"Wow. I get it now."

"You've never had one before?" he asked in surprise.

"I guess not."

He smiled, slow and possessive. "Well then. How about we do that to you again?"

He reached down between them to where their bodies joined. His thumb rolled back and forth across her slick, swollen bud, and she nearly spontaneously combusted. If her first orgasm had been an electric shock, this one was a bolt of lightning. It streaked through her like a million volts of pure sex. She arched up violently into him, her entire body spasming around the erection still buried deep within her.

He swore under his breath, and she echoed the sentiment. No common words could describe that. And then he was all restless heat within her and against her, his body growing ever more demanding of hers.

She had no inhibition left. The pair of orgasms had stripped all pretense of rational thought from her, leaving her a creature of sensation and delight, blinded by lust and hounded by greed for more.

She gripped his hips with all her strength and made ravaged sounds of pleasure as he lifted her hips in his hands and pounded into her with abandon. It wasn't elegant or sophisticated. It was raw and primal. And utterly glorious.

He slammed into her so deep she felt him in her throat as he convulsed against her, groaning from the depths of his being. At the sound of his pleasure, she met his release with yet another of her own.

It was so personal, so intimate, she had no words for it as she held him close and he panted over her, his body protectively covering hers.

He dropped his forehead to rest against hers. Even that seemed somehow more intimate than a mere kiss.

She was completely drained. Her entire being felt wrung out, her emotions and stress washed clean away, leaving behind a still, silent core of darkness deep inside her. But it was a peaceful dark. Quiet. Reflective.

Ashe's breathing recovered to something resembling normal much more quickly than hers did, but he did not move. He stayed right there—his legs tangled with hers, body sprawled against hers, torso propped up on his elbows, staring down at her for a long time after he was breathing slow and steady. He looked pensive, as well.

At long last, he murmured huskily, "What am I going to do with you?"

She stared up at him, not understanding the question.

He dropped a kiss on the tip of her nose and pushed away from her. He rolled to his back, an arm thrown over his face.

Frightened at the abruptness of his departure, both physical and emotional, she followed him, propping herself on his chest with her forearm. "What's wrong, Ashe? Talk to me."

He lifted his arm away from his face to stare at her bleakly. "That changed everything."

Full-blown panic tore through her. "How? How do I put it back the way it was?" she cried.

"That's the thing. Nothing will ever be the same after that."

"What was wrong with it?" She'd thought the sex had been spectacular. Beyond spectacular.

He made a sound that he'd probably meant to be laughter, but it bore more resemblance to a bark of disbelief. He shoved a hand through his disheveled dark hair. Swore. Then he asked, "Are you kidding? Nothing was *wrong* with it. That was…it was—" A pause. "Hell, there are no words to describe how perfect that was."

"Then what's the problem?" she asked in a small voice. He wasn't saying anything to alleviate her panic here.

He frowned up at her. Swept her hair back from her face. "I can't let you go after that. I can't walk away."

He'd been planning to walk away from her? When? Tonight? Tomorrow? In two weeks, after the club was raided? Or was it the fact that they hadn't used protection? Which had been really dumb. She was on birth control pills to regulate her cycle, but protection with a new sexual partner was Common Sense 101. Was he worried about that—?

"You're overthinking again, Hank. I can see it in your eyes."

"Then explain it to me. Why can't you walk away? Where were you planning to go? And when? Is there something wrong with me—?"

He pressed his fingers against her lips. "I already told you the sex was perfect. *You're* perfect. There's nothing wrong with you. It's me. I'm the problem. I suck at relationships. I don't do…this."

She spoke against his fingertips. "You don't have sex? You're pretty good at it for someone who doesn't do—"

His fingers tightened against her mouth. "Enough already," he growled. "Give me a minute to try to get the words right. I don't talk about this sort of thing often."

She backed off, frustrated but trying to be patient for his sake.

"My life, my job...hell, I suppose my personality... none of them are set up to include relationships. I have colleagues who are friends. When I get some downtime I occasionally hook up with a woman. But the real stuff— love and commitment and promises—I don't have time for all of that."

A sharp knife slid home in her heart, and she felt herself beginning to bleed out emotionally. She rolled away from him, onto her back, to stare up at the ceiling. God, she'd been an idiot not to tell him to stop when he'd given her a chance to. He'd known this moment was coming.

His voice floated out of the darkness from beside her. "But then you happened. This outrageous sex happened. I'm not the only one feeling some sort of...connection... between us, am I?"

"No," she answered in a quavering voice.

"Exactly. And now I don't know what to do about you."

He said that like she was a horrible and unwelcome complication in his life. The knife in her heart twisted, shredding more of the organ's fragile wall. The pace of the emotional bleeding increased. She was dying. Yet again, a man was rejecting her. Leaving her. First her father. Then her brother. And now Ashe.

Chapter 7

Ashe felt Hank withdrawing from him as surely as if she'd gotten up out of the bed and walked away. God, he was terrible at this emotion stuff. He propped himself up on an elbow to stare down at her.

"Listen to me, Hank. I'm not bailing on you. I'm trying to tell you that I think I need to do the whole relationship thing with you. Or try, at least."

"What?" She sounded as blank as her expression looked. Wow. She thought he wasn't relationship material, either.

"I can't promise to be any good at it. In fact, I can pretty much promise to screw it up royally. But there's something about you...you're different. Special. I'd be a damned fool to walk away from you."

A frowned puckered her brow. "Thanks—I think," she said hesitantly.

An ugly sensation skittered down his spine. It was bigger than apprehension. Bigger than doubt. But he couldn't name it. Didn't she feel it, too? Was he the only one feeling a crazy connection between them, like they'd known each other forever and were two halves of the same whole?

Fear. That was the thing crawling along his spine. He went into crisis mode, clamping down on the sensation as unproductive, setting aside and closing it in a little box in a corner of his mind. Now, to deal with the crisis that had provoked it.

He threw her own words back at her. "What's wrong, Hank? Talk to me."

"I'm not sure anything is *wrong.*" She laughed a little. Ruefully. "I just didn't expect you to be as scared of a relationship as I am. I guess we kind of are a perfect fit for one another, after all. We can be terrified together."

How did she do that? She'd known he was feeling fear almost before he did. He scowled down at her. "I don't do fear, dammit."

"Right. You're a highly trained Special Forces operative who can take on any threat...except a scrawny female who couldn't even put a dent in you if she tried," she teased lightly.

He had to grin at that. The tension of the moment broken, he gathered her against his side, her head resting on his shoulder. "I can show you some moves that would hurt a guy of my size and strength. You should probably know how to defend yourself from the jerks in the club, anyway."

"After you staked your claim on me the way you did earlier, I can't imagine any of the regulars will bother me," she reminded him. "And besides, Vitaly loaned me to you for your exclusive use. He won't let anyone mess with me."

"Huh. He and I agree on one thing, then."

"Well, yeah, but for totally different reasons."

He shrugged beneath her. "I'll take it. I'd hate to have to kill some scumbag and blow the whole operation."

"Don't do anything rash on my account!" she exclaimed.

"That place needs to be shut down for good and those girls rescued."

"The Who Do Voodoo is going down, regardless." He shrugged again. "But as for not doing rash things to protect you, that's not how I roll. You're mine now. And I protect my own."

"You do realize that sounds a little creepy and stalkerish, right?"

He dropped a kiss into her hair. "Look, I'm not trying to be a wacko control freak by making it clear to the people around me that you're my personal possession." Clearing his throat, he admitted, "Truth is, Hank, I don't actually see women that way at all. It's purely a safety thing for you. I'm merely making the rules of engagement with my enemy known. Mess with you—" he stroked her jaw lightly "—and you're messing with me."

She snuggled a little closer to him.

"My deal with Vitaly for you was just part of my cover story. That, and to give you some protection when you're in the club from now on. You're free to walk away from me anytime you want. I won't stop you."

"Really?" she asked, a slight hitch in her voice.

"Hey, don't get me wrong. I'll try to convince you to stay. But I would never force you to do anything against your will."

"And that's where you and Vitaly are different," she said quietly.

He sighed in relief. She got it. Thank goodness. Sometimes he forgot how different he was from most men, how weird most civilians would think he was if they actually knew how he thought and functioned.

"If you ever don't understand why I say or do something, promise me you'll ask me about it before you just walk away, Hank. I'll do my damnedest to explain myself."

It was her turn to press her fingertips to his mouth. "It's okay. We'll figure this out together. I'm not going to scream and run for cover just yet."

Easy for her to say now, in the afterglow of their lovemaking. But foreboding filled him at how she would react the first time she saw him do his job for real. He could harm—or kill—without blinking an eye. It wasn't that he was a monster. But in his world, sometimes people were in need of erasing. And sometimes he was the man called to do the job.

Hank woke up with a jolt. Light streamed in through the window. Too much light for her bedroom over the rug shop—

Not the rug shop. A hotel. A suite with...oh, Lord... Ashe's bed. She turned her head to look for him, and he was lying on his side facing her, his big body curled protectively toward her. The moment she moved, his eyes popped open, instantly alert. The man really was a warrior at heart. And apparently he slept as lightly as a feather.

"Good morning," he murmured.

She smiled at him sleepily. "'Morning. How'd you sleep?"

He grinned broadly. "Better than I have in months. You?"

She'd slept surprisingly well considering how much stress she'd been under and how worried she'd been when the power went out last night. Apparently, mind-blowing sex was good for a person's rest. Go figure. "I slept very well, thank you."

His voice was deep and smooth as he murmured, "You're welcome." He reached out with a hand to brush her hair back from her face. "In case I haven't told you today, you take my breath away."

"We've been awake ten seconds."

"I'm running nine seconds slow on the uptake, then."

Warmth unfurled in her tummy. For a guy who thought he sucked at relationships, he was doing pretty well so far.

"Do you have any plans today?" he asked.

"It's Sunday, so the Voodoo is closed. It's my day off."

"Excellent. You can come to brunch with me and meet my aunt Eloise."

"The owner of this place?" Alarm burst through her like an exploding firework. The only clothes she had with her were the trashy fake-leather miniskirt, skimpy tank top and red lace bra she'd worn to work last night at the Voodoo. No *way* was she meeting the owner of this elegant establishment wearing haute slut couture.

"She's awesome. You'll love her. And she's going to be fascinated by any female who can capture my attention."

Eloise wanted to meet the woman good enough in the sack to impress her nephew? Somehow, Hank doubted that.

Ashe rolled out of the far side of the bed in a quick, agile move, and Hank enjoyed the view as he strolled into the bathroom, naked and unconcerned. Why was it men were so uninhibited about their bodies? She would have given anything not to worry about how she looked.

He called out of the bathroom, "I'm going to take a shower. Feel free to join me if you want. Auntie El can wait a little while longer for breakfast."

She smiled ruefully. While she would love to join him and discover what athletic endeavors were possible with a man of his strength in a shower, making her escape while he was out of sight was more imperative. She was *not* having brunch with his aunt, and that was all there was to it. It would be disrespectful in the extreme to force any decent woman to dine with some chick dressed like a ho.

Hank jumped up, hurried to her bedroom, threw on her clothes, and slipped out of the suite as quickly and quietly as she could. The water in the shower was still running as she closed the hallway door behind her.

Afraid to wait around for the elevator, she raced down the stairs, all but running through the lobby to the street. A taxi was just dropping off someone at the hotel, and she was able to jump in the backseat and take off in under a minute. The driver looked at her askance when she gave him the address of her apartment. He must think she was the luckiest streetwalker in town to have landed a client this far uptown when she lived that far downtown. Traffic was light on a Sunday morning, and he dropped her off at her place in under a half hour.

It felt weird to step into the squalor of her apartment after the grandeur of the Hotel Fontenac. The dirty walls, threadbare carpet and worn-out furniture in her place looked more depressing than ever. It was all part of her cover, though. Until she found Max, she was a waitress in a strip club who couldn't afford a nicer place.

She took a quick shower and dressed in white jeans and her mint-green brushed-silk oxford shirt. It was the kind of shirt she wouldn't be ashamed to meet Aunt Eloise in. She was just heading to her refrigerator to see if the milk was still good when pounding erupted at her front door. She jolted, alarmed.

"Hank! Are you in there? Let me in."

Ashe. And he sounded pissed. She winced and reluctantly unlocked the door.

He loomed in the doorway looking more ravaged than she expected. "Really?" he said without preamble. "You couldn't talk to me before you just took off?"

"I didn't want to meet your aunt looking like a streetwalker."

He frowned. "You don't look like a streetwalker."

"All I had to wear was my waitress uniform. It was bad

enough walking through the lobby wearing that getup. I bloody well wasn't having lunch in the formal dining room with your aunt in those rags!"

"You could have told me."

"You're a man. You wouldn't have listened to—"

He cut her off sharply. "Back up. Inside your apartment. Now."

Startled, she took several steps backward. He followed her aggressively, closing the door behind her and crowding her away from the window with his body. "What on earth?"

"Close the curtain over the sink without standing in front of the window," he ordered her tersely. "I'll get the bedroom curtains."

"What's going on?"

He shook his head in the negative and didn't answer her. He emerged from her bedroom and commenced prowling along the back wall of her apartment, staring at it like he was looking for something. "What are you—?"

He turned fast, grabbed her by the shoulders and yanked her up hard against him, growling, "I didn't give you permission to leave my place."

She stared up at him, shocked. The expression in his eyes was completely at odds with his angry tone of voice. He looked at her almost pleadingly. *What the heck?*

"I don't understand…"

"What is there to understand? Vitaly gave you to me. You're mine. I say what you do. Where you go."

He let go of her, leaving her staring at him in complete confusion as he moved over to her kitchen drawers and commenced rummaging in them. What was wrong with him? He was acting like a crazy man.

He found a sticky pad and a pencil and brought them

over to her. He tore off a note and scribbled on it quickly and showed it to her. *Your place is bugged.*

She stared down at the words but they refused to compute. Snipers? Bugs? Her? None of it made sense.

He wrote another note. *Warehouse space behind your back wall?*

She nodded in the affirmative.

We need to break through the wall. Can't go out the door.

Ahh. He was looking for another way out of here. She moved over to the television cabinet perched against the back wall of the living space and gestured for him to help her move it. He frowned but crossed over beside her. The unit squeaked as they slid it to one side, revealing a door. It led downstairs into the back office of the rug store. The owner had no doubt used the stairway to slip up for visits to his mistress.

Ashe examined the nails holding the door shut and pantomimed using a hammer to pry them out. She nodded and moved over to the kitchen drawer to bring him a hammer.

He took it from her, and then perplexed her by taking off his belt and doubling it over. Speaking loudly and clearly, he declared, "I'm going to have to teach you a lesson, aren't I?"

She frowned, lost.

He slapped the belt against his thigh, and it cracked loudly. She jumped, startled by the noise.

He growled, "You'll howl before I'm done with you."

Oh. She was supposed to make noise to cover up whatever he was about to do. Got it. He handed her the belt. She slapped her thigh with the leather strap and cried out in fake pain. Ashe pried out the first nail in time with her shout.

She waited for him to position the hammer at the next

nail. He nodded, and she repeated the slapping-howling maneuver. There were a dozen nails in the door, and she was having to restrain giggles between her piteous cries by the time the door was freed. Ashe tested the doorknob, and it was locked.

He moved close to her, lifting the belt gently out of her hand. He kissed her temple lightly, breathing against her skin, "Go pack a few things in a bag you can carry easily while I pick this lock. It'll take me two or three minutes."

She stepped back and smiled up at him. Then she sobbed theatrically, "You're a beast. I hate you."

He called after her as she retreated into the bedroom, "I don't care. You're still mine to do whatever I want with."

She mouthed "I dare you" and then disappeared into the bedroom. She heard him chuckling in the living room as she tossed clothes and toiletries into a duffel bag.

When she stepped back out into the main room, Ashe had the door open and was pointing a small flashlight down a dark staircase. Of course he happened to have a flashlight stowed on his person. He was just that kind of man.

Ashe gestured her over to him and lifted the bag out of her hands. He tossed it over his shoulder as she passed by him, and they started down the steps with him leading the way. She pulled the door shut quietly and locked it before following the narrow beam of bright light into the bowels of the warehouse below.

She held the flashlight for Ashe as he picked the lock at the lower end of the staircase. Eventually they stepped out into a messy office with piles of paper everywhere. The rug merchant was apparently not much of a believer in using the filing cabinets lining the walls of the tight space.

Ashe picked up the receiver of the old rotary phone on the desk and dialed a number. "Hey, Catfish, it's Hol-

lywood. What are the odds you can get your hands on a
clean vehicle and bring it over to that rug shop I had you
check out night before last?"

Ahh. Ashe was talking to the cop. Bastien Something.
The police officer replied, but she couldn't make out the
words. Ashe replied drolly, "A van. The creepy kind with
no windows that kids are taught not to get into."

She heard tinny laughter, and then Ashe hung up. He
turned to face her. "He'll be here in an hour. Until then,
we're sitting tight and seeing if this place has an exit out
the back way."

"It does. Loading dock's at the back of the building,"
she supplied.

"Perfect."

"Care to tell me what the hell all that stuff upstairs
was about?" she demanded. "Why did you hustle me out
of there like that?"

"When you were standing in the doorway, a laser dot
pinged on your throat."

"A what?" Foreboding formed a knot low in her stomach.

"Laser dot. As in a little red light from a laser sight. It
shone on you for just a second. Right here." He reached
out and touched the base of her throat with his fingertip.
"Snipers use them to measure the distance to their target."

"You're telling me a sniper just pointed a gun at me?"
she cried. "That's nuts!"

"I'm telling you someone with a sniper's scope was
looking at you through it and measured how far away you
were from him or her. Whether or not it was attached to
a rifle, I couldn't say."

She opened her mouth to declare him mistaken, but
he forestalled her with, "This is my work, Hank. I'm not
wrong. I know what I saw."

She studied him closely. He didn't *look* crazy.

"But who?" she finally asked. "Why? And a sniper? What would someone like that want with me? I'm nobody. Is someone trying to send *you* a message?"

That made him study *her* thoughtfully. "Possible. But not probable. Most of the people I piss off are overseas. Or dead. No, that dot was for you."

"I ask again. Why me?"

He moved over to a red velveteen love seat that matched her sofa upstairs. "Come sit down. You look tense."

Frowning, she perched on the edge of the settee. He held an arm out to her, and she couldn't resist the invitation to cuddle against his beckoning chest and all those wonderful muscles.

"Why did you leave this morning?" he asked quietly. "Tell me the truth. I won't be mad no matter what you say."

"I was ashamed."

"Of me?"

"No! Of me. I didn't want your aunt to think I'm a cheap slut."

His arm tightened around her. "I would never sleep with a woman like that, and I certainly wouldn't introduce my aunt to one. Have a little faith in yourself."

She shook her head and didn't bother to argue. When she met his family, she wanted to look and feel like a lady. Assuming Vitaly and the Voodoo hadn't stripped that part of her completely away and destroyed it for good.

"You tensed up again just now. Why?"

Did Ashe have to be so darned perceptive? "It's nothing," she mumbled.

"We already discussed that. When you say nothing's wrong, it means something is wrong."

"Are you always this pushy?"

"Pretty much." He flashed her a wry smile that totally

derailed her irritation. He was so good-looking it was hard to maintain her train of thought, let alone argue with him.

She scowled. "I'm worried that the Voodoo has rubbed off on me."

"And done what?"

She admitted, "And made me...as dirty and unfeeling as Vitaly."

He laughed heartily at that. "You, my dear, reek of class. You'll never fit into that place. It's the thing about you that initially caught my attention. You were a pearl in a pig pen."

She pushed up from his side to stare at him. "You're not just saying that to make me feel better?"

The humor drained from his expression, leaving behind an intensity that would have been frightening if she didn't trust him already. "I have a bad habit of telling the unvarnished truth, Hank. It's part of why I don't do well in relationships with women."

She studied him as she considered that. After the last few months of living a double life among people like Vitaly who were wreathed in dangerous secrets, honesty sounded pretty darned good.

She nodded slowly. "I can live with you telling the truth, even if it hurts sometimes. But if I ever ask if something I'm wearing makes me look fat, you still have to answer no."

"Deal." He leaned down to kiss her and she sighed in delight, melting against him eagerly. She simply couldn't get enough of him. He was so masculine and confident, and he made her feel sexy and feminine and desirable. And he could kiss like a god. His mouth moved across hers like he genuinely enjoyed tasting her.

"I'm sorry I left without talking to you," she eventually murmured against his delectable mouth. "I should have trusted you to understand. Or at least to respect my wishes."

"I still don't understand, kitten. No one could look at you and see anything tawdry."

"Spoken like a man. Women are much quicker to judge on appearance than guys, apparently. And I've been wallowing in the mud for a while. I'm worried that some of it has rubbed off on me."

"Nah. You're just naturally classy, darlin'."

"That's me," she said wryly. "Class in a glass."

He stared down at her while she gazed up at him a shade apprehensively. "I'm serious, Hank."

"I know. You and that whole unvarnished truth thing—"

"Exasperating female. I'd make love to you right now to shut you up, but I don't know how soon Bastien will arrive."

"You can kiss me some more," she purred. "That might shut me up."

He grinned at her. "I like the way you think."

And that was the end of any talking for a while.

She loved the fact that he was willing to make out with her and not necessarily make love to her. Although he did groan when his phone vibrated in his pocket. "That'll be Bastien," he grumbled against the side of her neck.

Apprehension slammed through her as she abruptly recalled that a sniper was lying in wait for her outside. Although she was still halfway convinced the shooter was after Ashe and not her. "How exactly are we getting out of here without getting shot at?"

He held up a finger to tell her to hold that thought and answered his phone. "Hey, Bastien. You got it? Great. Pull up at the loading dock behind the rug warehouse. We'll meet you back there."

Ashe stood up and held a hand down to her. "Your chariot awaits, my lady."

"In case I haven't told you yet today, you're a pretty amazing man, Asher."

He froze, still holding her hand, and stared at her intensely for several long moments. "Thanks," he said gruffly. Like he was touched and not sure how to express it. Like he didn't entirely believe her.

Note to self: compliment Ashe until he believes that he is as special and lovable as he really is.

The office opened onto a short hallway. One end obviously led to the storefront, and the other probably went to the storage and cleaning facility she knew to be in the back. Ashe turned toward the rear of the building. The warehouse door was unlocked, and they stepped out into a dim space that smelled like wet wool. Rolled rugs were stacked around the edges of the room in tall bays.

Ashe snagged a baseball cap off a hook by the door and slapped it on his head before he lifted one of the big garage doors at the back of the space. A rusty, once-white van was just pulling up outside.

A big, good-looking guy cut from the same cloth as Ashe got out of the driver's seat and came inside.

"Bastien LeBlanc, meet Hank Smith."

Bastien grinned, flashing a killer set of dimples. "Pleasure, Hank. Interesting name—"

"This may be the future Mrs. Konig, dude. Think carefully before you tease her about her name. I would hate to have to kill you."

Hank's head whipped in Ashe's direction nearly as fast and hard as Bastien's did. *Mrs. Konig?* Her jaw dropped.

Ashe spoke blithely, ignoring their reactions to his comment. "I was thinking we could wrap Hank in a rug and carry her out of here. I don't think there will be sniper coverage on the back of this place, but I can't be sure. This Vitaly Parenko character is a slick sonofabitch. Suspicious as hell. Tightest security I've seen in a long time."

"And you say he's running a sex trafficking outfit?" Bastien responded. "NOPD wasn't aware of it. Which means his operation *is* tight as hell. We've got a pretty damned good informant network in this town."

"Either that or someone in the department is protecting him."

Bastien shrugged. "Let's just say rumors of police corruption in New Orleans are greatly exaggerated. That may have been true twenty or thirty years ago, but we've cleaned up our act. It works to our advantage to let criminals think we'll look the other way, so we help the reputation persist."

Ashe moved over to a bay holding a dozen rugs that were maybe eight feet tall. "Would one of these fit in the van?"

"With the girl wrapped in it?" Bastien looked at her appraisingly. "If we load it on the diagonal, it'll go."

Ashe hauled one of the rugs out and unrolled it on the floor. "In you go, Hank."

She stared askance at the thick Persian rug. "You do know I'm not fond of small, confined spaces, right?"

Understanding lit his darkly handsome face. She'd been trapped in a mangled car with her dying mother for hours. In a tiny, terribly confined space. "I'll let you out as soon as we're away from here. Just a couple of minutes. I promise. And I'll be with you the whole time."

She could do this. She knew where her fear came from and that it was unfounded. It was just a rug. Kind of like a really thick blanket. And Ashe would take care of her. She took a deep breath and lay down on the rug. Ashe and Bastien rolled her up gently.

Oh, God. It was tight. And hot. And she couldn't draw a deep breath. And wool dust made her need to cough. But she dared not give away that she was in here. Terror choked her as she was hoisted in the air.

"Okay in there, kitten?" Ashe's voice came to her muffled and distant.

"Uh-huh," she managed to gasp.

"We're heading outside now...and into the van..." She felt herself being lowered. A hard surface supported her once more. And then she was sliding. A door slammed nearby. Another door.

"Almost done, baby. You're doing great."

No. She wasn't. But there wasn't a thing she could do about it. She was suffocating, and she had to trust Ashe not to let her die.

An engine started. The floor lurched into motion. Bounced over a curb or something. She rolled to one side a little as the van turned. She counted from ten to one in her head. That was it. That was all she could take.

"Let me out, Ashe. I can't breathe. *Oh, God...*"

The rug unrolled, twirling her around and dumping her on her side as she emerged from the layers of her wool mummification. And then Ashe's arms were there, lifting her. Wrapping her in safety.

"I've got you, baby. You're fine. Breathe out slowly. In again. Now out." He coached her down from hyperventilating as if she were a frightened child.

"Better?" he asked.

She nodded against his chest. He held her protectively until she was finally able to look up and mumble, "Sorry about that."

"It's okay." And then he kissed her like he really meant it.

"When you two lovebirds come up for air, maybe you

could tell me where we're going?" Bastien complained from the driver's seat.

"Someplace we can talk," Ashe replied. "And it goes without saying to make sure we're not followed."

"I didn't fall off the turnip wagon yesterday, bro."

Ashe grinned down at her. "I trained him. I'd have kicked his ass if he skipped a basic operational procedure like that."

Bastien told him succinctly and crudely what he could do with his procedure, and Hank laughed in genuine amusement as the two men spent the next few minutes trading insults.

"Do you miss the teams, Catfish?" Ashe eventually asked.

"Nah. Plenty of excitement in my current job."

"Found a woman yet?"

"Who says I'm looking?"

Ashe rolled his eyes at her behind Bastien's back. "The ladies always hung all over you, dude. I figured one would've snagged you by now."

"Hah. Says the pot to the kettle, Hollywood."

"Yeah, but I mostly ignored the ladies. You were happy to take whatever they wanted to…offer you."

Hank had no trouble believing that their handsome driver was a ladies' man. She had a little more trouble believing that Ashe was not one also, however. "Tell me the truth, Bastien," she piped up. "Does Ashe really ignore women?"

The cop glanced at her in the rearview mirror. "Yeah, he actually does. He's always too busy being the job. Your boyfriend has a tendency toward suicidal heroics."

Her boyfriend? Was that what Ashe was? She looked over at him quickly, and he merely shrugged. She turned her attention back to Bastien. "What kind of suicidal heroics?"

"You'll have to ask him. I'll tell no tales, *chère*."

She turned expectantly to Ashe, who merely shrugged again. "Am I going to have to tickle the truth out of you?" she demanded.

"You can try," he replied evenly. Somehow the complete lack of threat in his tone managed to convey a world of threat.

"Oh, I think I know how to make you talk," she murmured.

His eyes glinted in challenge. "Be my guest."

"Here and now?" she squeaked.

"Bastien knows what sex looks like. He'll keep his eyes on the road. Won't you buddy?"

"Hey, leave me out of this domestic dispute. I'm just the wheel man."

Lord, these guys were unlike any she'd ever been around. No filters at all. She shook her head and subsided, leaning back against the side of the van with her arms crossed.

Ashe laughed under his breath. "Don't pout, kitten. I'll give you a chance to make me talk later."

"You are a bad, bad man. And you're embarrassing me."

Grimacing, he surged forward immediately to join her on her side of the van. "I didn't mean to embarrass you. I'm sorry."

"It's okay. Really." Intense, too, these special operators.

The van pulled to a stop, and Bastien turned off the engine.

"Where are we?" Ashe called forward.

"My place. And we're in the garage. You can come out and no one will see you."

Ashe opened the rear door, hopped out and held a hand

in to help her. She stepped out into a barnlike structure that resembled a fancy auto repair shop more than a regular residential garage. She looked around in amazement.

"I restore old cars," Bastien commented.

"So I gather," she replied.

"House is this way."

Off to one side of the large metal building was a walled off area. Bastien ducked through a door and held it gallantly for her. "After you, Mrs. Konig," he murmured as she moved past him.

Shock coursed through her as Ashe merely put an arm around her shoulders and pulled her close as they stepped into what turned out to be a small, but beautifully appointed, kitchen.

"I also like to cook," Bastien said a little shyly. "Speaking of which, are you guys hungry? You called me just as I was getting ready to eat."

She hadn't eaten since the picnic last night in the Hotel Fontenac. "Can I help cook?" she offered.

"Sit. I'm more efficient on my own. And this place is too small for two cooks."

Ashe sank onto the banquette seat and startled her by drawing her down onto his lap. He certainly wasn't shy about showing his affection for her in front of his friend.

Wielding a whisk, Bastien spoke grimly. "What's going on, Ashe?"

While the cop made what appeared to be an omelet, but stuffed with more veggies, chopped meat and grated cheese than she'd ever seen in one omelet before, Ashe filled in his old friend.

Bastien absorbed the entire briefing in silence until the part about the laser dot. At that, he burst out, "Why's a sniper targeting Hank? She's a small fish. Best used as bait to reel in the bigger fish. You don't kill the bait!"

Was she supposed to be comforted by that? Somehow the idea of being bait made her more nervous than ever. It made her sound entirely expendable.

Ashe shook his head. "Dunno."

"Unless she's rattled some cage you guys aren't aware of. I assume you've been asking around the Voodoo about your brother, yes?" Bastien asked her.

"Of course. But I never asked more than one or two people at a time. And I never made a big deal of it."

"Still. You brought up a name that someone might not have wanted to hear." Bastien asked Ashe, "You run his name through ops yet?"

"Yup. Waiting on Jennie Finch to get back to me."

"How about Vitaly?"

"Same."

"Then I guess we eat and wait to see what she comes up with," Bastien declared.

The two men made small talk, mostly about mutual acquaintances and a little about Bastien's work as a cop, while the omelet baked. Eventually a timer buzzed, and Bastien whisked a big cast-iron skillet out of the oven. A ginormous puffy omelet filled the pan. Their host plated a huge pile of hash browns and the ham steaks that had been sizzling on the stove.

After last night's romantic athletics and this morning's scare, she was ravenous. She dug in with gusto, as did the two men. She couldn't believe they ate everything on the table, but eventually an assortment of bare plates stretched away before her. She stood up to do the dishes, but Ashe and Bastien waved her back down. She relented and let the two men do cleanup duty.

They were both big, muscular men, but they moved with an easy grace that defied their size. It was not a hardship to sit here, stuffed to the gills on good food, and watch the two of them work together. And to think one of them actually liked her.

Mrs. Konig? Where on earth had that remark come from? It must be more of that territory-marking thing Ashe had mentioned last night. Relieved to have made sense of that mystery, she sat back and relaxed.

Ashe's phone rang just as Bastien was putting away the last dishes. He pulled it out and glanced at it. "Jennie," he bit out.

Bastien sat down at the table immediately, as did Ashe, who answered the phone. "You're on speakerphone, Jen. Everyone at this end is cleared to hear anything you have to say."

"Uhh, some of this stuff's pretty classified," a woman's voice responded.

"I'm with Bastien LeBlanc and Miss Smith."

"Hey, Catfish!"

"Long time no hear, Finchie. How come you no callin' me? You gotta man on de hook?"

Hank grinned at the sudden and thick Cajun accent.

"I may be heading that way sooner than you think, Swamp Boy," Jennie retorted. "You've walked into a hornet's nest, Ashe. I had no choice but to brief Commander Perriman, and he wants to talk to you. He's flying to Washington, DC, tonight, but when he gets there, he's going to call you. Keep your phone on."

Hank looked up at Ashe in alarm. That sounded serious. Some military muckety-muck was getting involved in this? What in the world was Max doing? Fear for her brother filled her lungs until she could hardly draw her next breath.

"What the hell?" Ashe muttered. "What's Hank mixed up in, Jen?"

Chapter 8

Crud. Perriman was taking a personal interest in the search for Hank's brother? Ashe seriously hoped it was to deal with whatever was going on at the Voodoo and not to fire him from the teams and yank him off active duty for good.

Jennie Finch spoke grimly. "You were right, Ashe. Vitaly Parenko is an alias. He's been Vitaly Parenko for going on a decade now."

Ashe asked somberly, "Is he actually Russian?"

"Most likely," Jennie answered. "You reported that he sounds like a native Russian speaker. I'm gonna go with the obvious and say he is."

"Did the Russian mob build his fake identity?" Ashe asked.

"Possible. They've got enough ex-KGB types to know how to do it."

"Has he got a record?"

"Checked it," Jennie replied. "Ran his face against the FBI and Interpol wanted lists. Nada."

Ashe frowned. "Okay, so he's a Russian mobster living under a fake name. Why a strip club in New Orleans?"

"Money," Hank piped up. "He complains all the time about his bosses taking all the money from the club."

"Who owns the club?" Bastien asked.

Jennie answered, "Public records indicate a man named Al Nichols owns the property. Can't find anything on him whatsoever. Another alias, if I had to guess."

Bastien frowned. "Who runs the whorehouse, then? Hank, does Vitaly run the upstairs operation, too?"

She shrugged. "He goes up there every hour or so like he's checking in on things. But he spends most of his time downstairs in the bar."

Ashe leaned forward, nodding at Bastien, who nodded back. They were thinking in the same direction. If Vitaly wasn't sitting right on top of the sex trafficking operation, then that meant somebody else was. Who was running the brothel?

Ashe turned to Hank. "Have you ever overheard anyone talking about the upstairs operation with Vitaly or with someone else?"

"No."

"How many regulars pass through the club to go upstairs? Do any of them look or act like management?"

"Lots of customers have a drink—or five—and then head upstairs," she replied. "The problem, though, is that there's a rear exit from the lap dance lounge. This theoretical manager of yours could be coming and going through that door, and I would never see him or her in the main bar."

"Sounds like a stakeout's forthcoming," Ashe commented with a heavy sigh.

"Be my guest, man. You're on your own tonight because I'm pulling a double shift, but I'm off tomorrow," Bastien replied.

Hank supplied, "Things shut down upstairs—or at least it gets quiet and customers quit coming and going—by about three a.m. most nights. If whoever runs the brothel leaves at night, it would happen around that time."

Ashe nodded. "What else have you got for us, Jennie?"

"About the missing man. Max Kuznetsov."

Hank visibly tensed and Ashe asked grimly, "What about him?"

"I've got his cell phone records for the last few weeks before he dropped out of sight. I'm still running names, but I thought maybe Miss Smith could take a look at the names and numbers and see if any stand out."

"Sure," Ashe replied. "And you can call her Hank. Email me the list of names."

"Just a sec…done."

"Anything else?"

"Yeah," Jennie said a little reluctantly. "His fake ID was nearly as good as Vitaly's."

"Fake ID?" Hank squawked. "What are you talking about?"

"That's not his real name, of course."

"Yes it is! I've known him my whole life. That's always been his name."

"Well, his alleged father, this Yevgeni Kuznetsov guy, doesn't exist. I can only conclude that his whole family history is a ruse."

Hank stared in disbelief, first at the phone and then at Ashe. She stammered, "I have pictures. Memories. I grew up with Max. With both of them. They existed."

Ashe reached across the table to grasp her hand. "We'll figure it out. Jennie's the best. She'll unravel this mystery."

"*I* exist," Hank said blankly.

Ashe and Bastien both laughed. "Of course you do."

"But if Max and my father were using aliases, then who am I?"

That was a damned good question. One thing was clear: her family was nowhere near as simple or straightforward as she seemed to think it was. Either that, or she was concealing a great deal from him very, very well. The notion worried him. He valued honesty above all else in life. It was one of the few things he and his father could agree upon without nearly coming to blows with one another. *Please, God, let her be on the up-and-up.*

Jennie had nothing more to report. Ashe ended the call as Bastien stood up, announcing, "Well, kids. I gotta get ready for work. I'll be home around dawn tomorrow. Make yourselves at home and don't have too much fun without me."

In short order, he and Hank were left alone in his friend's odd abode—a house within a shop. It had all the comforts of home: kitchen, living room, two bedrooms and bathrooms. It even felt like a regular house if he didn't stop to think about the huge auto restoration shop encasing it.

Hank spent the afternoon surfing the television. From the way she was switching channels with no interest in the shows on the screen, he gathered she wasn't paying the slightest attention to it.

He spent the afternoon formulating and discarding various plans for infiltrating the club. He did end up with a list of information they needed and supplies that would be necessary to launch a full-scale assault on the place, though.

He made a big salad for supper and carried a plate of it to Hank in the living room along with his own. He sat down beside her on the leather sofa. "Tell me more about your father."

Her expression went tight, closed off. Yeah, he knew

the feeling of having a difficult, distant relationship with a parent. Or maybe that was her shutting down on secrets she wasn't planning to share with him.

She muttered, "There's shockingly little to tell. I have vague memories of him living at home with us when I was really little. He traveled a lot for his work, and I was always excited when he came home."

"Did your folks fight a lot before the divorce?"

"Not that I remember."

"How did he react to the car crash?"

She frowned. "It took him a couple of days to get to the hospital. He was overseas when it happened. I remember my mom being surprised that he took care of all the medical bills. I guess we were still on his health insurance or something."

Or something. Ashe made a mental note to have Jennie look into how those bills had been paid.

"And your father was in the art business like your brother, right?"

"Correct. He imported pieces at the request of clients and auction houses. The antiques he generally got in the US. He had them trucked in when people wanted them. A lot of the art came from overseas."

"Do you know who any of his clients were?"

"God, no," she said quickly. "That was all strictly confidential. Even Max won't say a word about his clients to me."

Which might explain why Jennie could find no trace of the man. Ashe asked, "Where are his personal possessions?"

"I suppose they're stored with the other stuff from our house. When my mom died, there was an auction. The remaining stuff got packed up and put in storage somewhere."

Another mental note: have Jennie find that storage locker.

"What about Max's home? Where is it?"

She looked down at her plate, abashed. "I don't know. I lived in a dorm at Tulane, and he and I texted or called from time to time but didn't really see each other. He was busy. I was busy…"

Tears welled up in her eyes.

Regret. He probably ought to feel some of that regarding not seeing his father for so long before he died. Or for not making it home for the bastard's funeral. But he just couldn't work up any sense of remorse.

Sure, his father had made him into the man he was. For that, he could be grateful. But the other stuff, the coldness, the judging, the harshness…

Nope. No regret.

He yanked his attention back to the discussion at hand. "I'll have Jennie see if she can find out where Max was living. Maybe we can swing by and check it out."

Hank nodded miserably. Wow. Was that guilt, too?

"Kitten, your brother is a grown man. Whatever he got into is his responsibility. It's great of you to be so determined to find him, and I'm willing to throw every resource at my disposal into helping you. But none of this is your fault."

"I hear you, and my mind knows you're right. But my heart hurts too much to accept that."

He lifted the plate out of her hands and set it on the coffee table. "Come here."

She huddled against him, shivering, and he wrapped his arms tightly around her. "You're not alone anymore, Hank. A whole bunch of really smart people are going to help you figure this out."

"Thanks to you, Ashe. I'll never be able to pay you

back." She reached up to kiss him, and he lurched away from her.

"What?" she asked in worry.

"You do understand that I don't expect you to sleep with me to pay me back for my help, right?"

She blinked at him in shock. Clearly the idea had never occurred to her. Thank God. He leaned down and captured her sweet mouth with his. She tasted like orange slices and black pepper from the salad. Sweet and spicy. That was her, all right.

"Help me forget everything for a little while, Ashe."

He knew all too well the tactic of using sex to escape reality. Special operators employed it all the time. Sex as stress reliever, sex to erase grisly images the mind refused to forget, sex to feel a little less like a monster. Oh, yeah. He got it. And he was okay with giving that gift to Hank tonight.

As she rose from the sofa and drew him by the hand into the bedroom, he wondered if all the women he'd had one-night stands with over the years had exercised the same generosity. Had they known how much he had needed them? He sent out a silent thanks to all of them, wherever they were right now, and wished them happiness with someone less screwed up in the head than him.

Then Hank was undressing him and being quick about it, and he couldn't think about anything except returning the favor.

Her movements held a frantic quality he recognized all too well. She was absolutely focused on forgetting. On falling into a world of pure sensation. On feeling good, even if only for a little while. He gave her his body to use as her playground, and she threw herself into the venture with abandon.

But at some point, he found himself needing to call a

halt to her manic energy. "Relax, Hank," he whispered. "I'm not going anywhere. We've got all night. Why don't you let me take care of you for a little while, okay?"

"Uhh. Oh…okay."

He soothed her body with his mouth and hands, helping her to unwind when she couldn't do it herself. Finally, at long last, when she was moaning and writhing beneath him in genuine pleasure that had nothing to do with panic, he sank into her.

Intentionally, he kept the pace of their lovemaking slow and easy. Not only was he concerned that she might be a little sore already from last night, but he wanted her to stay present. Here. In this moment. With him for the sake of being with him.

Funny how he was the one who insisted that this be real. That was a change from his usual MO. But it felt right to him. He didn't want to be with Hank any other way except with full disclosure and total honesty. Damn. What did that say about the two of them as a couple? He'd never cared about such a thing before with any woman. Was this yet another signal that she was The One?

An odd sensation of…hopefulness…leaped in his gut at the notion.

Cripes. Had he been that lonely all these years and never known it? Amazing. His reflective train of thought was broken by Hank moving with more urgency against him, her body demanding more from him in no uncertain terms. Grinning, he turned his attention to the entirely pleasant task of driving Hank out of her mind with pleasure. He had to hand it to her. She was one wickedly responsive woman. Sex would never be dull with her.

"Earth to Ashe. Come in. If you don't get busy pretty much right now, I'm going to have to take matters into my own hands and ravish you."

He laughed richly. "I'll look forward to that some other time. But I've got this tonight. Hang on tight to me, baby. It's time to fly."

A vibration under his pillow woke him some time later. It was pitch-dark in the windowless room, and he could feel Hank's soft warmth in the bed beside him. Her breathing was light and quiet and slow. She was out cold.

He grabbed his cell phone and slipped out of bed carefully. The glowing screen announced that it was nearly 1:00 a.m., and that Commander Perriman was calling.

Ashe closed the bedroom door behind him and moved into the kitchen, as far away from Hank as he could get while staying in the house. "Hey boss." He pulled on a pair of jeans as Perriman apologized briefly for calling so late.

As if that had ever stopped the man. Hah. He was famous for calling his team at all hours of the day and night. But then, their job wasn't exactly the nine-to-five variety.

"Can you talk openly now?" Perriman asked. "Or is Hank within earshot?"

"No, she's not nearby. What's up?"

"Jennie just sent me a report on her old man. You knew his name was fake, right?"

"Yes."

"Turns out he was likely a big-time smuggler."

Ashe sat down heavily on a convenient chair. "What?"

"There's no concrete proof, but he's got all the signs. Multiple offshore bank accounts. Piles of cash in hand. He paid for his ex-wife's hospital bill in cash. We're talking upwards of a half-million bucks. He carried it into the hospital in a briefcase, apparently."

"He could've borrowed it from someone. Hell, from a bank, for that matter."

"His travel records are equally mysterious," Perriman told him. "The guy hopped all over the globe."

"He was an art dealer. Hank said he imported stuff. Couriered it around."

"Perfect cover for a smuggler. When Jennie dug into the records of the auction houses Kuznetsov Sr. worked for, there were frequent omissions and outright irregularities in the records around the objects he brought in."

That was damning. Still, his boss wasn't the kind to make a serious accusation based purely on circumstantial evidence. Ashe asked grimly, "What else have you got?"

"I think the son may have followed in the father's footsteps."

Ashe swore low and hard as Perriman continued inexorably, "I need you to treat the daughter as a possible suspect. It's entirely possible she's in on the family business and is using this supposed disappearance of her brother's to worm her way inside our organization. To find out what our capabilities are."

Ashe shoved a hand through his hair in dismay. Hank, a smuggler? *No way.* "I'm the one who randomly wandered into the bar where she works."

"That doesn't mean she and her boss didn't seize on the opportunity that your unexpected arrival on the scene represented and throw her at you."

He tried to recall if Hank and Vitaly had had any conferences in a back room together right after he showed up at the club. There had been one moment…Hank had disappeared into a storeroom for a couple of minutes and Vitaly had followed her inside. They hadn't been in there together for more than a minute or two, but that could have been enough for the Russian to give her orders to gain Ashe's trust and get in his pants.

Still. What were the odds?

That was, of course, his heart talking. His head weighed in with a reminder that Perriman didn't go around making accusations of criminal activity lightly. It made sense that the daughter would be like the father and son.

"What about the mother? Was she in the dark?" Maybe, just maybe, if the mom had been clueless, Hank would be, too.

"Doubtful. Jennie has reason to believe she acted as a mule for the husband, even well after they divorced. There were regular deposits in her bank account from an off-shore account over the years. She lived well beyond what her own income and child support would account for."

"Alimony from the ex-husband?"

"Maybe. Possibly it was more. Payment for services rendered."

Ashe realized he was shaking his head back and forth in denial.

"Keep your distance from this girl, Ashe. Be careful around her. She may be a black widow."

Hank, a hardcore criminal with killer tendencies? Now that was laughable.

Or was it?

Chapter 9

Hank woke to total darkness interrupted only by a thin strip of light on the floor. She lurched upright. *Door. Daylight beyond the door. Bastien's house.* And the terrible revelation from last night that her father was not who she'd always believed him to be. She supposed it might have made sense to hide his true identity as a matter of personal security. After all, he carried around priceless works of art and dealt in large sums of money on a regular basis in his line of work.

But why would he and her mother have falsified his name on her birth certificate, for crying out loud? That seemed a little excessive, even for the most paranoid person. Maybe they thought that as a little kid, she wouldn't be able to keep the secret and would spill his real name by accident. The explanation felt like a bit of a stretch, though.

Perhaps his deep paranoia about the internet and his hatred of electronic data were the reasons he didn't appear to exist when Jennie Finch had gone looking for him. Maybe he'd been too old-school to show up in a modern, computerized search. That must be the explanation.

God knew, her father had been a secretive man. He'd withheld almost every detail of his life, of his past, from Hank—and, to her knowledge, from Max. How much had her mother really known about him? Hank cast her mind back to the time before the accident. Her mother had never spoken about her father voluntarily, and had only with great reluctance answered any questions Hank remembered asking about him.

It had always been understood by Max and her that they did not talk about their father or his work. When asked, they were instructed to say that he was a furniture salesman. And if anyone inquired where he traveled, they were instructed to answer that they did not know. Which was largely the truth anyway.

She'd never really stopped before to think about how secretive her family had been. It had always just been that way, and she had accepted it blindly. She'd assumed that all families were the same. But apparently not.

She took a leisurely shower, extending it as long as possible in hopes that Ashe might join her. He had yet to show her what magic he could perform in one. And she had faith that, with his physical strength and sexual prowess, it would be epic.

He never joined her, however, and she eventually climbed out, disappointed, to dry her hair and dress.

Ashe closed a laptop computer when she stepped into the kitchen and said matter-of-factly, "Bastien's asleep. There are waffles on the counter if you want to reheat one in the microwave."

She frowned a little. He was all business this morning. She supposed she shouldn't take it personally, though.

Ashe's boss was probably breathing down his neck to resolve this mess and quit wasting government resources on it.

She drowned the reheated waffle in syrup and ate it without enthusiasm as Ashe announced, "Jennie found your brother's apartment and the storage unit he rented to store your mom's personal effects. I thought we'd swing by both and check them out. Then we need to get you fitted for a wire."

"A wire, as in a hidden microphone?" she blurted.

"No way am I letting you go back into the Voodoo without having some sort of monitoring device on you. I don't trust your boss further than I can throw him."

She smiled gratefully at Ashe. It was really sweet of him to be so concerned for her safety. She washed down the remains of the waffle with a big glass of milk, rinsed her plate, and declared herself ready to go.

Ashe led her to a pickup truck parked behind the garage. "Bastien lent me wheels. It may not look like much, but if I know him, this puppy will outrun just about anything street legal in all of Orleans Parish."

She hopped in the truck's cab and grinned as the engine did indeed rumble to life like a race car. "It's a beast."

Ashe just shook his head and backed the beast out of the driveway. They drove into the French Quarter and pulled up in front of a traditional building with a tall locked gate to what must be a courtyard. Beautiful wrought-iron balconies overhead looked down on the street. The building might not be much to admire from the street, but the courtyard was magnificently landscaped with fountains, brick-paved walkways and raised flowerbeds. Although, on closer inspection, she noted that the fountain needed cleaning and the beds could have used a weeding.

She followed Ashe as he let them into Max's home

using some sort of a lock-picking gun. Why hadn't she known this place existed? Was it just more of her family's over-the-top secrecy, or had she just been so self-absorbed through her college days that she'd never bothered to stop and think about where Max had lived? About what he did on a day-to-day basis with his life? Man, she'd been a crappy little sister.

The two of them had never been close. Their ages—they were almost seven years apart—had precluded that when they were kids. But he'd always looked out for her. She'd known in the recesses of her mind that he had her back.

Which was part of why his disappearance had been so disturbing. Her last safety net had been ripped away with his departure from her life. She'd been so focused on her need to have him back, to assuage her own selfish loneliness, she'd completely missed the fact that he'd had his own life to live.

A life that had been horribly interrupted.

Her brother's apartment looked about like what she expected a successful art and antiques dealer's home would look like. It was stunningly furnished, chic and elegant. A blend of Old World and New. Which was a bit hard to reconcile with the messy kid she'd grown up with. He couldn't keep his bedroom neat to save his life.

But then they stepped into Max's office.

It was smashed to smithereens. Not one piece of furniture was left intact, and the average size of the remains hovered at about the dimensions of a pencil. She gasped, appalled at the violence it took to create this level of destruction. Her fear for her brother's safety spiraled even higher.

Ashe was silent, picking his way through the destruction thoughtfully. "Can you tell what kind of furniture this stuff was?"

She leaned down to pick up a few slivers of wood. "Walnut. Old. Hand-joined. Eighteenth century, maybe. This inlay is exquisite. Italian if I had to venture a guess." She caught Ashe's startled look and rolled her eyes. "I did grow up around the antiques business." She looked at the cove-paneled ceiling and leather-covered walls now shredded into ribbons. "Knowing Max, he'd have gone for a traditional secretary desk. Lots of drawers and compartments."

"Okay. A desk. What else got busted up?" Ashe picked up a metal strip. "Drawer roller from a filing cabinet."

She moved over to look at the wall outlets. "There's a cable outlet over here. A computer or a television was over here. Some sort of stand or cabinet for that must have been here."

"Do you see any chair remains?" Ashe asked.

She looked around the debris in dismay. "I don't see anything that looks like chair legs or wheels. But I'm not sure that means anything."

"I don't see any upholstery or stuffing. Was he a padded butt kind of guy?"

Hank smiled reluctantly at him, grateful for his attempt to lighten the mood. "He liked his creature comforts well enough. So, yes, I'd take him for a padded chair man."

"Strange that there was no sofa in here," Ashe observed. "It's a big room. There'd have been plenty of space for a couple of armchairs in front of a desk, or a sofa in front of those bookshelves."

The same bookshelves that were completely emptied. "There aren't any wrecked books in here. Max loves books. Collects them rabidly. Where did they all go?"

Ashe frowned and shrugged tightly.

They picked through the remains of the office for a few more minutes but didn't learn much more about what an intruder might have been looking for or whether the guy had found it or not. The thoroughness of the destruction was impressive, however. Someone had to have taken a good, long time to destroy Max's office. And yet, not one other part of the apartment looked as if it had been touched. What was so special about the office?

A search of the rest of the apartment didn't reveal much besides the fact that her brother had become fastidiously neat sometime in the past few years, and that it was impossible to tell if any of his clothes were missing from the crowded closet. Who knew Max was such a clotheshorse? A toothbrush was waiting in a holder by the sink, a razor inside the medicine cabinet, but it would be easy enough for a man who traveled a lot to have duplicates of those items permanently in his luggage.

The more Hank saw of this place, the less she knew of her brother. She didn't recognize anything about the man who lived here. It was an appalling disconnect to realize what she was guilty of.

Ashe surprised her by handing her a key ring as they walked back down to the car. "Found these in the kitchen. Spare keys. That brass one works on the front door. I guess the place is yours until we can find your brother. Jen says it's paid off and the deed is in your brother's name."

Where in the hell had Max come up with the kind of money it took to own a place like this? Prime real estate in New Orleans was *not* cheap. Hank blinked down at the keys lying in her hand. "He'll be back. I'll look after it until then, but that's it." He *had* to come back. She needed to get to know this man her brother had become.

Ashe shrugged. "Sell it if you need the cash. This place should fetch a pretty penny."

As if she'd given a moment's thought to her financial future since this whole mess had begun. When her mother had died, the regular monthly payments to her mother's checking account had mysteriously started showing up in hers. It wasn't a fortune, but Hank had plenty of ready cash to deal with life.

In hindsight, she probably ought to have investigated where that money came from. She'd always assumed it came from some sort of trust fund or bank account her father had set up. Apparently she'd been so conditioned not to ask questions as a child that the mental prohibition from being curious had extended to the deposits in her checking account.

They climbed into the truck, and Ashe headed for the other side of town. Familiar streets and businesses passed by. This was the neighborhood where she'd grown up. It had changed a lot in the past few years, though. It was home and not home. Or maybe she just saw it with different eyes now. Older. More judgmental. Heck, more cynical.

What didn't she know about this place? Was she as clueless about it as she'd been about Max?

Thankfully, their route didn't take them past the house where she'd grown up. She would probably have cried if she'd seen it again. Too many painful memories were associated with the sprawling clapboard bungalow and its wide porch.

Ashe spoke up reflectively, jarring her from her thoughts. "And you had no idea your brother owned that place?"

"Nope. None."

"Is it possible, then, that there are other things you don't know about him and his life?"

"Of course it's possible. It's probable. I don't know everything about him any more than he knows everything about me."

"I'm talking about important stuff, Hank. Like who he works for. What he really does for a living."

The topic was already upsetting enough without Ashe poking at it. She stared across the truck cab at him, not wanting to continue this line of discussion, but asking anyway, "What are you trying to say, Ashe?"

"Are you entirely sure he wasn't involved in something…questionable?"

"Like what?" she asked a little more defensively.

"Like maybe he's tangled up in the Russian mob. Or doing something else criminal. I think you have to consider that possibility seriously. A fair bit of evidence points in that direction."

"You're telling me my brother is a *mobster*?" And she'd had zero clue? God. It was the last straw. She sucked as a sister.

Ashe shrugged.

Max? She tried unsuccessfully to picture her goofy brother as a suave, smart, dangerous criminal. *Nope.* "That's crazy."

"Actually, it's a lot less crazy than you might think."

It was too much. All these things he was saying about her brother simply couldn't be true. "No. I reject the idea."

"Hank, my boss and I think it's probable your brother is engaging in some sort of criminal activity."

She stared at him, completely stunned. "You can't just say random stuff that will turn my world on its head as if it's nothing."

"The truth is the truth."

"How would you feel if I told you your father was a great guy? That he had a big heart and a generous nature before he went off to war, and that's why your mother stayed with him for all those years after he got back, a broken man." A pause. "But you were always such a jerk around him that you never got to see that softer side of him. That you provoked his hard-ass side and that he was only trying to teach you some manners by being so tough on you."

Ashe looked over at her in shock. As if he'd never thought of his father in that way before. Ever. If she wasn't mistaken, the color slowly drained from his face. He stared at her long enough that she finally yelped, "Eyes on the road!"

The truck jerked and re-centered in the lane of traffic. Ashe looked ahead now, but his knuckles were white on the steering wheel, and the muscles in his jaw ridged tightly. Hah. The truth was not so easy to deal with when the shoe was on the other foot.

He turned onto a side street that ended in a storage facility. The gate was open, and they drove into a long alley lined by garage-door-style lockers. "What number is yours?" Ashe bit out.

As if she remembered off the top of her head. The last time she'd been here, her mother had been gone a few weeks and her life had been in a shambles. "You'll have to go to the office and ask—"

A squeal of tires behind them made her lurch in her seat and look around in alarm.

Ashe swore under his breath. "Hang on." He gunned the engine, and the truck leaped forward and screeched around the corner into another long alley. The row of orange garage doors flew by only inches from her side of the truck as it roared down the narrow drive.

They were maybe fifty feet from the end of the row when a black late-model muscle car pulled across the end of the alley, blocking their escape.

She heard a screech behind them. She looked out the

back window and cried out, "There's another car blocking the end of the alley behind us!"

Ashe all but stood on the accelerator. "Brace yourself!" he yelled.

Chapter 10

Hank slammed herself back in her seat, feet pushing against the floorboards with all her might as Ashe reached over to punch off the airbags.

The impact was tremendous. Their truck slammed into the front corner of the car, spinning it to one side and lurching in a ninety-degree right turn of its own. The vehicles were crunched together like they'd been welded into one. She stared in horror through the windshield at a driver and front-seat occupant staring back at her. The bastards had the good grace to look shocked.

As Ashe threw the truck into Reverse, she frantically took mental notes on their assailants. Two men. Dark sunglasses. Baseball hats. Both white. A crunching sound of metal tearing apart accompanied a backward jerk as the truck separated from the car. It looked as if they'd left the truck's fender behind, mangled into the car's bumper.

Ashe yanked the steering wheel, throwing the truck into

a Y-turn and flinging it down another alley that loomed beside them. He stomped on the gas and the truck lurched forward.

In front of them, the wrought-iron gate enclosing the facility began to slide shut.

"Bastards," Ashe ground out, flooring the truck.

She held her breath as the truck shot the gap with perhaps six inches to spare on each side. A squeal of brakes and screeching tires announced that their pursuers hadn't made it out before the heavy gate blocked their way.

"Who was that?" she gasped as they burst out onto a main street.

Ashe slowed to a saner pace as he gritted out, "Did you see anyone in the car?"

She relayed what little she'd seen of the two men, aware that it wouldn't be much help. He swore under his breath.

"But I did get the license plate," she added. "It's from Texas."

"That's my girl." He reached in his back pocket and tossed her his cell phone. "Hit speed dial number three and pass whoever answers the phone that license plate number."

A male voice rumbled in her ear, "What's up, Hollywood?"

"Umm, this is Hank Smith. I'm with Asher Konig— Hollywood—and he gave me this phone. Told me to call you. He wants you to run a license plate."

"Why can't he talk to me?"

"He's got his hands full driving right now. Our truck is kind of smashed up, and the guys we just hit may be following us."

The voice on the other end went terse. All business. "Say the tag number and state."

She relayed the information.

"Do you and Konig need backup?"

She pulled the phone away from her ear. "Umm, Ashe? The man wants to know if we need backup."

"Nah, I got this. Easy-peasy. Those guys were just testing me. It's no big deal."

"Are you kidding me?" she exclaimed.

"If those guys had actually been out to hurt us, they'd have shot at us. And they'd have disabled that gate before they jumped us."

"Did you catch all that?" she asked the guy on the phone.

"Roger. Tell Ashe the vehicle in question was reported stolen last month in Houston, Texas. Probably a burner car."

"Like a burner phone?" she asked in shock. An entire car that was a throwaway tool?

"Yes, ma'am."

"Umm, okay. I'll tell him."

She ended the call and passed along the information to Ashe. His response to the news was merely, "Garden variety thugs don't sit on burner cars. This is a high-end crew we're messing with, apparently. Big dogs. Plenty of resources."

"Like the Russian mob?" She would rather believe Max was involved with that gang than that he was an outright criminal in his own right. If he was involved with the mob, she could at least pretend he'd been sucked in against his volition and was still a decent guy at heart. Redeemable.

Ashe shrugged. "I don't know if your brother's in the mob or not. But it's obvious that you and I have kicked a hornet's nest. Clearly it is time to find out who Vitaly's bosses are." Sighing, he flicked a quick glance her way. "We've moved up the food chain of response from these jokers, and I want to know exactly what species of hornet we're messing with."

"How do you plan to do that?" she asked, curious.

"Identify the manager of the brothel."

"Are we going to do a stakeout?"

"I think it's time for more direct action. I'll ask Bastien if he wants to go in. I'm known around the Voodoo, so I can't make a visit upstairs. I'd hate to give them the impression that you're no good in the sack by my going upstairs."

She rolled her eyes. "That's what you're worried about? Someone just tried to run us down, and that's what comes to your mind? My reputation in the sack?"

He grinned over at her. "It's how I roll, baby."

"You're certifiable."

"Never said I wasn't."

They drove in silence for several minutes. "Where are we going now?" she asked.

"Back to Bastien's place. He's not going to be happy that I crashed his truck."

"At least we're alive for him to yell at us."

It turned out, however, that Bastien was much more interested in who had tried to screw with them than the damage to his truck. He mumbled something about having wanted to install some sort of reinforced winch assembly, anyway, and didn't seem overly concerned by an absent front bumper. Truth was, he seemed most bummed to have missed out on a good car chase.

Men. All of them were overgrown boys at heart.

After grabbing a quick sandwich, Hank announced, "Well, it's time for me to go to work."

Ashe shook his head. "Umm, no. That's a bad idea."

"Why?"

"Did you not just participate in a violent car crash with me?" he demanded sharply.

"Well, yes. But if I do anything off my normal routine, won't that make Vitaly suspicious?"

Bastien chimed in. "She has a point, bro."

Ashe scowled. "Can we wire her? Do you have the stuff here at the house?"

The cop shrugged. "Duh. Once a SEAL, always a SEAL."

Hank gathered that meant he did, in fact, have the gear she would need to wear a wire. "What's the point of me wearing a wire? Am I supposed to get Vitaly to confess to being some sort of crime boss or something?"

Ashe replied, "I'm actually more interested in you wearing a microphone and an earpiece so I can be in constant contact with you in case something goes bad."

Although trepidation crept along her skin at what would happen if Vitaly caught her wearing a wire, she had to admit she liked the idea of being able to holler for instant rescue. "If I wear my hair down and wear an ear cuff—which I sometimes do—Vitaly will never be the wiser, I suppose."

The earbud turned out to be a tiny wireless gadget that she wore like a hearing aid. The mike was equally teeny, and Ashe glued it along the top of her bra cup, with a flat silver-dollar-sized battery pack taped inside the cup. She was frankly a little disappointed at how impersonally he installed the microphone setup. She'd hoped he might linger at least a little bit as his fingers dipped into her cleavage. But he was once again all business.

Was he ticked off that she'd pooh-poohed his theory about her brother being a criminal? Or maybe he was annoyed at what she'd said about his father. Tough. If he insisted on everyone around him dealing with the truth no matter how much it hurt, then he could swallow a dose of his own medicine.

She was being immature, of course. But he'd hurt her feelings when he attacked her brother's reputation. Blood was thicker than water, thank you very much. Not to mention the past few months had been exhausting both physically and emotionally. She wasn't exactly at the top of her game just now.

"So where will you be while I'm working tonight?" she asked Ashe.

"Behind the Voodoo, one block over. I'll be staking out the alley. Bastien and I will put a new license plate on the van we used to get you out of the rug warehouse, and I'll be inside that."

"Won't that be a little bit obvious?"

He shrugged. "Best place to hide is often in plain sight."

She shrugged back, miffed that he continued to be so cold and impersonal with her. "Whatever you say, G.I. Joe."

"He was army. I'm a navy man."

"Same diff."

Irritated, she pulled on her skimpiest tank top. It was high enough in the front to conceal the microphone, but the racer back was deeply cut and showed off her hot-pink bra straps in all their sassy glory. The thin cotton fabric clung to her chest, leaving little to the imagination. The fuchsia lace of her bra showed through, clearly outlining the shape of her breasts.

Ashe's brows slammed together as he frowned. "You shouldn't wear something so sexy."

"Why not?"

"You're asking for trouble."

She laughed. "I'm asking for good tips."

"I don't like it."

She patted the center of his chest. "I can handle it, big guy. I've been working there for months."

"I still don't like it."

She shrugged. "I don't like wearing a wire nor do I like

you sitting in a van that screams of you being some guy on a stakeout. But we all do what we've got to do."

His scowl deepened. At least she had his undivided attention. Turning on her heel, she marched into the kitchen. "What are you up to this evening, Bastien? Keeping the mean streets of the Big Easy safe?"

"Nah. I'm getting laid." He suddenly caught sight of her shirt and shot her an appreciative grin that flashed devastating dimples. "Speaking of which, don't act like you recognize me if you see me tonight."

"Ohmigosh. You're not going upstairs at the Who Do Voodoo, are you?"

"Not only that, but the City of New Orleans is paying for it. How cool is that?"

"Promise me you'll be careful, Bastien," she implored. "Vitaly's smart and will be able to smell a cop from a mile away."

"I'm brand new to the department. Your boss won't have any idea who I am."

"You're assuming he doesn't have informants in the department who'll tell him you're coming."

That made Bastien's dimples disappear. "Thanks for the warning, but I'll be wearing a disguise and using an alias. This isn't my first time at the rodeo, you know."

That didn't make her feel any better. These two weren't taking Vitaly anywhere near seriously enough—

Bastien stepped close and took her hands in his. "Relax, *chère*. Ashe taught me everything I know. Just don't act like you recognize me, and I'll be fine."

She nodded, worried nevertheless, and fretted in the back of the van all the way to the Warehouse District. Ashe stopped the vehicle so she could walk the rest of the way to work. He joined her at the back of the van and, after a quick sound check of her microphone and earbud, crouched in front of the door.

"Be careful, Hank. If anything spooks you, leave. Just turn around and walk out. The cops and I have this thing in hand. We don't need your help, and we don't need you to take any risks whatsoever. Got it?"

She didn't need this terse-soldier side of him right now. She needed the reassuring lover from before. "I'm sorry I said that stuff about your dad. I was hurt, and I lashed out at you for no good reason. You were just saying aloud things about Max that I've already thought to myself but I've been too afraid to admit."

He frowned. "You don't owe me any apologies. Honesty goes both ways. What you said about my Dad aside, if I expect that you'll accept honesty from me, then you should expect me to accept hearing the truth from you, too."

"Umm, apology retracted, then."

He exhaled hard and then gathered her in his arms. "I don't care if your brother is a serial axe murderer. He's not you. And I refuse to believe that you're part of whatever he's mixed up in."

Did he have doubts about her innocence, then? Not that she would blame him for wondering about her motives. It wasn't like she'd been stunningly forthcoming with him about her life or her family. Even now, there were secrets she wasn't sharing. Lies she was letting him believe. But blood was thicker than water, right?

His arms tightened momentarily, and then he released her and moved to the other side of the tiny space.

Reluctance to let her go shone in his gaze as he reached for the door handle. "Promise me you'll be careful."

"Umm, of course." She wasn't sure what to make of his tension, but she appreciated his obvious concern for her. And then the door was open, and she stepped out into the gathering dusk. She looked around fearfully as the van pulled away from her, leaving her alone on a street no sane woman would dream of walking along alone. It shouted of danger to her with its many recessed doorways, dark alleys, and general air of sleaziness.

The Voodoo was just around the corner, and she made her way to it as quickly as her stiletto heels would allow. Vitaly insisted on all the waitresses wearing them. He said the patrons bought more drinks when the girls dressed sexy.

Taking a deep, calming breath, she walked inside. A football game on the big screen TVs meant the bar wasn't completely deserted on this Monday night. But it wasn't a big-drinking or a big-tipping crowd. The dancers had to time their sets for commercial breaks in the sports action or risk getting booed off their poles.

Halftime of the game started, and Vitaly sent out dancers as fast as their music could be cued up, no doubt to maximize the tips. Hank had to give the guy credit for being a hustler. He never missed an opportunity to squeeze more cash out of his customers.

Bastien came into the bar near the end of halftime. Thankfully, one of the other waitresses spotted him first and muttered on her way past Hank, "Check out the hunk who just walked up to the bar. He's as hot as your new boyfriend. Think I'll go get me a piece of that."

Hank glanced up and spied Ashe's friend an instant before she spied Vitaly watching her. She shrugged at her boss and turned away from Bastien, doing her best to look disinterested.

Her customers ordered a flurry of snacks and drink refills as the football game got ready to start again, and she was kept busy for the next few minutes serving tables.

When she looked up at the bar again, Bastien was gone. Thank God.

"How's our new friend?" a male voice asked from behind her. "You're keeping him happy, yes?"

She turned to face Vitaly. "He's great, actually. Thanks for hooking me up with him."

Vitaly moved closer and lowered his voice to a conspiratorial mumble. "Does he call people? Do business on the phone?"

Huh. Vitaly was going to try to extract inside information about Ashe from her, was he? She responded cautiously, "Well, yeah, he talks on the phone. And I guess it's business. I don't know. He talks in some foreign language."

"Which one?"

Crap. She had no idea. Did she dare make something up? A voice muttered low in her earbud, "Spanish, Hebrew and Farsi."

She mentally jolted. Of course. Ashe was listening in on this conversation. She'd forgotten for a moment in her panic.

She gave Vitaly her best dumb blonde look. "I've heard him speak Spanish. And maybe Hebrew. My best friend in middle school was Jewish, and she had to memorize this stuff to say at her big bat-mitten-thingy, or whatever it's called. And then he speaks this other language. It's kind of like Arabic. But he sounds like some guy from, I don't know, India or something."

"Is it Hindi?" Vitaly asked in surprise.

"As if I would know Hindi from Klingon." She snorted.

Vitaly rolled his eyes. "Ask him the next time you see him."

"Umm, okay."

"And let me know if you overhear anything in English about his business."

Ashe whispered in her ear again. "Tell him you've heard me talking about some sort of shipment and when it arrives."

"He did talk to some guy this afternoon about a shipment he's got coming."

"Did he, now?" Vitaly's eyes lit with interest. "Anything else?"

She hesitated long enough for Ashe to give her any further input. When he stayed silent, she shrugged at Vitaly. "Nope."

"Good girl. Keep an eye on him for me, okay? I reward loyalty well."

The bastard stroked her rear end as she turned away from him, and Hank barely managed to suppress a shudder in time. Right. Like the prospect of sex with him would turn her into a willing mob Molly. *Not.*

"Enough standing around," Vitaly snapped at her. "Get back to work."

She picked up a tray of drinks and trudged back out into the sea of tables.

At closing time, she and the other waitresses left together, and Hank peeled off to head for her place, like she always did. When she was well away from the other girls, she muttered without moving her lips, "Where do I go?"

Ashe's reply was immediate. "Back to your place. "I'll meet you there when I shut down here for the night."

"'Kay."

She hurried home, the dark, deserted streets making her nervous like never before. It had probably always been this dangerous, but she'd been oblivious to the risk to herself before now. She'd been so focused on finding Max that she'd never stopped to think—or to care—about what might happen to her.

Sheesh. She had great sex with a hot guy, and her priorities were suddenly skewed. Max. He was the only thing that mattered, darn it. She *had* to find him. Renewing her resolve to keep going until she succeeded, she marched home more boldly.

The next three nights were carbon copies of one another. She worked until closing and walked home to her apartment, and Ashe called her a little before dawn. Then she would sneak down the hidden staircase and out through the warehouse to the loading dock, where he picked her up in the van.

She could tell he was as frustrated as she was. The head of the brothel stubbornly refused to show himself, and there was still no sign of Vitaly's boss. The FBI had wiretaps in place, compliments of Bastien, and had apparently told Ashe's boss that they would be ready to raid the joint in a few days. She and Ashe were running out of time to catch a lead on her brother.

The next afternoon, they sat at Bastien's kitchen table while he cooked what he promised would be the best gumbo they'd ever tasted. Both natives of the Big Easy, she and Ashe had expressed skepticism, and the cookfest was on.

"We're getting nowhere with finding my brother," she groused over the sizzle of sausage browning in a cast-iron skillet.

Ashe frowned. "I think it's time for a change of strategy."

"Meaning what?"

"It's time to go on the offense."

That raised her eyebrows.

Bastien came over to sit down at the table, a big grin on his face. "'Bout damn time."

Hank looked back and forth between the two men. It

felt as if they were having an entire silent conversation that she was being completely left out of. "What? What do you guys have in mind?"

Ashe shrugged. "If Vitaly were suddenly to misplace the weekly payoff to his boss, I'm thinking that might be cause for the head honcho to make a visit to the club. What do you think, Catfish?"

Bastien nodded, his grin even wider.

For her part, Hank stared. "Are you suggesting that we *rob* Vitaly? Are you *nuts*?"

Chapter 11

Ashe pulled out a pad of paper and drew what he knew of Vitaly's office from memory. He pushed the pad at Hank. What else can you fill in?"

She rolled her eyes at him and shocked him by casually remarking, "If you're trying to figure out where Vitaly hides his safe, it's in this cabinet here. It has reinforced steel doors. The right side houses weapons—a couple of big machine gun things and two or three handguns. I think the body of the safe is actually sunk into the wall. But the door and the combination lock are right there."

A slow smile spread across his face. "You don't by any chance know the combination, do you?"

"The first number is 54. Last number is 12. No idea what the middle number is."

Ashe actually felt his jaw sag. "Are you kidding me?"

"No. Those are the numbers."

Bastien let out a bark of laughter. "Next time I rob a bank, I want her on my crew."

No lie. "Okay, then. This is going to be a piece of cake. All we need is a diversion out in the bar or maybe in the lap dance lounge to draw Vitaly away from his office for two or three minutes, and we can empty the safe."

Bastien nodded, but Hank stared at him in dismay. "You're serious about this idea?"

He nodded. "Of course."

"He'll kill you."

Bastien interjected, "It would make most sense to have you do the actual break-in, Hank. Your boss won't think it's weird if you hide in the office to avoid a bar fight or the like."

"No way. I'm not a thief."

Ashe spoke right on her heels. "No way. I'm not putting Hank at risk."

"But she's the obvious choice. She's our inside man—woman—"

"No!" Ashe bit out.

Bastien threw him a look of patent disbelief as if he couldn't believe Ashe's vehemence. Frankly, neither could he. The guy was right; she was the obvious choice to get into Vitaly's office and rob the safe.

Hank, apparently oblivious to the silent exchange of *what the hell* and *no eff-ing way* glares he and Bastien were exchanging, asked, "Aren't you guys supposed to uphold the law, not break it?"

"Is it stealing to take money that a criminal has collected from illegally trafficking in young women?" Ashe countered.

She shook her head in the negative. "He'll replay his security cameras and see who robbed him. Or he'll notice I'm the one who slipped into his office. Either way, he'll figure out it was me. He'll kill me…" She was wringing her hands again so he reached out to grasp them in his bigger hands, stilling them momentarily.

"Nah. He'll be too busy tap dancing for his boss over why the money disappeared. And then the FBI will raid the club, and he won't be in any position to care about a few thousand bucks that went missing from his safe."

"He keeps more than a few thousand bucks in there," she told him. "I overheard him brag once that the brothel brings in fifty grand in a bad week. Quadruple that during Mardi Gras."

Ashe whistled.

"What do you suppose his boss does with all that money?" Hank asked curiously.

That was a damned good question. Although the weapons Vitaly was proposing to buy from him would account for a whole lot of bad weeks' worth of income. Which led to the next obvious question: What did Vitaly need with a minor arsenal?

Bastien commented, "He's not likely to report the robbery, at any rate."

Ashe nodded. "The first order of business will be taking out his security cameras. He runs them from his laptop computer and has them all over the joint. I've spotted at least ten of them downstairs."

Hank gasped. "He has so many?"

Bastien snorted. "I'd estimate he's got at least twice that many upstairs. Do you suppose Jennie could hack into his system?"

Ashe turned to Hank. "Does Vitaly get onto the internet from his laptop?"

"Absolutely. He plays fantasy football online all the time. Says he makes good money at it, too."

Ashe grinned. "Excellent. I'll give Jennie a buzz. She's never met a firewall she couldn't bust through."

He and Bastien spent the next hour picking Hank's brain about Vitaly's routines and behaviors in various scenarios at the bar. Gradually a picture unfolded of the best time to hit the safe. If they could create some sort of bar fight that carried over into the lap dance lounge, particularly if certain influential, regular customers were in the lounge at the time, they could guarantee Vitaly's absence from the office for five to ten minutes, if not more.

Apparently, Vitaly carried out the money every Saturday night after the club closed. They would make their move just before that, then, when there would be maximum cash in the safe. The distraction would have to be low-tech, however. Nothing that would raise KGB-trained Vitaly's suspicions.

Ashe made copious notes and enlisted Jennie's help. She was insulted at the insinuation that she might not be able to teach them how to take down Vitaly's security cameras from the guy's laptop computer. They rehearsed the plan until Hank looked like she might scream if she had to walk through it again.

And then it was time for Hank to go to work on Friday. Robbery day minus one. It was also time for Ashe to make another appearance in the club, too. He dressed in a black-on-black suit tonight. His tie, gunmetal gray, was the only relief from the black dress shirt, black trousers and impeccably tailored black jacket.

"Wow," Hank breathed as she emerged from the bathroom in her usual slut-kitten ensemble of skimpy tank top and pleated leather miniskirt. "You look fantastic, Ashe."

"You like the dark, dangerous criminal type, huh?"

"No. I just like you." Her gaze skittered away shyly from him.

Something warm and possessive seeped outward from his belly toward his extremities. He reached out to stroke her jaw with the back of his knuckles. "I like you, too, kitten."

Pink flushed her cheeks as she stared down fixedly toward their shoes. He would love to take her to bed right now. To make slow, sweet love to her all night long. To hell with Vitaly and his damned club. Let the FBI deal with the guy—

Whoa. Since when did he get an urge to just walk away from a job? He lived for the job, dammit. Finding her brother mattered to Hank. Therefore, it mattered to him. Privately, he was convinced either the guy was part of the mob organization Vitaly worked for, or the same organization had killed her brother and dumped his body somewhere it would never be found.

Either way, the outcome was going to suck for Hank. If only he could talk her out of pursuing her brother with such dogged determination. Whether he would call it loyalty on her part or sheer stubbornness, he didn't know and could care less. His first and only priority was to keep her safe. Hence, his refusal to let her act as the safecracker.

He tipped her chin up to kiss her. He'd intended only to brush her lips gently, but the moment their mouths met, she surged forward into him and up into the kiss. He caught her up against him, savoring how warm and vibrant her body felt in his arms. How alive she made him feel.

Her tongue stroked at his mouth, and he wasn't about to deny her. He opened his mouth, and their tongues and teeth clashed in rapidly growing passion. One of his hands slid down and then back up again, underneath her sassy little skirt. Her tush was pert and firm, and he cupped it with pure masculine appreciation.

Her hips rocked forward, pressing her belly against the zipper of his dress pants. "I want you, too," he muttered into her mouth. "We'll be late—"

"Let Vitaly wait. He told me to keep you happy."

"By having frequent hot sex with me?"

"Yes. That," she panted, her hand fumbling at his zipper.

He backed her up against the wall and tore her panties down her luscious thighs. She kicked them off one of her feet. And then he was lifting her to him as her hands frantically freed him from slacks and boxer briefs.

Her right leg wrapped urgently around his waist, and he found her entrance with his throbbing erection. He thrust deeply into her and she groaned under her breath, imploring him to do *that* again.

He withdrew and thrust up hard, lifting her almost off her lone foot supporting her weight. He pressed so deep within her he thought he might not be able to stand it. Her body was hot and tight and slick and clutched at him like she never wanted to let him go. Another hard thrust and another long groan. Although whether it issued from her throat or his, he wasn't sure.

Bless her, she merely wrapped her leg more securely around his waist and held onto his neck even more tightly with her slender arms. She was leaving her body entirely open to him in blatant invitation to take all he wanted from her.

Except tonight, he wanted to give something to her, too. He withdrew once more, this time plunging to the hilt more deliberately, drawing out the stroke for her maximum pleasure. Again and again he stroked her body, fanning it into a frenzy upon his flesh.

Her limbs moved more restlessly, more disjointedly. The sounds issuing from her throat grew hoarser and took on a quality of raw delight that drove him out of his mind. He had no intention of finding release alone, however, and gritted his teeth as his own body began to demand relief from the torturous pleasure threatening to engulf him.

Hank tensed against him. Her breath caught and her entire being went still. And then all of a sudden, she shuddered violently against him, crying out wordlessly as a massive orgasm overtook her. It was, bar none, the sweetest sound he'd ever heard, and it sent him over the edge without warning.

He muffled his own shout of pleasure against her neck as even their heaving breaths synchronized. Their bodies were completely simpatico with one another.

Hank gradually went boneless in his arms. He kissed her neck softly and lifted his head to stare down at her sleepy eyes. "You're going to have to do your hair again. And your lipstick."

She laughed a little. "I can see. You're wearing all of mine. And may I say, it's a fabulous shade on you."

Ashe gently lowered her leg to the floor, and they crowded together into the small bathroom to set themselves to rights after their impromptu sex. He backed out to give her some extra privacy and strolled into the kitchen to have a word with Bastien.

"Hey, Catfish. I've had an idea for how we can create the diversion we need to break into that safe…"

Bastien was chuckling by the time he finished explaining his idea. "I'll get the stuff we need, Hollywood, if you'll talk Hank into doing her part."

"She'll do it for me."

"I'll do what for you?" she asked from the doorway.

He looked up quickly, taking in the slightly swollen lips and sleepy look of satisfaction lurking in her gaze. He knew the feeling.

"You're going to help Bastien set up the diversion tomorrow night at the club."

"How?"

"You're going to drop ice cubes in a few drinks."

She frowned. "I put ice in drinks all the time. How's that going to start a fight?"

"You'll see." He grinned mysteriously at her. Yup, this was going to be fun. He turned his attention back to Bastien. "Last thing we'll need is a digital descrambler to figure out that middle number in the safe combination."

"I got you covered, bro. This is my town, remember?"

Ashe grinned. "Don't let me down."

"Have I ever?"

"Nope. And that's why I trust you."

Hank winced at the exchange between the two men. Ashe wasn't kidding when he said he valued honesty above all else in the world. Too bad she couldn't be completely upfront with him. But no way would he help her find her brother if she spilled all her family's secrets.

They weren't her secrets to tell, though. They'd belonged first to her father and now to her older brother. She seriously doubted that Ashe would forgive her if and when he found out the depth of her deception. She turned away, heading for the van lest he spot the worry in her eyes. He was far too perceptive and read her far too well for her to hide it from him. What was she going to do?

Every day she waited to tell him the truth, the worse it got. She should have told him that first night when she'd pepper-sprayed him and he'd barged into her apartment. But he'd been so intimidating, and so crazy attractive, that she hadn't wanted to say anything to chase him away. At the time, she'd thought not being forthcoming was for a good cause. She really did need to find Max, and she really did need Ashe's help.

But now, she wasn't so sure she'd done the right thing.

One thing she knew for sure: it was a huge mistake to rob Vitaly. Ashe and Bastien were so confident in their own skills that they continued to underestimate her boss. The guy was really dangerous. Even if Ashe was equally dangerous, which she sincerely hoped he was, a direct clash between the two men could destroy them both.

In a pensive mood, she rode across town beside him. After a quick sound check of her microphone and earbud, Ashe helped her out of the van. He walked with her the last few blocks on foot to the Who Do Voodoo, which was a nice change. With him beside her, she didn't worry about who might be lurking in the shadows in this section of town. He carried a box about the size of a shoebox under his left arm. He said nothing about it, so she didn't ask. She'd grown up knowing how not to ask questions that might have awkward answers.

Ashe paused across the street from the club. "Ready?" he murmured.

She took a deep breath. She hoped in a few more days she would never have to lay eyes on this place again. She just had to take it one day at a time.

"Let's do it," she mumbled back.

"You may be the bravest woman I've ever met."

"Hah. Then you never met my mother. She never complained, not once, about her paralysis. She was completely helpless and lived in constant pain, and she never did anything but smile and put up a hell of a fight to live."

"She'd be proud of you now," he said softly.

"God, I hope so."

Ashe smiled down at her. A genuine smile, filled with pride. She blinked up at him, more than a little stunned. Words of praise and looks of approval like the one he was giving her now were completely foreign things to her. She honestly didn't know how to react to them.

"You remember what you're supposed to do tonight?" he murmured.

"Plant that radio thingy somewhere in Vitaly's office where he won't spot it. Ideally, close to the safe at or above the level of its lock, so you can help me hack the safe combination tomorrow night."

"Perfect. And don't get caught."

"Duh." She rolled her eyes at him.

Smirking, he dragged her up against his side and growled playfully, "Don't get fresh with me, young lady."

And so it was that they were laughing at each other when they stepped into the Voodoo. Ashe's arm only reluctantly peeled away from her side after she caught Vitaly glaring at her and muttered something about having to go to work.

"Nice of you to join us," her boss snapped as she hurried toward the storeroom to get her apron.

"You told me to keep him happy. He got frisky and made me late for work." A week ago, she would never have dreamed of being so bold with her boss. Funny how Ashe's courage and fearlessness were rubbing off on her.

Which was not necessarily a good thing. She was already too impulsive for her own good. And even though he was one heck of a man to have at her back, she was wary of developing a false sense of safety with him around to bail her out of any messes she got herself into. Still, gratitude and affection flowed through her that he would try to save her from herself.

"Wow. That's the smile of a woman in love," one of the other waitresses teased.

Hank started. "Oh. Sorry I'm late and that you had to cover my tables. I'll cover yours if you want to take an extra break."

"Nah, that's okay. There's a new dancer, and the patrons are drinking and tipping like crazy tonight."

"How old is she?" Hank asked drily.

The other waitress pulled a face. "I swear this one's not older than sixteen. She's barely sprouting breasts, for crying out loud." She lowered her voice to a bare whisper. "If I didn't need this job so bad, I'd turn in the bastard myself."

Hank murmured back, "I'm looking for a new job. If I hear of anything promising, I'll send it your way."

"Thanks. You're a peach."

"Hey!" Vitaly shouted from the bar. "You two chicks gonna wait tables or is that Waitress Wanted sign going back in the window?"

Hank and the other waitress shared eye rolls and waded out into the grope-fest.

Like the last time Ashe had come in here, the quantity and intrusiveness of gropes tailed off rapidly to nearly nothing. Only the drunkest and most oblivious patrons in the club even threw her lewd looks, let alone touched her.

How Ashe did it, she hadn't the slightest idea. He never spoke to any of the other men, never did anything physical to stake a claim on her. He just sat in the corner and... watched her. And all the other men backed the hell away. Her tips sucked, but she wasn't complaining. The evening was blessedly without incident.

At about midnight, there was some sort of fuss in the lap dance lounge, and Vitaly left his office to take care of the problem. Hank happened to be standing right by the office door when her boss strode out of his office, and it was a piece of cake to slip into the abandoned office and push the door mostly closed. It didn't hurt that doing such things had been second nature to her since childhood, after all.

She looked around fast, searching for a hiding place near the safe. Up high. Out of sight. She spied an old-fashioned radio backed into the corner of a tall wooden bookcase, right next to the cabinet that hid the safe. A thick layer of dust on both radio and surrounding shelf indicated that Vitaly never touched the boxy antique.

Being careful not to disturb the dust, she slipped her hand behind the radio, setting up the transmitter, which was about the size of a pack of cigarettes. She stepped back to check her work. Not a trace of disturbance in the gray dust. She hurried back to the door to peek out. Crap. Vitaly had just stepped out of the lap dance lounge and was headed straight this way. Panic leaped in her throat.

She muttered into her microphone, "Crud. I need Vitaly distracted."

"Hey, Vitaly, my friend!" Ashe called loudly as her boss walked past his table. "Drink with me."

Vitaly turned to face Ashe, and she used the moment to slip out and put the door back to where it originally had been. Bless Ashe for the quick reaction. Heart racing, she slid down the bar away from the incriminating door.

"Hank! Chilled vodka glasses for us!" Ashe called to her.

She nodded and hurried to fill a bowl with crushed ice. She was surprised to see the box that Ashe had carried with him open on the table. A bottle that looked like cut crystal was nestled in dark blue velvet inside the box.

She listened as Ashe explained in Russian that this was the special reserve vodka served to the elite insiders at the top of the Kremlin hierarchy. Apparently it wasn't for sale at any price to any outsider.

"Then how do you have a bottle of it?" Vitaly demanded.

Ashe shrugged as he broke the seal and poured two shots of vodka. "It is all in who you know, my friend, is it not?"

Vitaly took the shot glass Ashe offered him and raised it. "To good friends. And profitable business dealings."

Ashe grinned and tipped back his shot glass.

Vitaly swore in Russian and then breathed in English, "Nectar of the gods."

Ashe spared a glance in her direction. The question in his eyes was clear. Had she successfully planted the transmitter? She nodded infinitesimally. "Keep the ice coming, baby. Makes the vodka bite all the hotter. Like you. Cool on the outside. Sizzling hot on the inside."

She blinked at him, startled. He was dropping compliments in front of her boss?

"You like my girl?" Vitaly asked in Russian. "Maybe I should think about moving her upstairs when you're done with her."

Hank's horrified gaze shot to her boss. Only belatedly did she realize that she was not supposed to have understood what he'd just said. Thankfully, Vitaly was looking at Ashe, studying him intently, in fact, as if measuring Ashe's reaction to that comment.

To the vast credit of his iron self-control, Ashe merely shrugged. He commented lightly, "She's too classy for a two-bit whorehouse like this. She'll bring in big money if you move her uptown."

Vitaly leaned back, nodding slowly. "It is a thought. Perhaps I will suggest it to my…associates."

Hank turned away fast lest she dump the whole damned bowl of melting ice in Vitaly's lap. Two days. And then this place would be out of business for good. Suddenly she was feeling a whole lot less ethically challenged by the idea of robbing her boss blind. She hoped they took him for a freaking fortune.

Chapter 12

Ashe and Vitaly drank together until closing time. Sheesh. She could've opened the safe herself in the amount of time that her boss sat out in the club tossing back fancy vodka.

Ashe declared his intent to take her home and not let her stay behind to help the other waitresses clean up. Hank surreptitiously slipped all of her evening's tips into the other girls' purses by way of thanks and then left the club with Ashe.

Ashe had to be drunk, but he walked arrow-straight down the sidewalk. When they were perhaps two blocks away from the club, she ventured to breathe, "Where are we going?"

"Take me to the French Quarter. No way should I be driving right now. Your boss can hold booze like nobody I've ever seen before."

She snorted. "Then you obviously haven't done much drinking with Russians. They grow up on vodka. Sometimes I wonder if Vitaly's immune to the stuff."

Ashe grinned a little crookedly at her. "I ate a bunch of bread before we left the house, but I think I caught him on an empty stomach. He should feel like crap for most of tomorrow."

Her eyes narrowed vindictively. "Good."

Ashe's smile widened. "Remind me never to make you mad. Hell hath no fury like a ticked-off female."

"I think that's supposed to be no fury like a woman scorned," she corrected him.

"Yup." He sighed. "I'm drunk."

Smiling, she guided him to the French Quarter and hailed them a cab. Ashe was alert enough to watch carefully out the back window and declare them not followed before she finally gave the driver Bastien's home address.

The cop was working all night again, so she poured a bunch of water down Ashe, got him to gulp down some preemptive ibuprofen for tomorrow morning's headache, stripped him out of his suit coat and shoes, and let him collapse across their bed. She barely managed to get the covers pulled down before he crashed. He was unconscious by the time his head hit the pillow.

She covered him and crawled in beside him, cuddling up against his big, relaxed body. She bunched up a pillow to make herself comfortable and then settled next to him with a sigh of contentment. She could really get used to sleeping with him like this. Even passed out cold, he still made her feel safe and protected. He was a good man. Better than she deserved.

A sense of creeping foreboding intruded upon her contentment, and no amount of ignoring it made the feeling go away. Her fretful thoughts turned to tomorrow night's heist, and any remaining sense of peace was destroyed. She lay next to Ashe for long hours, counting his gentle snores and wondering darkly how many more times she would get to lie beside him like this before her deception was exposed.

Max, what have you gotten mixed up in? More to the point, what had her brother dragged them all into?

Ashe's shoulder shifted beneath her ear almost as if he'd heard her thought and was reacting to it. Truth be told, she and not her brother had been the one to drag the government operative into this whole mess. And she had no doubt she was going to live to regret that decision.

If she knew what was good for her—and good for Ashe—she would break off this relationship with him first thing in the morning. She would thank him for his help and invite him to get on with his regularly scheduled life. Somewhere else. Although the idea of never seeing him again caused physical pain in her stomach, she resolved to be strong and end things between them. Tonight, though, she would enjoy feeling safe one last time.

But she woke up the next morning to discover that her resolve had evaporated. When her eyes opened and she stirred, he woke immediately and smiled down at her. Not just any smile, either. It was hot enough to curl her toes and sweet enough to melt her heart. She would never find another man like him. What was she thinking to contemplate breaking up with him? She was riding this train all the way to the end of the rails.

Sadly, she knew the ride of their relationship couldn't last forever. When he found out how much she'd been withholding from him, that would be it for them. But she was as trapped in her course as he was in his.

Maybe it was the realization of impending doom that gave their lovemaking such a bittersweet quality that morning. She actually felt tears tracking down her cheeks when they both fell back to the mattress panting. How on earth was she going to give him up when the time came?

"Are you okay, sweetheart?" he asked in concern, using the pads of his thumbs to wipe away her tears.

"Oh, uhh, yes. Fine. I'm just happy to be with you. It's all a little overwhelming how fast things are moving between us."

He tucked her close against his side while she silently kicked herself for letting a chance to come clean with him slip away.

Ashe left immediately after breakfast, murmuring something about needing to go over to the naval air station to pick up a few supplies.

Hank made her own preparations for tonight's caper, walking through her part of the plan over and over in her mind. She tried to envision every single thing that could go wrong and how she would respond if it did. Odds were the only thing she hadn't thought of would be the one to go wrong, but her father had always said that mental preparation was the key to success in any endeavor.

Ashe was gone a long time. When he returned, he was all business and spent nearly an hour teaching her how to use the electronic number descrambler that would be critical to breaking into Vitaly's safe. She still couldn't believe they were going through with this madness.

"Ashe, I have to try one more time to talk you out of this robbery. It's a bad idea."

He grinned rakishly at her. "Honey, bad ideas are my middle name."

"I'm serious. It's too dangerous. One of us could get hurt or killed."

"Only if we get caught. And we're not going to get caught."

"Speak for yourself," she grumbled under her breath.

"My middle name is Klutzy. If there's a way to screw this up, I guarantee I'll find a way to do it."

He chuckled at that. "Hence the careful preparation now."

It wouldn't be enough. Nothing was enough to overcome her natural tendency to mess things up. Ashe just didn't know her or her history well enough to understand that.

The afternoon passed all too quickly. Her misgivings mounted with every passing minute. Long before she was ready, Bastien and Ashe sat down with her at the kitchen table for one last walk-though of the heist. And then it was time for her to dress in her usual sleazy attire.

Had some cosmic force sped up the passage of time? It seemed as if it had been only the blink of an eye, and she was crawling out the back of the van a few blocks from the club. A giant lump of lead lodged in her stomach, and foreboding weighed heavy on her mind. She had a bad feeling about tonight's subterfuge.

As the club filled with patrons and the alcohol flowed, her apprehension continued to climb. It attempted to claw its way out of the back of her throat with sharp talons embedded in her flesh.

The plan was to wait until the bar was at maximum capacity and maximum drunkenness, a little after midnight. It would be late enough for the diversion they had formulated to work and early enough to give them a few hours to get away before Vitaly discovered the theft.

In theory.

The clock over the bar raced toward the witching hour, and then…well, before she was mentally prepared to become a safecracker, it was time.

Bastien, who'd been drinking and socializing randomly for a couple of hours, caught her eye and requested a round of rum and diet colas for two big tables of patrons. *The signal.*

She ordered the drinks and told the bartender to go light on ice. The harried guy merely nodded and moved away to mix the order. When her tray was filled with the drinks and the bartender had turned away to respond to someone yelling for him at the other end of the bar, she unobtrusively slipped into the storeroom and opened the small soft-sided cooler hidden in her purse. Into each drink, she dropped one of the special ice cubes Bastien had prepared last night. Several Mentos candies were frozen into each cube.

When the cubes melted and the Mentos mixed with the diet cola, the drinks should commence exploding all over the patrons. With an assist from Bastien, the idea was to initiate a massive brawl that would spill over into the lap dance lounge. If all went well, Vitaly would be forced to dive in and help break up the fray. Which would be Hank's cue to slip into his office and crack his safe.

Easy-peasy. Except a million things could go wrong. The drinks could fail to fizz. A fight might not break out. Vitaly could refuse to get involved. For all she knew, her boss had already discovered the little radio transmitter hidden in his office. He could be lying in wait to catch whoever was targeting him.

However, if everything *was* going according to plan, Ashe was messing with the wireless security camera feeds to Vitaly's laptop right about now. The idea was to make the pictures flicker in and out for a few minutes before Ashe finally cut off the feeds entirely, using the radio transmitter she'd planted in the office yesterday to block the signals.

Hank moved to the storeroom door and peeked out. There. Vitaly was just heading into his office. Her gaze swung to her right. The bartender was turning away from her, moving down the bar in response to someone yelling for a drink. *Now.* The coast was clear. She slipped outside, tray of doctored drinks in hand.

Now to wait for the next dancer to start before she delivered the drinks. The idea was for the ice cubes to melt into relatively full glasses of cola. The new girl, who did look extremely young, started to dance to hoots and whistles. Perfect. The patrons were completely distracted and not drinking.

Hank set the drinks down on the table in front of the very boisterous and particularly drunk crew that Bastien had hooked up with. He'd chosen well. This bunch had just reached that belligerent level of drunk where they were all spoiling for a fight and pretty sure they were invincible. She backed away from the table and turned to take another drink order as a patron grabbed her elbow.

She figured she had five minutes before all hell broke loose. Ashe should be upping the intensity of the signal problems from the wireless security cameras by now. She served a few more tables and did her best to act nonchalant while the dancer gyrated, the ice cubes melted, and Bastien stirred up controversy between his two tables of drunks over which college football team was the best in the South this year.

She had to smile to herself. He'd chosen his topic well. In this part of the world, football was serious business. Insulting someone else's team was fighting words in this town.

Bastien had the tables of drunks nearly in a row even before the drinks started to explode. There had been quite a bit of discussion between Ashe and Bastien last night on how to suspend the Mentos identically inside each ice cube so the drinks all went crazy at approximately the same time.

Whatever Bastien had eventually done worked, because within about ten seconds of each other, a half dozen drinks erupted, spewing soda everywhere. It was an easy misdirect for Bastien to roar something about the other guys having thrown their drinks on him and his buddies, and the fight was on.

More drinks exploded in quick succession, adding gasoline to the fire of the evolving brawl. The result was the entire first table jumping the entire second table.

A last few drinks exploded just to add to the general confusion. Drunks at the surrounding tables took umbrage at getting sprayed with sticky soda and seemed happy to use it as an excuse to jump into the fracas. In a matter of seconds, what seemed like the entire bar was a madhouse.

When Vitaly didn't immediately emerge from his office, Hank opened his door without knocking and said urgently, "All hell's breaking loose out here."

Her boss, who'd been frowning hard at his laptop, surged up from his desk, swearing, and shoved past her.

Something—a beer bottle, she thought—sailed past her head and slammed into the wall. She ducked and slipped into Vitaly's office and closing the door, using her hip to shut the door and making sure not to touch the knob.

She yanked on a pair of latex surgical gloves and then locked the door. Ashe doubted that Vitaly would call the police to report the theft, but he might know how to collect fingerprints and run them on his own. Hence the gloves. No sense making it easy for her boss to figure out who'd robbed him.

"I'm in," she whispered.

Her earbud came alive instantly. Ashe's deep voice murmured, "Hey, hot stuff. Do you have the descrambler I gave you?"

"Yes." She moved over to the cabinet and opened it to

reveal the safe. Following his directions and using tiny magnets embedded in its case, she stuck the electronic device to the front of the safe beside the numeric keypad. Red numbers began to flutter across the descrambler's face.

"This should only take a minute or two, since we already have most of the combination," Ashe reassured her.

Hank started counting, and it had never taken so long to get to sixty in her life. A particularly loud shout went up outside the office at about forty seconds, and she muttered, "Can we hurry this up?"

"Sorry. The device is having to test every single number between one and ten thousand in combination with the other digits we already have."

Too nervous to be still, Hank moved around behind Vitaly's desk. "Ashe, can you let the security cameras run again?"

"Sure. In fact, that's a good idea. Just a sec. How's that?"

On Vitaly's laptop, a video feed flickered into existence. It showed a view of the main bar from one of his security cameras. The brawl appeared to be in full swing and showing no signs of slowing down.

She reported under her breath, "The fight's still going strong. We've still got a couple of minutes."

"Great. Lemme turn off that feed, then. No sense giving Vitaly too much video footage to be able to analyze."

Relieved, she started to step away from the computer. But then she froze. Vitaly's cell phone was lying right in front of her on the desk. "Ashe, Vitaly's phone is here. Is there a way for me to download its contents to you?"

"With the right equipment, sure."

"Do we have that equipment here in the club?"

"No. I have the gear here in the van, but that won't help you now."

"Can I email files from it to you?"

"No!" Ashe bit out sharply. "Not only are files likely to be encrypted—assuming you could even get past the phone's security code in the first place—but you would leave behind a record of who you had sent the files to and which files you had sent. Vitaly would get wise to us in a second."

"Rats," she replied. "Getting into his phone would be the mother lode of information on whoever he's working for."

"Eyes on the prize, baby. We take the money, draw out his boss, then track the boss to your brother."

Ashe was right. But the phone was sitting right there. She'd been angling for weeks to get a look at that phone. And it was on the desk, in plain sight, taunting her with its closeness. She made a quick decision.

"Change of plans. I'm taking the phone. I'll bring it out to the van when I dump the money with you. You can copy the data off the phone, and then I'll bring the phone back."

"No, Hank. Stay on task. We're cracking the safe."

Something big, like a body, slammed into the door. She lurched in alarm. "You don't understand," she whispered urgently. "All his finances are on this phone. It's the key to the whole operation behind the Who Do Voodoo."

"Hank—" Ashe said in warning.

"Save it. I'm doing this, and you can't talk me out of it. Besides, the thingy on the safe just beeped."

To the sounds of Ashe swearing in her ear, she raced over to the safe. "Hush, Ashe. You're distracting me."

With a last curse of frustration, he clammed up. Stony silence filled her earbud. Tough. She knew what she was doing by taking that phone. Quickly she followed the steps he'd taught her for opening the safe. The descrambler had done its job, and it was an easy matter to punch in the combination displayed on its electronic face and swing open the safe's door. A small, crowded compartment yawned before her.

"Is there cash inside?" Ashe asked brusquely.

"Oh, yeah. Stacks of it," she muttered as she commenced stuffing rubber-banded bundles of cash into her purse. "This is a *lot* more than the fifty thousand we were expecting." On impulse, she riffled through one of the bundles of cash. Mostly twenty-dollar bills. Some hundreds. She estimated fast, guessing that she was looking at upwards of four hundred thousand bucks. "Apparently Vitaly's been a bad boy and is holding out on his bosses."

"Take it all."

She smiled wolfishly at Ashe's terse order. "I was hoping you'd say that."

"Like I'd have stopped you from doing whatever the hell you want, anyway," he grumbled.

The problem was that several hundred thousand dollars in cash turned out to be bulky. They hadn't been expecting anywhere near this much to be here, and her purse bulged full to the gills by the time she wrestled it shut and barely managed to zip it. She would just have to hope Vitaly didn't notice the dramatic change in the size of her purse.

She closed the safe and pocketed the descrambler. Now to escape. Adrenaline surged through her body, and the urge to flee was so strong she could barely contain it. The tricky part of the heist was going to be getting out of Vitaly's office unnoticed.

"Can I get a peek at the security cameras again?" she breathed.

"Coming up."

Vitaly's laptop showed static for a moment, and then a picture flashed into view. Crud. The bar fight was starting to wind down. She had to get out of here fast. She searched the computer screen and spied Vitaly facing toward his office. Damn. If she left now, he would spot her for sure.

She spoke into her microphone. "Is there any way Bastien can get Vitaly turned around facing away from his office?"

Ashe answered, "I'll relay the request to Catfish. Stand by."

"When I leave, you'll need to deactivate the cameras so Vitaly doesn't see me slipping out of his office."

"I'm on it. I'll give you the word when it's safe to leave."

Hank moved over to the door, and while she waited for Ashe's signal, she stripped off the latex surgical gloves and stuffed them in her bra. Searching around for something to protect the doorknob from fingerprints, she spied a bar napkin on the floor. She picked it up and palmed it.

"Go," Ashe bit out.

It was an act of pure faith to assume that Bastien had done his job and cleared the path for her to sneak out of here. She eased the door open a crack and, crouching low, slipped out. Closing the door behind herself, she crawled the few feet to her right to hide behind the bar.

She jolted when another waitress already there turned to mutter, "I swear. This place is the toilet of humanity."

Hank winced. Had the girl seen her come out of Vitaly's office? She muttered back, "I had to hide under a table until the fight moved away from me. Are the other girls okay? I couldn't see a thing from where I was hiding."

"Yeah, I think so. Crap. I gotta pee."

Inspiration struck Hank. "Me, too. Let's sneak into the lap dance lounge and use the restroom back there while this mess clears up."

The girl nodded and started moving toward the back of the bar. Hank followed, letting the other waitress run across the long, open space between the end of the bar and the door to the lap dance lounge. The girl waved at Hank to join her, and she darted over to her. Perfect. If Vitaly happened to see the two of them, he would think Hank had been behind the bar the whole time.

She followed the other waitress through the lounge, moving fast. "You use the bathroom first," Hank offered. "I'll wait."

"'Kay. Thanks."

While the other girl hurried into the tiny single restroom, Hank took a quick look around the lounge. No one was in sight. Perfect.

She ducked out of the lounge's rear exit and came up short as the broad back of a bouncer loomed in front of her. The guy wasn't one she recognized. She'd had *no* idea Vitaly posted a man back here. Damn. Was he some sort of guard to prevent girls from escaping out here? The plan had not included avoiding this guy. Now what? Did she go back into the club? Abort her escape? Or should she take her chances and try to distract the guy? Maybe get him to go inside? Either way, he would be able to tell Vitaly he'd seen her back here.

She improvised fast. "There's a huge fight in the bar. I'm scared that the other girls and I are gonna get hurt. Vitaly could use your help out front to break it up."

The guy swore in Russian, ending with an imprecation about damned Americans who couldn't hold their booze. Hank backed into the club and prayed the other waitress wouldn't emerge from the bathroom before the bouncer disappeared from sight.

The toilet flushed as the bouncer made his ponderous way across the lap dance lounge. *C'mon, c'mon. Please God, let the girl wash her hands.* Just a few more seconds. A few more steps from the big Russian...

There. He was gone.

Hank slipped outside fast. Just as the exit door closed behind her, she heard the bathroom lock turn. Man, that had been close.

She raced down the dark alley as fast as her high heels would allow her to go. Ashe and the van should be just around the corner. Sure enough, the rusty white van was parked only a dozen feet beyond the mouth of the alley.

She leaped into the passenger seat. Ashe reached for the ignition, but she gasped, "I've got to put his phone back."

He looked up sharply. "There's no time. Bastien says the fight's winding down."

"You said you had the gear in here to copy the data off his phone."

"I do. But we're out of time."

"If I don't put his phone back, he'll know he's compromised. By dawn tomorrow, all the girls will be moved out of here, and any evidence of his operation will be erased."

Ashe made a sound of disgust but did not disagree with her assessment.

"Copy the stuff off his phone," she urged him. "I'm telling you, it'll have everything you need to bust open Vitaly's operation." Ashe stared at her doubtfully and she added, "Trust me. I've been watching the guy for a long time."

A moment's more hesitation, then a terse nod. Ashe swore low and hard as he slipped out of the driver's seat and headed for the bowels of the van. He took the cell phone she held out to him as he passed by. He dug around in a gym bag in the back and came up with some sort of device that he plugged into the bottom of the cell phone. It looked like a credit card swiper on steroids.

Meanwhile, she upended her purse on the floor of the van beside him.

"Jeez! You didn't say you'd robbed a flipping bank!" Ashe exclaimed.

She grinned. "Apparently Vitaly kept a private stash of cash for himself. And I'm betting his bosses don't know about it. He's always complaining about how they leave him no money of his own. What do you want to bet he's been skimming this cash and holding it on the side?"

"That's a bet you'd win," Ashe muttered, concentrating on doing something to Vitaly's phone.

"Are you getting the data?"

"That'll take only a few seconds to copy. Right now, I'm trying to get past his security code and get into the damned phone."

The little device plugged into the phone must have done its job, though, because in a moment, Ashe made a sound of triumph. He pulled out a second gadget that looked a lot like a thumb drive and plugged it into the phone.

She stared down at the pile of money speculatively. "I'm guessing there's more than four hundred thousand dollars here. I figured I'd better take it all so he can't cover this week's receipts out of his personal money. Besides, what self-respecting thief would leave any money behind?"

"Who in the hell is this guy? Small-time thugs don't have that kind of dough just lying around."

"It wasn't exactly lying around—" she started.

The new gadget flashed a green light, and she broke off as Ashe quickly unplugged the external drive. She held out her hand for the phone, but he said roughly, "I'll take it back in."

"You can't. We don't want him to suspect you of the theft. You can't be seen anywhere near the club tonight. I'll take it back inside."

"No. It's too dangerous."

"Bastien is still in there to keep an eye on me. And Vi-

taly will be less suspicious of me than you. Besides, I'm
the one who took it."

"I don't—"

She snatched the phone out of his hand. "There's no
time to argue about this. You know I'm right. Oh, and
there's a guard at the back door. Don't try to come in
after me."

She jumped out of the van before her courage could
fail her. This was insanity. She should let Ashe drive her
away from here and never look back. The thing was, if
Vitaly lost both his phone and his money, he would know
he'd been found out and flee. By daybreak tomorrow, he
and all those poor trafficked girls would disappear. She'd
been crazy to steal his phone. But it would be crazier not
to put the stupid thing back.

Hank paused at the mouth of the alley and peeked
around the corner. Dammit. The beefy guard was back
at his post. No way could she stroll past him back into
the club. Even if she could come up with a decent excuse
for having been outside, Vitaly would know for sure that
she'd carried his cash out of the club and passed it off to
someone.

She would have to go around to the club's front door. It
would cost her precious time, but she had no choice. Running as best she could in her tottery high heels, she made
her way around the block.

On the assumption that Vitaly's hypothetical sniper
would be watching the entrance, she slowed to a walk as
she turned the corner to approach the club. There was no
help for Vitaly's gunman spotting her. She could always
claim that she'd run out of the club to avoid the fighting,
she supposed. But it was a flimsy excuse, and Vitaly would
still suspect her of having been the thief.

The bouncer was not back at his post outside the front

door, which she took to mean that the mess inside was still getting sorted out. Patrons were starting to emerge from the club and standing around in clusters, recounting their part in the fight.

She slipped through the patrons unobtrusively and made her way inside the club. She moved as unassumingly as she could around the edge of the main room toward the bar. She slipped behind the near end of it, dropped to her knees and crawled her way down the length of it toward Vitaly's office.

Just as she reached the end of the bar nearest his office, though, her boss materialized in front of her. Or at least his knees did.

She stopped in chagrin.

"What are you doing down there?"

"Picking up broken glass," she lied

"That's what brooms are for. Get out there and help put the place back together. What a damned mess," he growled.

Hank nodded, his cell phone all but burning a hole in her skirt pocket. She stood up, slid around Vitaly and went out into the club. It was *destroyed*. With a sigh, she picked up the nearest intact chair and set it upright. How was she going to get Vitaly's phone back onto his desk? He was hovering near his office door, glowering at the staff scuttling around picking up broken pieces of chairs and tables, and he didn't look inclined to move away from that spot for a good long time.

If only the phone had fallen out of his pocket. Then she could "find" it…

Wait. That could work.

She cleaned her way over toward where Vitaly stood. She would have to find a spot he couldn't see from where he was standing to stash the phone. Someplace it might have slid to…there. Half-under a shelf unit at the back of

the bar used for storing extra glasses. It was just to the left
of his office door. He would be standing no more than three
feet from her if she tried planting it there.

It was wildly risky. But she didn't see that she had any
other choice.

Heart racing, she bent down to pick up an imaginary
piece of trash, the cell phone palmed in her hand. A quick
drop, a nudge with her toe, and the phone was tucked almost entirely out of sight. She moved away slowly, cleaning as she went.

When nobody was near, she muttered toward her chest,
"Phone's planted."

Ashe's reply was instant. "Then get the hell out of there."

"Can't." Moving a few feet away from the bartender,
who was righting a table, she mumbled, "It would look
weird."

"You can't stick around till the end of your shift, Hank.
He's going to figure out the money was stolen and go crazy.
You have to be out of there before then."

"I can't just walk out now. He's watching."

"I'm giving it a half hour, and then I'm coming in to
get you," Ashe warned.

She crawled under a table to pick up some broken glass
and to give herself privacy to mutter, "Call him. Tell him
to send me to your place because you need me for something."

Ashe made an exasperated sound. "And if he says no?"

"You okay under there, Hank? Be careful you don't
cut your knees. There's a lot of broken glass on the floor."

She looked up at the bartender. "I noticed. I was just
picking up some of the big pieces."

"Don't worry about that stuff. I'll sweep it all up once
we've got the tables upright."

"Okay," she replied, pasting on a fake smile.

The fight had chased out all of the patrons, and the place was deserted as she and the other staff finished the worst of the cleanup. Vitaly griped at length about the lost business and how much money the fight had cost him. Hah. He had no idea how much he had really lost.

Hank got an unpleasant bit of news in her ear when Ashe murmured, "Had to move the van. Some guy took a hard a look at it just now. I'm about ten blocks away, but I'll come back and pick you up when you leave the bar. Hank, can you give me an estimate of how much longer you'll be in there?"

"Gimme ten," she replied.

"Huh?" one of the waitresses asked her.

Hank looked up quickly. "Oh. Nothing. I was just thinking out loud that Vitaly's gonna have to buy a bunch of new chairs. I figure at least ten."

Ashe snorted in her ear. "Good recovery."

She sent him a mental eye roll and carried a sack of trash toward the back of the club, where the bags were being collected and hauled out to the back alley by the bouncer.

The bartender waited until a pause in Vitaly's ongoing tirade and asked, "Any chance you'll close early tonight? I don't mind giving up a couple hours' pay. And the place is empty."

A couple of the waitresses chimed in, offering to forego their last two hours' worth of pay for an early night off. None of them would make a dime in tips with the club deserted and trashed, and their actual pay was pitiful. It wasn't much of a sacrifice on anyone's part.

"Okay, fine," Vitaly bit out. "All of you. Get out. Go. Before I change my mind."

Wow. The Russian accent was thick tonight. A little stressed out, was he? Hank smiled to herself as she and the other girls hurried out of the club before he could change his mind about shutting down early.

Thank God. She peeled away from the other girls like she usually did to head toward her apartment. "You caught that, Ashe? I'm out."

Ashe let out an audible sigh of relief. "Bastien's three blocks north and two blocks east of your position. Make your way to him on foot. He's driving a red Chevelle. I want to keep the van well away from the club. That guy who cruised past to look at it worried me."

"Okay."

Maybe it was because she was so relieved to have gotten rid of Vitaly's phone and to have made it out of the club that she let down her guard. But the man had jumped out of the shadows and had his arm around her neck almost before she registered his presence. Something wet slapped over her face, and her last thought was that this was not good. Not good at all.

Chapter 13

Ashe jolted when Hank's cry of surprise in his earbud cut off sharply. "Hank. Talk to me!"

Nothing. All he heard were some rustles as if Hank's clothes were moving around against the microphone.

"You need to say something right now, Hank. Anything. Just make a noise."

Nothing at all.

Ashe's pulse spiked even harder than it already had. "Something's wrong, Catfish. Go get her. And hurry, for God's sake."

The gunning of a huge engine and a squeal of tires across Bastien's throat microphone announced that he'd followed Ashe's order to the letter.

Into his own microphone, Ashe said urgently, "Talk to me, baby. What's happening? Where are you?"

If she could hear him, she didn't answer. Perhaps her earbud had been knocked out. Her microphone continued to work, though, and a noise similar to something heavy being dragged across pavement transmitted. Ashe heard a grunt.

Dammit. A *male* grunt. The kind a guy made when he hoisted up something heavy. Like a body. *Hank's body.* Horrible certainty ripped through him. Someone had snatched Hank. It had to be one of Vitaly's men. With all the drunks recently exiting the Voodoo, no common street thug would be hanging around the area. Too many people had been milling around too recently for petty crime to be safe.

"A man has grabbed Hank," he reported to Bastien. "She was about one block from the club, headed in your direction. Look in an alley. It sounded like he dragged her somewhere. There's been no talking between accomplices, so I'm pretty sure it's just one guy. But the takedown was fast as hell."

"A pro, then," Bastien replied tersely. "Say your ETA."

"Estimated time of arrival…three minutes," Ashe snapped. But he and Bastien knew that was a lifetime in special operations terms. A man could be killed in three seconds. Quietly and efficiently.

"Hurry, Hollywood."

No kidding. He already had the van floored and was squealing around corners like a drag-racing lunatic. It was madness to take the van back to the vicinity of the club so soon after robbing the joint, but it wasn't like he had any choice. Screw busting up Vitaly's operation. If anything bad happened to Hank, Ashe would never forgive himself.

Hang on, kitten. I'm coming.

God, he hated this helpless feeling. By the time he could get back to her, whatever was happening to Hank would be long over. "Hurry, Bastien."

"I'm on it," his friend bit out. The engine noise stopped and Ashe heard a car door open.

Ashe cursed silently in a steady mental stream when he wasn't concentrating on driving at breakneck speed or on hearing something—anything—to help Bastien find her. Hank's mike had since gone silent. Either her assailant had found it and disabled it, or she was stationary at the moment.

Why would the bastard knock her out, drag her someplace and then just leave her? It didn't make sense. Not that he was wishing any further attack on her, but still. It was strange.

Unless Vitaly's spotter had grabbed her. Ashe and Bastien never had proven that Vitaly actually had a man watching the Who Do Voodoo from another vantage point along the street, but Ashe was convinced the guy was lurking out there somewhere. What if the spotter had seen something that made him suspicious of Hank? Would he snatch her off the street?

More to the point, would the guy have reported in to Vitaly and gotten orders to snatch Hank first, or would the guy have just taken the initiative and done it himself?

If Vitaly was wise to Hank, would he give the order to kill her immediately, or would her boss want to question her? Find out who she was working for?

Ashe gripped the steering wheel tighter, his mind reeling, when the street the Voodoo was on finally came into sight ahead. He slowed to a sane speed to take the corner. No sense bringing Vitaly himself out into the street to check out a giant squeal of rubber on concrete. The guy had to be jumpy as hell after the events so far this evening. And as far as Ashe could tell, Vitaly hadn't even realized he'd been robbed of four hundred thousand bucks. The guy was going to go crazy when that happened.

He reported tersely to Bastien, "Something metallic just

banged close to Hank. It sounded big. Hollow. A Dumpster, maybe. Or a garage door."

"I'm moving in," Bastien breathed. "Second alley on the left, east of the club. I spotted a pair of sharp tracks, like those stupid high heels she wears being dragged."

"I'll be there in sixty seconds."

"Come in quiet. I'm going dark."

Which meant Bastien was going to stop talking. "Roger." Ashe pulled the van over to a curb just behind Bastien's red muscle car. He jumped out of the van and was careful to lock the door and set the van's special alarm system behind himself. No point in making it easy for Vitaly to get his money back.

As Ashe slunk toward the alley in full stealth mode, he surprised himself when a prayer drifted through his mind. He was not a religious man by nature, and most of the time on missions he was too busy staying alive to invoke higher powers. But tonight, a prayer emerged from the dark recesses of his subconscious. She *had* to be okay.

Ashe eased into the narrow gap between darkened buildings. The parallel stripes of what did indeed appear to have been a pair of high-heeled shoes being dragged along the gravel and dirt alley came into sight.

He drew his pistol and breathed to Bastien, "I'm in your six and packing. Standard field of fire." Which was shorthand for telling his partner that he was right behind, carrying a gun, and to be careful not to shoot Ashe by accident.

The two of them had practiced maneuvers like this a hundred times and knew the drill cold. But procedure was procedure. And it wasn't like Ashe was functioning at his best right now. His entire body jangled with barely controlled nerves, and he was so jumpy he could hardly contain himself. Now, of all times, it was important to rely on the standard protocols they'd spent so many hours drilling into their bones.

A doorway yawned in the wall ahead. As he drew close to it, Ashe saw it was slightly ajar. Bastien was making it easy for him to follow. Good man. Ashe slipped into the darkness.

His heart just about leaped out of his chest, and he struggled to get enough air into his lungs. It was the most awful and unfamiliar feeling. He hadn't been this scared since he'd been a kid. Never in his military career had this body-enveloping panic come over him. And he'd come damned close to death a *lot*. Hell, he'd killed and seen other men die more times than he cared to count.

But it had never been Hank. Not sweet, beautiful Hank.

He paused for a moment to slow his breathing forcibly. To allow his pulse to settle the hell down. To clear his mind. Hank's life depended on him finding that emotionless, focused state of a warrior. C'mon. He could *do* this.

It was a fight, but he got there. Senses on full alert, he continued into the bowels of the darkened building. The interior was carved into a series of smaller spaces. Some looked light industrial, some looked like artists' studios and others looked like storage lockers. How in the hell was he going to find Hank in this mess? It would take hours to clear the place cubicle by cubicle.

Bastien was in here somewhere. In breaching a room, the first guy in always swept right. On the assumption that his counterpart had headed right, he turned to the left and commenced checking doors and spinning into the spaces behind each unlocked one. It was tense work, particularly since silence was required lest he and Bastien give themselves away.

Ashe spotted a steel staircase and hesitated. Should he go up? The attacker had been dragging Hank's body. Nah.

He wouldn't have taken her up there. She was down here on the main floor. He continued onward.

A scrape alerted him to the presence of someone else just ahead. His pistol swung up before him into firing position as he eased forward, rolling onto the balls of his feet with each stealthy step. Bastien or the bad guy? His finger cupped the trigger of his weapon, ready to deliver instant death.

A voice muttering low in Russian answered the question of the identity of the man ahead. Using the conversation to cover the noise of his approach, Ashe raced forward.

The man spoke again, impatiently. He was urging whoever was on the other end of the line to pick up his phone. A pause, then the guy left an impatient message to call him back immediately. It was urgent.

Ashe would bet it was. The bastard had seen fit to snatch Hank off the street. A movement down the hallway made him swing his weapon in that direction. Bastien. Closing in fast.

Using hand signals, Ashe indicated that they would use a standard room-clearing entry, going in hard and hot. The idea was to surprise Hank's captor for just long enough that Ashe and Bastien would gain control of the situation.

Bastien signaled that, from his angle, the room appeared to have clean sight lines. Which meant there were no visible obstacles that would impede their ability to see and shoot Hank's captor.

Ashe signaled that a live capture was preferable. Bastien pulled a disgusted face but nodded.

A quick countdown with his fingers, and then Ashe surged around the corner, shouting. Bastien came in on his heels, swinging left and also bellowing commands for the guy to freeze.

A man bending over a prone form. Reaching for his waistband. Dropping to one knee. *Shooter.*

The impressions registered so fast that Ashe didn't consciously process each one of them. He and Bastien fired simultaneously, and the target spun to one side and fell to the floor, swearing.

Ashe charged forward and planted a foot on the guy's neck. "Stay down," he snarled in Russian. Bastien kicked away the guy's pistol, which had fallen from his hand, and knelt by Hank, who was sprawled on the floor beside her kidnapper.

"Strong pulse, no visible injuries," Bastien reported tersely.

"Then I guess you get to live," Ashe growled at the man under his boot. The guy grunted, which Ashe took to mean the man understood English. Bastien pulled plastic zip ties out of a pouch on his belt and quickly immobilized and frisked their prisoner.

Ashe handed the guy over to Bastien and gathered Hank into his arms. She stirred slightly against him, as if even unconscious, she recognized him. "What the hell did you use on her?" he demanded over her head.

The guy shrugged. "It'll wear off soon. Bitch fought hard and didn't get much of a whiff of it before I lost the damned pad."

Ashe assumed the guy meant a pad he'd used to cover her mouth and nose, soaked in the chemical he'd knocked her out with. "Who do you work for?"

"Nobody. I was just messing around."

Bastien snorted in patent disbelief. "Is this an arrest, Hollywood, or is this off-book?"

"Oh, it's completely off the record. This guy's gonna talk if I have to pull all his teeth and fingernails out one by one."

Bastien shrugged at Hank's kidnapper. "Too bad, dude. My friend here is the meanest sonofabitch you've ever had the misfortune to cross paths with."

He moved away from Ashe and the prisoner and disappeared behind a tall wooden crate. Ashe understood what Bastien was doing. The cop needed plausible deniability later. To be able to claim that he'd no idea what Ashe had done to the prisoner and he hadn't been present to stop it.

Ashe heard footsteps jogging up what sounded like steel steps. His friend's voice floated downstairs, muffled. "You know that sniper you thought was covering the street? We found his hide. Nice rig he's got. Modified Russian rifle, Israeli sight. State-of-the-art stuff. I'm impressed. If this op's off-book, I may have to take this baby out for a test fire myself."

"Be my guest," Ashe replied mildly.

The sniper trussed on the floor flailed, irritated. No shooter ever let anyone else mess with his rig. It screwed up the sighting and made the weapon feel funny. Ashe made a sympathetic sound. "Sucks for you. Not that you're gonna walk out of here in any condition to shoot a gun for the foreseeable future, man."

The shooter subsided on the floor, eyeing him warily.

"How about we skip the questions and I just tell you who you are?" Ashe announced. "You work for Vitaly Parenko. He's a low-level lieutenant in a much larger and more powerful operation. You technically work for that larger group and are annoyed at being stuck in this hellhole day after day, keeping an eye on his two-bit whorehouse. How am I doing so far?"

The sniper's eyelids flickered faintly. Ashe was spot-on. He continued pleasantly. "You saw the girl, here, walk down the street toward the club hours after she normally shows up for work. That caught your attention. Made you a little suspicious. Then she acted tense when she left the club tonight. Tense enough to trigger full-blown warning bells in your head. Being a highly trained operative, you trust your gut, and it was shouting at you that she was up to something. Am I still on track?"

The sniper's gaze slid away from his face guiltily. And that would be a yes. Ashe was spot-on so far.

"Bored off your ass and spoiling for a little action, you get the bright idea to snatch the girl. Question her. Maybe have some gratuitous sex with her before you hand her over to your boss. If she's up to no good and you bring her in, you catch the attention of the big bosses and they let you out of this godforsaken job. If she turns out to be just an innocent waitress, you—what—kill her? No one will miss her anyway. You have your fun and dispose of her body in one of the Dumpsters downstairs, with no one the wiser. Yes?"

The sniper glared up at him defiantly.

Ashe punched the guy in the face with all his strength, crushing the guy's nose into a bleeding mess. The sniper screamed.

Hank stirred but did not wake. Good. Ashe wanted to be done with this little interrogation before she came around. She was too soft-hearted and kind to be able to witness what he had to do to this guy. He, on the other hand, had no such compunction. The bastard had intended to kill Hank.

"Who's Vitaly's boss?" Ashe asked the bloody sniper.

The guy looked faintly surprised at that question. "No idea," he spit out on a mouthful of blood.

"Wrong answer." Another punch. Another scream. A couple of teeth spit out at his feet.

"Let's try that again," Ashe said patiently.

It took a couple more minutes and a couple more body blows that left the sniper with a half dozen broken ribs, but the guy finally thought better of protecting his employers. He grunted, "Vitaly reports to a guy called the Butler."

"Name?"

"I don't know!" the sniper answered with enough urgency that Ashe was inclined to believe him. "They call him that because he likes to wear nice suits, and they're always perfectly tailored and pressed."

"The Butler, huh?" Bastien's voice floated down from overhead. "The butler *always* did it. Bad rap those dudes get. Everyone's afraid of a meticulous murderer."

Leave it to Bastien to inject a note of lightness into the proceedings as a gentle reminder to Ashe to be chill and not get carried away. "Message received, Catfish."

He had just one more question for the sniper. "Ever hear of a guy named Max Kuznetsov?"

Fear exploded—literally exploded—in the guy's stare. Even with one eye swollen most of the way shut and the other side of his face puffing up fast, there was no missing the genuine terror that flared at the mention of Hank's brother. *What the hell?*

Hank made a faint moaning noise, and her hands twitched a bit. Ashe stepped away from the sniper quickly to kneel down next to her. He pushed the tangled hair off her forehead gently. "Hey, baby. I'm here. You're safe."

Hank's eyes fluttered open. Drifted closed.

He tried again. "Can you wake up for me? Open your eyes, kitten. Let me know you're okay."

Her eyes didn't open, but she sighed. "You came."

"Of course I came. I'll always come for you." He realized with a start that he meant it, too.

"I'm...okay. If you're here, I'm okay."

It took her a few more minutes, but gradually she emerged from the stupor the sniper's chemicals had induced. She was able to sit up with Ashe's help, and she looked around in confusion. "Where am I?"

Propping her upright with an arm behind her shoulders, he explained, "Your friendly neighborhood kidnapper, here, dragged you into this place. Catfish and I found you and apprehended him."

He helped her to her feet and winced as she faced her assailant. "Looks like you worked him over pretty good," she commented.

Ashe shrugged. "He resisted capture."

Hank glanced at him drily. "Right. Let's go with that explanation."

"Only reason he's alive is because I figured you'd get mad if I killed him."

She nodded slowly. "A small fish like this isn't worth killing. I want the big sharks. If they've hurt my brother, you can kill all of them you want."

Bastien came downstairs and joined them now that Q&A time was over. "What do you want to do with him?" He jerked his head in the direction of the prisoner.

Ashe studied the guy. "I suppose the gators would find him tasty." He reached down and tore the guy's shirt off his back and was not surprised to see copious tattoos, including symbols that traditionally indicated kills. "The FBI might enjoy all this pretty artwork, though."

"I do believe they would. Quite the art connoisseurs, those feds." Bastien pulled out his cell phone and made a call suggesting that he had a gift for whoever was at the other end of the line.

"They'll be here in twenty minutes," he reported.

They used most of that time to search the sniper's hidey-hole and to copy files off the guy's laptop computer and cell phone. Regretfully, Bastien left the sniper rig for the

FBI to confiscate since it would help implicate the prisoner as a mob assassin.

Sirens became audible in the distance and Bastien announced, "That's our signal to go."

Ashe nodded, then bent down to whisper, "Can you walk, kitten, or do you need me to carry you?"

Hank frowned. "I can walk." But as he helped her to her feet, she wobbled slightly. He wrapped his arm around her waist, and she seemed happy to lean against his side as they made their way out of the building.

They reached the alley and he asked Bastien, "Do you need to stick around and make a statement?"

"Nah. I gave the tip to a buddy of mine. Told him to consider the guy he'll find inside an early Christmas present from an anonymous friend."

Ashe and Bastien traded grins.

"You bringing her back to my place?" Bastien murmured.

"Nah. I think we'd better go to ground for the night. Vitaly's gonna figure out he was robbed any second, and he's gonna be pissed. When he figures out he's lost his sniper, he's going to be doubly annoyed."

"Keep your head down, Hollywood."

"You, too."

Ashe gently helped Hank into the van and started the engine as Bastien's red Chevelle pulled away from the curb. He steered the van away from the alley and was just turning, a block down the street, when the first federal car rounded the corner.

"Where are we going?" Hank asked.

He glanced over at her, frowning. That was an excellent question. They needed someplace quiet where she could sleep off the rest of the drugs and where no one would find them for the next twenty-four hours. That meant no credit cards, no hotel registers where employees could be paid off to give out guest names. He knew one place that fit the bill, but it was the last place on earth he wanted to go.

Dammit.

Chapter 14

Hank woke up slowly. Stripes of light on a white ceiling spoke of venetian blinds. Not Bastien's place, then; his bedrooms had no windows. She turned her head and saw that she was in a rather old-fashioned bedroom. The furniture looked like it came from the early 1960s. Sturdy construction, uninspired design. Mid-century American decor, her father would have classed it.

And dusty. Everything in the room was covered in a thin film of gray. How did she get here? Wherever *here* was.

She remembered being attacked with vivid clarity. Then everything after that went fuzzy. Indistinct. A dark room. A bloody man. And Ashe. He had rescued her. She thought she remembered Bastien being there, too. And then…nothing.

She sat up carefully. She was a tiny bit dizzy, but nothing outrageous. She swung her feet to the floor and stood up. Again, a bit off kilter, but functional. She looked down in dismay at the flannel granny nightie she was wearing. It reached only her midcalves and was yellowed with age. Where on earth had this relic come from? *Whose* was it?

"Ashe?" she called.

She opened the hallway door and was surprised to see that she was in some sort of house. She wandered down a short hallway, ducked into the restroom, and then continued her exploration. A living/dining room opened up, and she spied a kitchen beyond it. And good smells were coming from the kitchen.

Following her nose, she opened the swinging door.

Ashe looked up from a stove and moved toward her quickly. "I was going to bring you breakfast in bed."

"I'll go back to bed if you want."

He gathered her into his arms, gazing down at her tenderly. "How are you feeling this morning?"

"Physically fine. Still a little shaken emotionally, I guess."

His jaw tightened. "I could still find him and kill him for you—"

"No. That's fine. But thank you for the offer. How are you holding up after last night?"

A shadow of something she might call fear if she didn't know him so well passed through his eyes. "I gotta say, you gave me a scare. When I heard that bastard snatch you...and I wasn't close enough to save you...I had a few rough moments, there."

She buried her nose against his chest while he wrapped her arms tightly around her. She held on to his waist almost as tightly. "The worst of it was thinking that I might never see you again. I finally found a man like you, and then I was going to up and die. It just wasn't fair."

"Nobody's dying any time soon. Got that?"

She nodded against his chest wishing she was half as sure as he sounded.

"Sit. Keep me company while I finish cooking breakfast. Here, let me help you."

"I'm fine," she protested. But it didn't dissuade him from treating her like an invalid and handing her into a vinyl-covered chrome chair. She plucked at the voluminous cotton nightgown enveloping her. "Whose nightgown is this?"

"I found it in a drawer. I think it was my mother's."

"Should I be creeped out at that?"

"Nah. She was great. She'd have been happy to lend it to you."

His mother. Which made this his parents' house. And made her a wee bit slow on the uptake this morning. She asked, "Is this the house you grew up in?"

He glanced around the room. "Yup. I guess it belongs to me, now that my old man is gone."

"No brothers and sisters?"

"Nope."

Intrigued by this glimpse into his past, she leaned forward. "Tell me about your family."

His expression closed up tightly. "Not much I haven't told you already. My dad was a jerk, and my mom was a saint."

"And you? How would you describe yourself?"

He shrugged. "I guess I came out somewhere in the middle. Maybe I tend toward being a jerk like my dad."

She laid her hand on top of his. "Ashe, you most certainly take after your mother."

He smiled sadly. "She was a fine woman."

"And you loved her a lot."

He shrugged. Slipped his hand out from under hers and

moved back to the stove. "Mustn't burn the pancakes," he announced.

She studied him as he moved around the kitchen. The set of his shoulders was stiff. Tense. He was uncomfortable being back home. "How long has it been since you were here?"

He frowned. "Seven years, give or take. I came back for the funeral when my mom died."

Whoa. "Didn't your father die fairly recently?"

"Yeah. Last winter."

"And you didn't come home for his funeral."

"I was downrange. Couldn't get back."

She didn't buy that excuse for a minute. But it helped explain why he was so wired now. She let the subject drop and kept the conversation light throughout breakfast. The bracing meal helped her feel like her old self, and she insisted on helping with the dishes. She dried while Ashe put the dishes away. They were just finishing up when she asked casually, "Do you need to go through your father's personal possessions while we're here? I could help if you'd like."

He glanced at her, bleak emptiness yawning in his eyes. "I've got no use for any of his stuff."

"Look, Ashe. We're not all blessed with perfect parents. And sometimes they do a crappy job of raising us. But I have to say, your father must have done something right because you turned out fantastic. Whether it was because of him or in spite of him, I don't particularly care. I only know I approve of the end result."

Ashe stared at her hard for a long time, and she let him. She knew all too well how hard it was to forgive parents for their sins.

He spun away, gripping the edge of the counter until his knuckles turned white.

"Are you sure you won't ever want anything to remember your parents by?" she asked gently. "What if you have kids someday? They'll want to know who their grandparents were. You should at least keep some pictures and hang on to a few keepsakes."

Ashe's jaw tightened, but he didn't utter a word. He merely put away the last skillet and banged the cupboard door shut. Then he disappeared from the kitchen.

She didn't follow.

Sighing with frustration, Hank shoved a hand through her hair. Granted, she might not have been close to her father, but at least she hadn't engaged in open warfare with the man.

A little while later she wandered out into the living area, but there was no sign of Ashe. Curious, she moved down the hallway into the bedroom she'd woken up in. It had to have been his parents' room. She poked around and found a sturdy suitcase and laid it open on the bed. Carefully she wrapped the photographs from the walls in shirts from his father's drawers and laid them in the suitcase. She opened the desk and went through the drawers one by one.

Into the suitcase went his father's wallet. Military discharge papers. Marriage license. Ashe's birth certificate. More pictures—some of Ashe as a boy, others of a man who looked a lot like Ashe in what looked like Vietnam, some of a beautiful, laughing young woman who must have been Ashe's mother. A stack of citation certificates that went with military medals: service medals, four Purple Hearts, and a half dozen medals for valor awarded to Ashe's father, Walter.

And then she hit the mother lode. In the bottom drawer of the desk lay a scrapbook. It was stuffed full of memorabilia from Ashe's life. The mementos and pages devoted to his childhood were written in a feminine hand.

But as Ashe's military career commenced, the handwriting changed. Walter had maintained this scrapbook when his wife passed away.

The last entry was less than a year ago, a newspaper clipping about the heroic rescue of a pair of aid workers from a foreign war zone. Ashe wasn't named in the article, but Walter had obviously known his son had been part of the mission.

She closed the scrapbook gently, stroking the leather cover lightly. She could feel the love that had gone into making this. The love the couple had had for their only child.

Should she show it to Ashe? It was doubtful that he would appreciate it. Not yet, but maybe someday. Although she'd been upset with him earlier, she understood his anger toward his father and had to respect his right to feel that way. Only time could heal the wounds of the past, and instinct told her that Ashe's father was too newly gone for him to be ready to see this book.

Her own father had thrown expensive gifts and money at her over the years by way of apology for his lack of attention, and none of it had helped her feel more charitably toward him, either.

She tucked the scrapbook carefully in the suitcase with his mother's jewelry and the other bits and pieces of his parents' lives. It seemed sad to her that their whole lives had come down to a single suitcase. At least her parents had left behind a magnificent collection of art and antiques for her and her brother. Each piece had been lovingly found and repaired if necessary. Her mother had been brilliant at restoring the distressed paintings her father had brought home over the years. Every time Hank looked at one of the paintings, she saw her father's taste and her mother's loving hands.

All Ashe had was the scrapbook. She would see to it the thing was kept safe until he was ready to really see the love collected in its pages. She closed the suitcase and carried it to the kitchen. Over the next several hours, she went through the house in search of valuable and unique objects that were worth preserving for posterity.

Eventually, Ashe asked her impatiently, "Do I want to know what you're doing?"

"I grew up in a house full of antique dealers. I'm collecting all the decent pieces for you to hang on to for later. I know you don't want any of this stuff now, but later you'll thank me for saving something for you."

He just rolled his eyes.

"Help me carry this stuff out to the van."

He stood up, frowning. "And what am I supposed to do with it after that?"

"You can put it in the storage unit with my mother's stuff. I just don't want this place getting robbed or a hurricane hitting it when you're not here to protect it from harm."

"It's just a house, Hank. And some stuff. I already told you I don't want any of it."

She stepped close to him and laid her palm gently on his cheek. "Just trust me on this one, okay? I lost both of my parents, too. And someday, you're going to wish you'd kept a small piece of them."

He turned away sharply, cursing. Then he snapped over his shoulder, "Fine. What goes out to the van?"

He carried out the suitcase and a laundry basket full of old sterling silver pieces. She packed his mother's collection of porcelain dolls and his father's service uniform in a small trunk that went out to the van, too.

Hank was just eyeing the small hutch in the dining room and pondering whether or not she dared suggest that he keep the antique piece when the living room window cracked. She flinched, badly startled.

A fast-moving large object crashed into her from behind and she slammed onto the floor. If the breath hadn't have been completely knocked out of her, she would have screamed. But as it was, she lay silent, crushed beneath Ashe's large body, too shocked to struggle.

"Don't get up, Hank. Stay on your belly and start crawling toward the bedrooms."

"What's happening?"

"Someone's shooting at us."

"The sniper from last night?" she gasped.

"Not a chance he's out of FBI custody yet. Nope. We kicked a hornet's nest yesterday. Vitaly or his guy must have planted a tracker on you. I burned your clothes, but I must have missed it." He added tersely, "Start crawling."

"What are you going to do?"

"Shoot back and kill this bastard."

Terrified, she crept away from Ashe. She hated not being plastered to his side. But she would only get in his way if it turned into a shoot-out.

Why hadn't he told her to head for the kitchen? He must be worried that a bad guy would come in the back door. If the house was surrounded, they were in big trouble. She pulled out her cell phone and pushed along with her feet and free hand as it rang.

"Bastien," she whispered, "Someone's shooting at us. We need help."

"Where are you?" the cop asked quickly.

"Ashe's folks' house. I don't know the address."

"I do. Tell him to hold on for five minutes. And keep your head down, Hank."

She relayed Bastien's message just as the dining room window exploded in a shower of flying glass. Ashe popped up from behind the sofa and fired a pistol through the front window. The sound of the shot was deafening and spurred her to hurry down the hallway, away from the unfolding madness.

She'd seen a big metal box in his father's bedroom closet that looked like an ammo container. On the off-chance that she was right, she headed for it once she reached the bedroom—and took the opportunity to hide in the closet while she was at it.

She fumbled at the latch in the dark and lifted out a layer of foam. Her fingers encountered steel. Exploring the shape, she recognized a revolver. Gratefully she pulled it out and kept exploring the box's contents. A pistol and several boxes of ammunition later, she backed out of the closet.

"Ashe! I found your father's guns and ammo. Do you need them?"

"Stay put. I'll come to you," he called back.

A flurry of gunshots from outside announced that his movement was drawing fire from whoever was surrounding the house. Ashe dived through the door and hit the floor beside her.

"We'll head for the bathroom. All the tile and ceramic in there will protect us a little extra. Then we'll sit tight until the police get here—"

"What's that smell?" she interrupted. A strong odor of gasoline abruptly hung in the air.

"Sonofabitch," Ashe muttered. "They're gonna burn us out."

"*Who* is?"

"Doesn't matter right now. Survive first. Identify attackers later."

"Now what?" she asked in mounting panic. The bad guys were going to set the house on fire? This was an old home. No doubt all-wood construction. It would go up like a tinder box. "How soon until the police get here?"

"It won't matter. The bad guys will back off. Get out of sight. Cops won't enter the house with it on fire. They'll wait for the fire department to get here. And in the meantime, you and I will be smoked out or forced out by the heat. And when we show ourselves, the shooters will pick us off."

She thought fast, purely an act of self-defense against the panic clawing at her belly. "They've had to move in close to douse the house in gas and light it on fire, right?"

"Yeah."

"Then they're having to back off. If they're doing that now, this is our window of opportunity to get out. While their backs are turned and they're not looking. They won't expect us to make a break for it yet, will they?"

"It's risky," he warned her.

"It's better than getting cooked. Or shot."

"Okay. Let's go." He talked as he rapidly jammed a clip into a handgun and chambered a round. "Van's out back. You take the pistol. It's the smallest weapon. If you see anything move, shoot at it. You don't have to hit it. We just want to make the bastards duck for cover."

She nodded and took the weapon he handed her. "Safety's off," he muttered. "Point and shoot. And hang on. It'll jump hard in your hand."

She didn't bother to tell him that she knew exactly what it would feel like. Spying a couple of extra clips she pocketed those, as well. He loaded the pair of revolvers quickly and nodded to her. "Ready? Stay on my heels. I'll be moving fast."

"Got it."

He opened the bedroom door and raced down the hallway to the kitchen. He was not lying. She had to run hard to keep up with him. He didn't even pause when he hit the back door. He just barged through the screen door, tearing it off the frame as he went. A gun in each hand, he burst outside. He fired left and right simultaneously.

The sound was painful, it was so loud. Something moved behind the tree in the backyard and she fired at it, double-tapping the trigger from a shoulder-height stance. A man crumpled to the ground beyond a big oak tree.

Ashe dived into the back of the van, and she dived in right behind him. While she rolled to her belly and turned to face the back door, he scrambled for the driver's seat. From the floor, he turned on the ignition and used his hand to push the accelerator.

The vehicle leaped forward. It careened to one side in a sharp turn, and she slammed into the side of the van. The back door swung open and a man came into view, a rifle poised at his shoulder. She fired and the man's rifle spun to one side. Whether or not she'd hit him or he'd just ducked, she had no idea.

The van picked up speed down the driveway. It bumped over the curb and swerved into the street. A flurry of gunshots pierced the side of the van over her head, and she plastered herself flat against the floor. The van engine revved as it raced away from the house. A third armed man came into view, stepping out from behind a parked car, and she was ready for him. She sent three rounds at the guy in quick succession. He went down as if she'd hit him in the leg.

And then they were turning violently again, and Ashe's home disappeared from sight. She ejected her clip, which couldn't have had more than a couple of rounds left in it, and slammed in another clip. All the while, she watched alertly out the back for any sign of pursuit.

After a couple of minutes, Ashe pulled the van over to

the curb, and she closed the back door and crawled into the passenger seat beside him. But she kept the pistol handy in her lap.

"Jeez, Hank. Are you okay?" Ashe bit out.

"Yes. You?"

"Fine. You're not hurt, are you?"

"No, Ashe. I'm fine. I swear."

"Thank God," he breathed. He reached over to squeeze her hand tightly for a moment, but then he pulled away from the curb and into traffic once more.

They drove in silence after that until they merged onto the highway.

Then Ashe looked over at her grimly. "Care to tell me how you know how to handle a firearm like that?"

She shrugged. "My dad showed me and my brother when we were kids."

"Was your dad military, by any chance?"

"Not to my knowledge."

"And he taught you kids how to prone fire and double-tap when you aim at a human?"

She shrugged, not fond of this line of questioning. It skirted too close to family secrets she'd been warned never to share. "Where are we going?"

"Naval Air Station New Orleans. I'm done having you attacked and shot at. I'm stashing you on a military installation, where I know Vitaly and his buddies can't get at you."

That sounded just fine with her. The van stopped at a guard shack, and Ashe passed an ID card out the window. The guard looked at it and saluted Ashe smartly as he passed the card back.

He drove to a nondescript pink brick building and ushered her inside. A bunch of men in uniforms stared back at her while she stared at them. "Why are they all looking at me?" she whispered to Ashe.

He grinned lopsidedly. "They don't see many civilian women, and rarely as hot as you, and never with me."

Her gaze swung to him. "Don't you like girls?" she blurted.

The roomful of men erupted in laughter, startling her more than a little.

"Who've you got there, Hollywood?" A handsome blond man with icy blue eyes stepped forward.

"Sir, this is Hank Smith. Hank, this is Commander Cole Perriman. My boss."

"I'm so sorry," Hank said gravely to the naval officer.

He smiled warmly at her. "I like her."

Ashe asked cautiously, "What brings you to New Orleans, sir?"

"You brought me to New Orleans," Perriman answered tartly. "What's going on?"

"Someone just tried to burn us out of my home and gun us down. The van outside should have some rounds lodged in it for forensic purposes."

At a glance from Ashe's boss, a guy near the door opened his desk and pulled out a box about the size of a fishing kit. Guy and kit disappeared out the front door.

"Come with me," Perriman replied tersely.

Ashe rolled his eyes at Hank behind his boss's back, and everyone else in the room rolled their eyes at Ashe. Worried all of a sudden, she let Ashe lead her into a conference room and close the door.

The commander waited until Ashe seated her politely in a chair at the long table, then turned on him sharply. "Start talking, Hollywood. What the hell have you gotten yourself into?"

If a sense of foreboding had been hanging over Hank's head since she met Ashe, it now blossomed into a thundercloud of impending doom.

Chapter 15

Ashe had given enough mission debriefs over the years to get through this one quickly and smoothly. But he couldn't shake a sinking feeling that Perriman knew more about the Who Do Voodoo than he was letting on. Frosty sat mostly silent through the debriefing, listening to Ashe but watching Hank.

Why was his boss so interested in her? Sure, she was beautiful enough that it was hard for a guy to take his gaze off her. But Perriman was staring at her like he'd love to crawl inside her head and uncover her secrets.

His boss could get in line on that one. This was the first time since the shoot-out at his folks' house that he'd slowed down long enough to process what he'd seen. Where did she learn how to fire a pistol like that? To reload so quickly and efficiently, like she'd handled a lot of weapons before? Why hadn't she completely panicked when the firefight broke out?

That kind of skill with weapons came from years of handling them. Had her father been her teacher? Or maybe her brother. Either way, the questions about her past continued to stack up.

Not that he was complaining that she'd stayed calm and focused, remaining fully functional under extreme duress, but that sort of behavior was just weird for a civilian. Even macho soldiers often froze up during their first firefight with bullets flying overhead.

Ashe caught up to the present, finishing up with a brief description of the gunfight at his parents' house, running away with Hank and driving over here.

Hank surprised him by interjecting, "Could someone remove the stuff from the back of the van and put it somewhere safe for Ashe? It's a collection of memorabilia from his family. And given that the house was on fire when we left, they're likely to be the only articles he retains from his past."

Commander Perriman picked up a telephone and relayed her request to someone at the other end of the line.

Ashe appreciated her concern over the items she'd collected for him. And he got that her family had been all about preserving the past. But frankly, he'd been a whole lot more concerned with getting her out of the house alive than a suitcase full of junk.

Perriman opened the folder he'd brought in here with him. Aww, crud. Jennie Finch had already briefed his boss, after all. And the guy was obviously armed with a pile of background material. Which meant there would now be a crap-ton of questions.

Ashe took a mental deep breath and prepared for an intense interrogation.

Except his boss didn't speak to him. Perriman turned, instead, to Hank. "So, Miss Kuznetsova. How much do you know about the car accident you and your mother had when you were thirteen?"

She looked as startled as Ashe felt. What did *that* have to do with anything?

"Since I was there, I know a fair bit about it," she replied a shade defensively.

"Do you know who hit you?"

"The police never found the hit-and-run driver."

"Who told you that?" Perriman asked.

Alarm bells went off in Ashe's head. Perriman knew more about the accident than he was saying. But his boss wanted to find out how much Hank knew before he showed his cards.

Hank frowned. "I spent all my waking hours at my mom's side in the hospital for the first few weeks after the crash. She was touch and go for a while, and then we were waiting to find out how bad her paralysis was as the swelling around her spine went down. My father was the one who told us the police never caught the guy who hit us."

"Did you see the vehicle that struck you?" Perriman asked.

"Sort of. It was big and dark. Tried to pass us, but a car came from the other direction and the guy swerved into us. We went off the road and hit a huge tree." She added drily, "The tree won."

"How fast were you going at the time of the impact?"

"Pretty fast. When the SUV came up behind us initially, it tailgated us, and my mom sped up to try to get it out of her backseat. I remember she complained about the guy's headlights shining in her rearview mirror."

Ashe leaned forward, worried. Worse, he saw where Perriman was going with this line of questioning. Sure enough, his boss's next words were, "Did your mother say anything or did you see anything that might give you reason to believe that the SUV intentionally ran you off the road?"

"Who would do something like that?" Hank demanded.

Ashe sat back in his chair, shocked. That was evasion in Hank's voice. What wasn't she telling Perriman? He laid his hand on top of hers where it lay on the table. "Hank, you're among friends. We want only to help you. Anything you have to say won't go beyond these walls. It's safe to be candid with us."

Her eyes were a deep, turbulent shade of blue, and she wouldn't meet his gaze.

"If we're going to find your brother, you have to tell us everything."

She made a sound of distress and pulled her right hand out from under his to wring her left hand with it.

He sent a subtle hand signal to Perriman that he should leave the room. But his boss did an odd thing. He studied Hank a moment more and then shook his head in the negative. Ashe trusted his boss's judgment completely. The guy could read body language like nobody else he'd ever met. Now why did Frosty think she would be more inclined to talk with both men present?

Although, it wasn't like she'd been forthcoming with him from the start. Hell, she hadn't even admitted that Max was her brother at first.

Perriman picked a piece of paper off the stack in front of him. "The police report indicates that you and your mother were run off the road by a skilled driver at a carefully chosen location that would ensure maximum harm to the occupants of your car and minimum chance of your vehicle being discovered in a timely fashion."

"You're saying someone tried to kill us?" Hank exclaimed.

Ashe stared first at his boss and then at Hank.

"Let's talk about your father," Perriman said briskly.

That was an abrupt change of subject. Ashe knew the technique—give your subjects mental whiplash and maybe they slip up and say something they shouldn't.

"What about him?" Hank leaned back in her seat and crossed her arms as if she knew the technique, too. *What the heck?*

"Who did he work for?"

"Himself. He found and bought art and antiques—"

Perriman cut her off. "Yes. I'm familiar with the party line about his job, and your brother's, for that matter. But that's not what I asked. *Who* did he work for?"

"Do you mean which auction houses? Or are you asking about specific clients?"

"Both."

"My brother would know those. But I don't. My father and I weren't close."

"How about your mother? Would she have known the names?"

"I guess so. At least until my folks divorced. But again, I wouldn't be privy to any of that." Hank shoved a hand through her hair and frowned. "To be perfectly honest, Commander Perriman, I don't see why you're asking me all these questions. How is this supposed to help you figure out who tried to kill us just now?"

"I'm trying to understand who you and your missing brother are. Who would want to harm one or both of you, and why. What aren't you telling me? Both of you are keeping secrets that could get you killed. Why is that?"

Ashe couldn't stand by any longer and let his boss browbeat Hank without coming to her defense. "Sir, her brother disappeared and she's worried about him. Trying to find him. What's so secretive about that?"

"She's lying to you, too," Perriman snapped. "And if

you hadn't fallen for her like I told you not to, you'd see it, too."

"Can we step out into the hall for a moment, sir?" Ashe asked quietly.

His boss pressed his lips together tightly but rose to his feet. Ashe moved down the hallway, well away from the door, before turning around to face Perriman. "With all due respect, sir, what the hell is going on?"

"I have reason to believe her father was much more than a simple art dealer. If I'm right, that casts serious doubt on just how innocent a player her brother is. For that matter, I think the mother was in on it before she got in that accident—which wasn't an accident, by the way."

Ashe stared at him, shocked. Perriman was hardly the kind of man to fling around accusations lightly. "What do you think her father was involved in? Who was he?"

"That's what I'm trying to find out. And while I'm at it, I'm trying to figure out if your girlfriend was in on the family business, too."

Dread lodged in Ashe's throat and refused to let go. Exactly what family business did Perriman think Hank's family was in? Not that it took a rocket scientist to answer that one.

His boss spun on his heel and marched back into the conference room, leaving Ashe no choice but to follow. He'd had his own suspicions about Max's involvement in the Russian mob. Did Perriman think the connection went back further than just the brother?

Perriman started in on the questions again without preamble. "Did your parents ever have Russian-speaking visitors?"

"Yes. All the time. They were immigrants from Russia and knew most of the Russians in this area."

"Did your father have a special room in the house that you kids weren't allowed to go into?"

"His office. He said we messed up his paperwork. And goodness knows, he used to leave huge piles of papers sitting around everywhere in there. It drove my mother crazy."

"Was there a big radio in your house?"

"You mean like a shortwave radio?" Hank asked. "My brother and my dad built a ham radio when Max was about ten. It was out in the garage, though."

A chill ran through Ashe. God almighty. Perriman didn't think her father was a mobster. He thought the man was a spy.

"…speak Russian or English in your home when other people weren't around?" Perriman was asking.

"Some of each. My parents spoke Ukrainian or Polish when they wanted to talk without us kids understanding them." She laughed a little. "Not that it helped. Max and I are both pretty good at picking up languages, and Polish and Ukrainian are very close to Russian as languages go."

"Did you ever overhear anything that would lead you to believe your father had some other job or employer besides the ones he worked with in the art and antiques business?"

Perriman asked the question casually, but Hank's re-action to it was anything but. Her entire body went still, her face closed, the expression in her eyes grew stubborn.

He leaned toward her. "Hank, you're not in trouble, and no one in your family is in trouble. If we're going to find Max, though, we have to know where to look. Anything you say in this room will go no further."

She smiled sadly at him. "You can't guarantee that, Ashe. Not when you don't know everything."

So. There *were* secrets in her family's past that she was not divulging. And Commander Perriman was apparently on the right track with his line of questioning. Ashe swore under his breath. He glanced at his boss, silently asking permission to dive in. Perriman nodded slightly.

"Kitten, your parents are dead. Anything you say about what they did in the past cannot hurt them. And if we're going to be brutally honest here, your brother may also be dead. If he's not already, he could be soon if we don't find him." Taking her hand in his again, he stared intently into her eyes. "So if you know *anything* about what he's involved in that might tell us where to find him, now's the time to share."

The set of her shoulders remained stubborn. Mentally wincing at what he was going to have to say to get through to her in front of his boss, he dove in.

"I know it's hard for you to trust people. But can't you trust me at least a little? After all we've shared and all we've been through together? Have I ever given you reason to believe that I would abandon you or give up on finding Max with you?"

Her shoulders slumped. "No," she answered in a small voice.

"Please, Hank. Let me help you. I care about you too much to stand by doing nothing while you lose the only family you have left."

It was a low blow. But she *had* to talk if they were going to find Max, and furthermore, figure out who was now trying to kill her, too.

She let out one of those big sighs of hers that presaged a confession. Praise the Lord. "My family was always secretive. It was the nature of my father's work. Some of the art pieces he was commissioned to find were, well, stolen. And he worked in large amounts of cash. We weren't supposed to tell anyone how much money he kept in the house. He was terrified that someone would rob him."

"He worked out of your home, then?" Ashe asked.
She nodded.

"What can you remember about his clients?"

"They tended to be old and rich. And...furtive."

Ashe smiled. If they were dealing in stolen art, they had good reason to be furtive. He pressed a little harder. "Was there any one client who came to the house often? Maybe over a period of years?"

She frowned, thinking back. "Yes. His name was Romulus. I always thought that was such a silly name. He used to call my father Remus. It was some sort of inside joke between them."

Or a code name. Was it possible that Perriman's intel was right? That her father had been a spy?

"What language did Romulus and your dad speak?"

"They whispered with each other a lot. But always in Russian. And always when they thought my brother and I couldn't hear."

"What about your mother? Did they whisper when she was around?"

"Oh, no. She always sat at the kitchen table with them into the wee hours of the night."

"What did they talk about?"

She shrugged. "I recall them griping a lot about how nobody respected Russia anymore and how all of their friends had lost their jobs and their homes and their pensions."

Ashe traded looks with his boss. Those might be the sorts of things Russian spies would talk about.

"What did Romulus look like?" Perriman asked.

Hank spent the next few minutes describing the guy in detail. Then she surprised Ashe by saying, "If you'll get me a pencil and a sketch pad, I'll draw you a picture of him."

"You can draw?" Ashe blurted.

"My college degree is in art restoration. I've studied

painting and drawing techniques extensively. Of course I can draw."

Perriman made a phone call, and as he stuffed his phone back into his pocket, announced, "The guys are going to scare you up a proper sketch pad and some charcoals. And while they're at it, they're bringing us food. I don't know about you, but I'm hungry."

Now that he mentioned it, Ashe was famished. Sandwiches arrived in a few minutes, and the three of them ate companionably. They chatted about nothing in particular—the weather, what it was like to be back in New Orleans after being gone for a while, the latest movie that depicted SEALs inaccurately.

The art supplies finally arrived, and Hank pulled them in front of her eagerly. "This is going to take a while, gentlemen. And I'll work better if the two of you aren't hovering over me watching every stroke that goes onto paper."

"I'll leave you to it, then," Perriman said.

Ashe rose to his feet and Hank did the same. He gathered her in his arms and buried his nose in her hair. "Look. I know this is hard for you. But we'll do everything we can to help you. Just trust me, okay?"

Something that sounded suspiciously like a sob slipped out of her throat. Poor kid. She was wrung out. He kissed her forehead gently. "I have to go talk with my boss, but I'll be back in a little while."

Reluctantly, he released her and strode down the hall to the ready room. Normally this was a security police unit populated entirely by marines. But Ashe recognized several of the men lounging casually around the big, open space. They were SEALs. Why had Perriman called them here like this?

He turned to his boss and muttered, "What the hell's going on that you're not telling me?"

"Both of your girlfriend's parents were spies for Mother Russia. And I have reason to believe her brother followed in the family tradition. All that's left is to determine whether or not Hank's one of them, too."

Hank? A spy? That was crazy!

Or was it?

Chapter 16

Hank worked quickly, capturing the general outline of Romulus's features. She would fill in the details later. But first, the basic bone structure—

She started when her cell phone buzzed. Why was Ashe bugging her? He knew she was working... She glanced at the face of the phone. She didn't recognize the name on the caller ID, but it was Russian.

Crap.

Cautiously she answered it. "Hello? Who is this?"

The male voice at the other end spoke in hushed Russian. "If you want to see your brother alive, come to the Jefferson Pier. Tell no one and come alone."

"When?"

"Now."

"I have no idea where the Jefferson Pier is or how to get there."

The man sounded exasperated. "It's on Bayou Rigolettes. Drive south to Lafitte and take a boat from there. Hurry."

She was only vaguely familiar with the area south of New Orleans. It was isolated, and she would be far from help. Not to mention it was a great location for a secret meeting. Or a murder. Was she walking into a trap? For there was no question about her going. It was the first actual lead she'd gotten on Max since he disappeared, not to mention the first suggestion whatsoever that he might still be alive. She had to take the chance and check it out.

The first order of business, of course, was to get out of here and ditch Ashe and his scary boss. This room wasn't any good. It had no windows and only the one exit. She poked her head out into the hallway and asked the first person she saw—a nearly bald young man with an insanely fit physique—where the ladies' room was. He pointed further down the hall. She headed for it.

When she stepped into the small room, she was relieved to see a window. She locked the bathroom door behind herself, opened the window and hopped out into the night. Now to get a car and get off this base.

She headed for the big paved area behind the building she'd just exited. It looked like some sort of parking lot for all kinds of utility vehicles. Everything from staff cars to dump trucks was parked there. It took her longer than she would have liked to find a vehicle that was unlocked, a heavy-duty pickup truck with dual rear wheels, a diesel engine and a gooseneck hitch in the rear truck bed. Whatever. Beggars couldn't be choosers.

It had been a long time since her brother showed her how to hot-wire a car, and she didn't know if a diesel vehicle worked differently from a regular one or not. But she had to try. Sitting awkwardly on the truck's floor and working in the dark, she pried off the panel covering the ignition wiring and stared at the jumble of electrical wires. She needed ignition wires. Working as much by feel as by sight, she traced the wires coming off the back of the ignition switch. She yanked two random wires loose and touched the ends to one another.

Nothing. Rats.

She pulled free another wire and tried it with each of the first two. Still nothing. It took her several more tries before she finally got a spark and a momentary growl from the engine. She tried again, holding the wires together this time as she pushed down on the gas pedal with her elbow. It was as awkward as could be, but the engine caught and roared to life.

Cripes. The navy apparently didn't believe in using mufflers on their trucks. How the vehicle hadn't woken everyone on base and brought them running, she had no idea. And she didn't plan to stick around long enough to ask. Now to get off this stupid military base and go find her brother.

That turned out to be much easier than she expected. She simply drove out the front gate and smiled at the guard who waved her through as she rumbled past him. And then she was free and clear.

She pointed the truck south. As she recalled there was really only one road to speak of all the way down to Lafitte. All points beyond that into the bayou required transportation by boat.

It took her a few wrong turns and backtracks, but she finally found Jean Lafitte Boulevard and signs pointing south to Lafitte. Any minute now, Ashe was going to discover that she wasn't in the conference room working on that drawing. And he was going to be *pissed*. She glanced down at her cell phone lying on the seat beside her. She expected it to ring momentarily and for him to chew her up one side and down the other for going on this wild goose chase without him.

She probably ought to turn the phone off in case Ashe and his boss had some way of tracking it, but she was worried that she might miss another call from the anonymous man who'd called before. Swallowing hard, Hank drew a deep breath. She would just have to trust that her head start in leaving New Orleans was enough to get her to Lafitte and the rendezvous before Ashe caught up with her.

It took her over an hour to make the drive, but it was dark and she was unfamiliar with the roads. Finally, houses and businesses came into view, and then a big sign welcomed her to Lafitte, Louisiana.

She glanced down at her phone in worry. Why hadn't Ashe called? Surely he'd discovered her escape by now. His silence was almost more worrisome than an angry phone call.

It was obvious that Ashe and his boss thought her father was a spy. Which was ridiculous. Sure, her family's secretive life looked suspicious. And her father's work hadn't always been exactly on the up-and-up. But her parents had also been immigrants to a country known to be hostile to their native land. Her father had just wanted to make a living and not attract any attention. That, and he had handled large amounts of cash. On more than one occasion when she'd been little, she'd seen briefcases full of money sitting open on the kitchen table or spotted her mother counting and bundling stacks of currency. Shady? Yes.

But spies? Not her parents. Surely she would have known if they were.

She jolted as she saw a sign for the Jefferson Pier. She slowed the truck and turned in to the parking lot. Here went nothing.

It was a little past 4:00 a.m. There wouldn't be anyone here to rent her a boat at this hour, would there?

She parked the truck and pulled the ignition wires apart. The engine died, and silence fell around her. She climbed out of the cab and was assaulted by the smell of fish and the vibrant sounds of night insects.

"Hey, Missy. Can I he'p y'all?"

She turned in shock to a man striding toward her from the direction of the dock. "Umm, I need to rent a boat, actually."

"You goin' fishin'?" He looked at her skeptically. Given her complete lack of fishing gear, she probably couldn't pass for a fisher.

"No. I've just got to meet someone. At Jefferson Pier. Do you know where that is?"

"Yeah, sure. Jeff'son Pier's 'bout three mile' down de bayou from heuh. What you wan' wit' dat place, *chère*?"

"I'm meeting a friend. And it's urgent that I get there as soon as possible." She'd always considered herself to have a fairly thick New Orleans accent, but this guy's Cajun drawl put hers to shame.

"You know how ta' steer a boat?"

She shrugged. She knew it involved a rudder and not much more, but she wasn't going to admit that to this guy.

"C'mon, then. Don' wan' ta' keep yo' frien' waitin'."

She followed the guy to a small office. He unlocked the door and ushered her inside. Then he swiped her credit card and made a photocopy of her driver's license while she fidgeted, antsy to get out of here before Ashe arrived and put a stop to this madness. He might not have called her, but she could feel him pursuing her. It was as if his presence was drawing closer with every passing minute.

"All righ'. How 'bout a nice bass boat for ya? Gots a fancy chair that won't get yo' nice clothes wet. Comes wit' a life vest an' a full tank o' gas. Y'all fill it up befo' you return an' it'll cost you less. I gotta charge y'all fo' a full tank otherwise."

"Okay. Fine," she replied, standing up eagerly.

The guy took a set of keys off a pegboard on the wall and strolled down to the dock with her all but jumping up and down behind him in frustration at his leisurely pace.

The guy must have sensed her complete unfamiliarity with boats because he boarded the vessel first, helped her aboard, and then gave her a maddeningly thorough tutorial on starting the engine, moving in reverse, steering, where the fishing map of Bayou Rigolettes was stored, and even basic boating traffic rules.

He handed her a life vest, which she shrugged into and tightened, and then, at long last, he put the keys in the ignition and started the engine for her.

"'Kay then. Y'all be careful. Y'heuh?"

"I will. Thanks."

The eastern sky was starting to lighten and she'd nearly had a stroke in her impatience, but finally she backed out of the marina slot and pointed the prow of the boat out into open water.

The boat guy had painstakingly pointed out a half dozen landmarks along the eastern shore of the bayou that would help her navigate down to Jefferson Pier, and as night faded into dawn around her, she was belatedly grateful for his thoroughness. The entire shoreline looked the same— green and thick and impenetrable.

Every now and then a home interrupted the wall of green. Sometimes a nice house sat back from the shore with a mown lawn, and other times the dwelling was no more than a tin shack on stilts at the water's edge. Further out into the open water of the bayou, shrimp boats passed by her.

Was this where her brother had been hiding all this time? Why? Had he crossed a client who posed a threat to him? If so, why hadn't Max at least let her know he was alive and lying low? If he'd had a way to get a message to her last night, surely he'd had the means to reach out to her long before now.

Although the pier that was her destination was supposedly only three miles down the coast, she made the trip cautiously. It was one thing to get a phone call and decide it was a good idea to go rescue her brother. It was another thing entirely to be all alone in the middle of a creepy bayou with no backup and no safety net, meeting a potentially dangerous stranger who could be leading her into a lethal trap.

If only Ashe was here. He would know exactly what to do and take charge of the situation. Nope, this had not been one of her more brilliant moves. But there was no turning back now.

Finally, as morning light broke over the open water in a glorious spill of gold and pink and peach hues, she spied Jefferson Pier.

It was just like the guy back in Lafitte had described: a long dock running parallel to the shore with tie-ups for boats ranging from flat-bottomed mud boats to a plush yacht with sleek lines and black-tinted windows. The yacht definitely looked closest to her brother's style of all the vessels at the pier.

She slowed her little boat, letting it glide slowly toward the dock. Nobody was visible on shore, and no movements caught her eye. But as she searched for an open spot to tie up to the pier, a figure came out onto the aft deck of the yacht and waved at her. The man gestured at her to bring her craft over to the yacht directly.

In the blinding glare of the sun at the man's back, she

couldn't make out his facial features. But he seemed to know who she was.

She steered the boat over to the yacht, and a lean, darkly tanned, middle-aged man called in Russian for her to toss him her mooring line. She looked around and spied a neatly coiled length of nylon rope near the front of her boat. She made her way precariously to the line and gave it a heave in the Russian's direction.

He caught the pile of rope and lashed it around a metal cleat mounted on the yacht, reeling her boat up tight against the side of the yacht in the process. He shoved a pair of foam tubes between the hulls of the two vessels and tied off the line he snagged from the back end of her boat.

In under a minute, her boat was completely tethered to the yacht whether she liked it or not. Then the man growled, "The boss wants to talk with you. Follow me."

Ashe opened the door to the conference room carefully, a cup of tea the way Hank liked it in hand. Where was she? He backed out and stuck his head into the common room. "Anyone see the woman I brought with me?"

One of the guys piped up from his desk, "She asked where the restroom was a while back."

A sinking feeling was festering in Ashe's gut. *What had she done?* He headed down the hall to the ladies' room and knocked on the door. No response. Swearing commenced in a steady stream in the back of his mind. He pulled out his pocketknife and popped the simple lock with a twist of his blade. *Empty.* And the window was open.

Son of a—

He whirled and sprinted down the hall to the main room. Perriman looked up sharply as he burst into the ready room. "She ran. Went out the restroom window."

"How long ago?"

The kid she'd asked about the restroom was consulted, and Ashe was dismayed to realize she had nearly an hour's head start on them. Worse, somebody volunteered the fact that a vehicle depot was behind the building. If she'd gotten hold of a set of wheels, she could be long gone by now.

A quick inventory of the vehicle lot revealed that a pickup truck was missing. A phone call to the front gate confirmed that it had left the base a solid half hour ago. Panic and anger warred with one another inside Ashe. To Perriman he said, "Her cell phone has a GPS tracker in it. Can Jennie get us a location?"

His boss made the call. Ashe was surprised when the ops specialist reported back a few minutes later that the phone was still turned on and on the move. It would take Jennie a few more minutes to pinpoint an exact location, but the phone was headed south from New Orleans.

"South? What's down there?" Perriman asked in surprise. "I thought it was just swamps and the Mississippi delta."

"You're mostly right. There's a little solid land south of New Orleans and a few small communities. And then there are a number of waterways and settlements in the bayou that are flotation-based."

"Why would she head down there? Any ideas, Ashe?"

He shrugged. "I dunno. She's a city kind of girl and not a bayou stomper by temperament. The good news is I have to head down that way today, anyway. My meeting with Vitaly's boss is down in the Bayou Rigolettes this evening—"

He and Perriman stared at each other.

What were the odds? No way was it coincidence that Hank had taken off in the direction of the very people he was supposed to meet tonight.

Perriman asked grimly, "Does she work with them? Has she been the insider all along, spying on us for them?"

It wasn't possible. She couldn't be a mole. Everything they'd had between them couldn't have been an act. But doubt made his breathing hitch and his heart clench.

"Once she gets out into the bayou, we'll never find her unless she wants to be found. That place can swallow a man whole."

"I'm calling in reinforcements," Perriman announced.

"Anyone in particular?" Ashe blurted. None of his teammates were nearby, as far as he was aware.

Perriman smirked. "I've got a pair of topflight snipers training a few hours from here along with a couple other operatives." He glanced around the ready room. "And I'd lay odds there are a few old Marine Force Recon guys around here who know their way around a covert op, too."

Several of the cops in the room stood up, grinning.

Ashe's blood ran cold. Perriman was fielding an ad hoc team of Special Forces operatives to…what? Apprehend Hank? Kill her? "What do you have in mind, sir?"

"You've got a meeting to go to this evening, right?"

"Correct."

"And we now know to expect Hank there. Furthermore, we can use her cell phone signal to pinpoint the location of the meeting right now. We've got almost eight hours to brief up, gear up, and get a team into position before the meet goes down." Perriman gave him a pointed look. "I'm not sending you in cold tonight, Hollywood. You're going in with a full support package."

Truth be told, Ashe was relieved. He'd already seen Vitaly's security procedures, and the guy was no amateur. A meeting with the guy and his bosses could prove extremely risky if he went alone.

But what about Hank? She could so easily get caught

in the crossfire. He didn't worry about his guys shooting her. But the Russians? Would they put a bullet in her head to shut her up and prevent her from revealing everything she knew? What were the odds he could talk Perriman into treating this op as a kidnapping recovery mission with Hank as the victim?

Unfortunately, he already knew the answer to that one. *Zilch.*

A strange ache in his chest caught Ashe's attention. What was up with that? Was this why people called it a broken heart? He swore viciously under his breath. He had no time for hurt feelings right now. They had a ton of work to do to pull together an intel briefing, build a plan, rehearse it with their impromptu team and then get everyone into place before the meeting.

The good news was that Perriman would be able to pull strings and turn the whole naval air station inside out to get everything the team needed. Still, the next few hours promised to be chaotic. And Hank's life hung in the balance. He only vaguely registered that his own life was also on the line. He was too worried about her to see beyond that.

As the op began to take shape, Ashe made plans of his own that did not fit in with the team's agenda. He needed to get to Hank and figure out a way to speak with her in private. To find out for himself if she was a prisoner of or conspirator with the Russian mobsters. He had faith that if he looked her in the eye and asked her the question, he would know if she was lying or telling him the truth. Although, apparently, she'd successfully lied to him before. The doubt resurfaced, worse than ever. Did he dare trust her...or would she betray him if he tried to save her?

What in the *hell* was he going to do?

Chapter 17

Hank's how-colossally-stupid-am-I-being quotient notched up even higher as she stared at the sailor waiting impatiently for her to follow him. But hey... she'd run off to some deserted corner of a remote bayou on her own. Why not board the big, scary yacht all by herself, too?

The hallway the man led her down was narrow and dim, but she made out beautifully polished wood paneling of the highest quality. The sailor stopped at the foot of a short flight of stairs and gestured for Hank to go up alone.

Lord, she felt like she was stepping out to face a firing squad. Hesitantly she climbed the steps and found herself in a spacious salon. At the front of the triangular space a man stood, looking out the windows. She couldn't make out his features, though, for he was silhouetted against the sunlight.

She stepped further into the room, and the man took several steps toward her, also. And that was when she saw his face.

"Max!" She raced forward and flung her arms around his waist tightly. "Oh my God. I thought you were dead!"

He chuckled a little. "I assure you, I am not dead. At least not yet."

She leaned back to glare up at him. "Where have you been? How come you didn't call me to let me know you were okay? I've been so worried. Who broke into your house and trashed your office? And what have you been—"

"Whoa. Back up. Someone trashed my office? In my house in New Orleans?"

"Yes. How come you didn't tell me you owned a gorgeous place like that? Sheesh. I'd have come to visit you more often if I'd known. I thought you lived in some junky bachelor pad with empty pizza boxes and dirty socks strewn everywhere."

That made him laugh. "I was never that big a slob."

"Yes, you were."

"God, I missed you. How have you been, sis?"

"Fine. Well, not fine. Worried sick about you. But other than that, fine."

He took her by the arm and led her outside through a sliding door onto a teak deck. A brisk breeze ruffled her hair and blew it around her face. Max leaned in close and spoke under his breath. "What's this about you working at the Who Do Voodoo? Are you nuts?"

"I was looking for you. It's the last place I could trace you to."

He shoved an exasperated hand through his tousled hair. "Cripes. You've walked into the middle of a den of vipers, Hank. You have no idea what goes on at that place."

"Actually, I do. I'm not stupid, Max, and I have eyes. I saw plenty." She likewise leaned in close and lowered her voice. "What have you gotten yourself mixed up in? Are you in trouble? I know people who can help you—"

"Stay away from this, Hank. I'm telling you."

"Too late. You're involved, and I'm not losing you again."

He huffed. "Did you at least bring some backup with you?"

"What do you mean?" she asked, perplexed.

"*Backup.* Please tell me you didn't actually come out here all alone."

"Well, yes, I did come alone. The man on the phone said to."

Max swore under his breath long and hard. She waited him out, confused. Wasn't that what he'd wanted?

"Well, that's that," her brother announced. "I guess I don't get to come home with you today."

"What's going on? I'm not a little kid anymore, Max. After everything you've put me through these past few months, you owe me the truth."

"Not now," he muttered.

The door slid open behind them, and Hank whirled around to face a man with silver hair and crow's-feet that belied his athletic build. He wore a golf shirt and crisply pressed khakis…and a black leather shoulder holster holding a snub-nosed Makarov pistol.

"Who's this, Maximillian? Wait—don't I know you?" the man said to her in Russian. "Yes. You're that waitress from the Who Do Voodoo club in New Orleans."

Hank caught the faint eye roll of disgust her brother shot her, but said politely to the man in English, "Hello. My name is Hank. Have I seen you before? You look familiar." She'd pretended not to know Russian at the Voodoo, and her gut told her to keep up the charade here, too.

The man turned to Max and spoke in rapid Russian. "Vitaly used her to keep an eye on the arms dealer. She was hanging all over the man last time I saw them together."

Max's eyebrows shot up. Then he answered in Russian, "This is my little sister, Evgeniya Hankova."

"And she speaks no Russian?" the man exclaimed in surprise. The guy still spoke in his Russian tongue, but she vaguely recalled from the club that he spoke English, too.

"She hasn't heard the language or used it since she was very young. Unlike me, she spent little time around our father after our parents separated. My mother refused to speak Russian after the divorce."

"Ahh. A shame your father let Deena get out of control like that."

Max shrugged. "My mother was a stubborn woman. Acclimated a little too much to American culture."

"Still. Look what happened to the daughter. Your father should have kept a firmer hand on them both."

"She's my problem, now, Remi. I'll keep her in line."

Narrowing his eyes disapprovingly, the Russian reminded Max, "She didn't look in line when she was sashaying around half-naked and throwing herself at that American."

"I'll have a talk with her about it. If Vitaly put her on the guy to watch him, though, wouldn't it make sense that she was sticking to him like glue?"

"She didn't have to like it so much," Remi snapped.

Fascinated by the exchange, Hank had to work actively to keep her face passive and her eyes blank. Max knew, of course, that she was fluent in Russian. Interesting that he'd chosen not to give away her knowledge of the tongue. Games within games were afoot here, apparently.

"Have you eaten breakfast, Hank?" Max asked her abruptly in English.

"No," she replied docilely. No need to tick off the raging chauvinist Russian dude by making a sarcastic comment about haring off into the bayou in the middle of the night because some guy had called with a message from her missing brother.

"Will you join us, Remi?" Max asked courteously in English.

"No. You two catch up. I have places to go. People to see." Hah. The man was as fluent in English as he was in Russian.

"The meeting is at nine tonight," Max reminded him.

"I know. I know. I'll be here." A quick switch to Russian. "And then we'll see if this American of your sister's is real or dead."

Hank's entire being stiffened. Were they talking about Ashe? What did Remi mean, real or dead? That sounded ominous. With great difficulty, she released a pent-up breath and even managed a wan smile at the silver-haired Russian.

"I'm going to have some food brought up, sis, and we can eat it on deck. And you can tell me about this American guy you've been making a spectacle of yourself with in New Orleans."

Remi harrumphed and excused himself from the room. The same guy who'd tied up her boat brought in a tray of steaming scrambled eggs, bacon and stewed tomatoes. They were just sitting down at a table to eat it when a sleek cigarette boat roared away from the dock with Remi at the wheel. Tension visibly eased from her brother's shoulders.

"Who's that?" she asked Max.

He spared a brief glance at the guy laying out their breakfast and murmured, "A business associate. No need to concern yourself over him."

"Oh...okay." She shrugged casually and took a seat across from Max. The door slid shut, leaving them alone on deck again. Pasting a smile on her face, she asked lightly, "What's up, bro? Talk to me or I'm calling my friends."

"Don't make any calls from the boat," Max responded sharply. He took a bite of eggs and mumbled around it without moving his lips, "All transmissions are monitored."

"Are you tangled up in the mob?" she asked back, sotto voce.

"It's complicated. I'm sorry I dragged you out here and got you in the middle of it. I was hoping you'd bring the cavalry with you."

"Is the American you were talking about with Remi a big, dark-haired guy named Ashe?"

"If he's an arms dealer, yes. That's the guy."

"And he's coming here tonight for a meeting?" Hank asked.

"Yup."

She grinned. "Then your cavalry's coming after all."

Staring at her intently, Max barely breathed, "Who is he?"

"US military. Special ops."

Max swore under his breath. "You don't mess around, do you, little sister?"

She smiled broadly. "Not where my big brother is concerned."

He just shook his head. "I don't know if Remi will want you at the meeting tonight. If he does, I need you to play dumb like nobody's business. It's your best defense. I'll do whatever I can to convince Remi and his buddies that you know nothing."

"About what?"

"About anything. About tonight's deal. About the Voodoo operation. About the whole organization."

"Why would Remi want me at this meeting of yours?"

"Leverage," Max replied grimly.

"Against Ashe?"

A nod. "He's planning to use you as a hostage to ensure that your boyfriend delivers what he promised."

"Or else what?" Hank asked in alarm. She knew darn well that Ashe would not hand over actual weapons to a bunch of Russian mobsters, even to save her life.

Would she and Ashe both be killed? Oh, dear. This was not good. Not good at all.

"I don't like this, Frosty," Ashe muttered. "I'm telling you. I don't think Hank is part of the setup. I think they're using her as bait to lure me in."

"They don't need bait. You're already scheduled to walk in their front door tonight."

"Insurance, then. Maybe they want to be positive that I'll come."

"Then why hasn't someone called you to let you know they've got her and that she's at the boat waiting for you?"

"I don't know. I just know what my gut's telling me."

"Look. I know you like this girl. Maybe even a lot. But you've got to get your head in the game, Ashe. Logic doesn't lie. She's one of them."

"How can you be so sure?" he bit out.

"Come on, Hollywood. Get with the program. Why else would she have fled in the middle of the night, stolen a vehicle and made her way down there? Not to mention, you didn't tell her where the meeting is going to be. How else did she know if she's not one of them?"

Ashe sighed. It didn't help the roiling mess of nerves in his gut to have his boss voice aloud the very same possibilities he was thinking to himself.

"Set aside your feelings for her. She's a target. Nothing more."

Easy for Perriman to say. He hadn't made love with her and bared his soul to her. And Ashe thought she'd bared her true feelings to him, too. But was all that a lie? Aloud, he said heavily, "I'll try to distance myself from her."

"I need you to do more than try, Hollywood. I have to know I can count you not to flake out on me. I can't have you taking any stupid risks or going off script. Got it? You stick to the plan. That's an order."

Jeez. Cole Perriman pretty much never gave direct orders. His men respected him too much not to do exactly what the man politely requested of them. Ashe replied tightly, "I understand, sir."

He might understand, but that did not mean he was going to comply with the order. It would cost him his career and maybe get him locked up in the brig—or killed—but he was not throwing Hank to the wolves. Period.

Hank wandered the ship, learning the passageways and paying an unintended visit to a compact but amazingly tricked-out kitchen—a galley, the guy cooking in it called it. She hung out on deck for most of the afternoon, napping in a shaded hammock. But mostly, she fretted about Ashe. Why hadn't he called her when he discovered her missing? Did he believe his boss's insinuations that her family was full of spies and maybe she was one of them?

As the sun dipped into the west and bled across the open water of the bayou, Max stepped outside to join her. He muttered softly, "You're clear on tonight? You don't understand Russian. If the deal goes down in English, you still don't understand anything. Everyone who'll be here tonight is dangerous and likely to be armed. But Remi's the one to watch."

"Why him in particular?"

"Because he's a psychopath, sis. Won't hesitate to shoot you for no good reason and won't bat an eyelash doing it. Don't draw his attention and don't piss him off."

"Umm, okay," she mumbled, alarmed.

"If tonight's meeting goes bad, get off the yacht, Hank. Jump over the side if you have to. Shrimp boats sail up and down the bayou all the time. You'll be able to flag one down and make your way to safety."

"I'm not leaving you behind," she declared. "I lost you once. I'm not losing you again."

"There's a great deal more than meets the eye going on here. You have to do as I say. If I tell you to run, I need you to do it. No questions, no hesitation. Just go."

"*What* is going *on*, Max? Just tell me once and for all. Are you involved with the mob?"

"Yes and no. I told you. It's complicated. Promise you'll run if I tell you to."

She stared at him intently. Did she trust him? With her life? He was her big brother, after all. He'd always looked out for her in the past. Had set his life and his dreams on hold to care for their mother and then for her. The Max she knew would never do anything to hurt other people. He was an honorable guy. Decent. Kind. If he was tangled up with the mob, there was a reason for it. He might not be in a position to tell her, and goodness knew, he probably shouldn't tell all while standing on a mob yacht that was en route to some sort of big mob powwow.

But at the end of the day, she trusted him. Deep in her gut, she was dead certain he would do the right thing. He and Ashe were a lot alike in that regard.

She nodded firmly. "If you tell me to run, I promise I'll go."

Max's shoulders sagged in relief.

"However," she added, "you'd better not go incommunicado with me again, or I'll come looking for you again. And now I know where to look, buster."

He grinned ruefully at her. "I'll get in touch with you when I can. No more communication blackouts."

She stepped forward to hug him. "Love you, bro."

"Love you, sis."

Max jerked away from her at the sound of a motorboat approaching at high speed. "That'll be Remi and his crew. Remember, be invisible. Your life depends on it."

Chapter 18

Ashe powered down the racing boat's throttles, a little out of breath. The hull settled gently into the water, and the twin engines rumbled like contented lions. Holy cow, this baby could flat-out fly. He had to have been pushing a hundred miles per hour just now, and the boat had still been accelerating when he throttled back. Commander Perriman hadn't been messing around when he told the powers-that-be at the naval air station to cough up the fastest boat they had for this operation.

Speaking of the operation, he needed to do a quick radio check out here in the bayou. He muttered, "One, two, three. Check. Check. How do you copy, anyone?"

Bastien's voice crackled in his tiny earbud, "Loud and clear. How about me?"

"Loud and clear, Catfish."

"You ready for this, Hollywood? Head in the game. Calm thoughts. Focus."

Ashe appreciated Bastien's concern. His former team-mate knew how much Hank meant to him. Bastien, of all people, was also likeliest to suspect that Ashe had an alternate agenda of his own for tonight's meeting.

He throttled down the powerboat even more. The vessel still barely touched the water as it skimmed across the open water. He'd opened her up out here at the north end of Bayou Rigolettes to get a feel for her, and he'd actually scared himself a little.

If it came down to a race tonight, he would win, hands down. Even captured drug-running boats he'd piloted before weren't as muscular as this sleek lady. One of the keys to a successful hostage rescue was a good escape plan, and this vessel would make for a hell of an escape.

The second piece of a successful rescue was good intel on the location of the hostage. Hank's phone hadn't moved more than a few dozen feet all afternoon. She was definitely on the yacht, their satellite telemetry had revealed, along with a pile of Russian mobsters.

The last piece of a successful rescue was a clean insertion of the rescue team. They needed to get close to Hank undetected and then be prepared either to sneak her out by trickery and stealth...or to blast her out with surprise, superior firepower and overwhelming speed. He sincerely prayed the trickery-and-stealth route worked.

He glanced down at the wooden crate at his feet. It was packed with a sample of weapons from his supposed shipment that had just arrived in New Orleans.

A team of gunsmiths had spent all day modifying each of the semiautomatic rifles inside, carefully filing the firing pins so they would fail after firing approximately a hundred rounds. Conveniently, none of the extended clips included in the crate held more than fifty rounds. If tonight's buyers wanted to take the weapons out for a test

fire, the rifles should be fully functional. *Should* being
the operative word. It was a risk to offer tampered weapons to criminals who were also gun experts. But the only
legal alternative was to sell them completely inoperative
weapons, and Ashe had been adamant that Vitaly and his
associates would be far too knowledgeable for that to work.

Ideally, this crate of firearms would secure Hank's release and get both of them off the yacht alive. He had no
doubt that Vitaly's bosses were holding Hank as a hostage
to ensure his follow-through with this deal. How they knew
he cared about her deeply enough for her to be an effec-
tive hostage, he had no idea. The fact remained that the
bastards were right, though.

She'd blasted into his life like a hurricane, sweeping
away everything that had come before and leaving him
scrubbed clean. And she'd gone and filled the void with
her joy and courage, her sexiness and stubborn loyalty. She
was the perfect woman for him. Assuming she wasn't a
spy for the other side, of course. Hell, even then, she might
just be his one true love.

"A high-speed vessel is docking beside the yacht now,"
Jennie reported across the secure team frequency being
piped into his ear. She was watching tonight's op via live
satellite feed. "I count twelve souls aboard the yacht. Hank
plus eleven."

Damn. They'd been hoping for no more than four or so.
Ahh, well. They'd contingency-planned for this many hostiles. And the good Lord willing, it wouldn't come down
to a firefight, anyway.

But a sinking feeling in his gut warned him that a
peaceful exit for him and Hank was unlikely to unfold.

"I have visual on Vitaly Parenko," Jennie announced.

He winced, not thrilled to have to see the Russian again.

Ashe had no way of knowing if Vitaly had pieced together the who and how of his safe being emptied.

Ashe glanced at his watch. He wasn't due at the yacht for nearly another hour. Huh. Maybe the club owner wasn't here to confront him after all. Maybe. Vitaly had been called on the carpet for losing all that money out of his safe.

"Have we got audio on the yacht?" he asked into the micro-microphone sewn into the collar of his shirt.

"Coming online momentarily," Bastien replied. "Parabolic microphone is just being moved into position."

This entire operation had been a huge scramble. Eight hours wasn't even close to enough time to plan and launch a rescue mission, so he had to give Perriman credit for having pulled the whole thing together so quickly.

A new voice came up on the frequency. A female voice. "I have visual on Hank."

Ashe had been surprised when Perriman's pair of snipers turned out to be SEALs he'd worked with before—a guy named Ford Alambeaux…and a girl. A girl SEAL, to be more precise. Her name was Trina Zarkos, and Ford assured him that Trina was as badass as they came and a hell of a shooter.

Ashe got the distinct impression that Ford and Trina were more than just a shooting team. Sexual sparks flew between them every time they looked at each other, let alone got within arm's length of one another.

Trina continued, "Hank is topside, on the foredeck. With a male matching the photograph of Maximillian Kuznetsov."

Ashe felt a jolt of surprise. Hank's brother was aboard the yacht? Could that mean she'd been in cahoots with him all along? Or was this some sort of reunion? Perhaps Max's presence explained why she'd snuck off last night without a word of explanation to him. Now that he thought about it, that actually made logical sense. Ashe knew she would do pretty much anything to track down her brother. But did that include getting into bed with the Russian mob?

He bit out, "Can we get confirmation of the Kuznetsov ID?"

It took about sixty seconds, but Commander Perriman's voice came over the radio very quietly. "Confirmed."

Son of a gun. Well, didn't that just complicate things all to hell? Of course, all missions had their share of monkey wrenches, and they were what his SEAL team trained for by the hundreds of hours. But Max's appearance was a giant wrench in the gears of this op, and the mission hadn't even gotten rolling yet.

Ashe transmitted to the team at large, "Be advised. We may be rescuing two hostages and not just one. Repeat: two possible hostages. Hank *and* her brother."

Ashe guessed that Perriman wasn't in a position to be chatty at the moment, given how quietly he'd confirmed Max's identity and given that he didn't dive in and start rebriefing the mission now. So as the second most senior member of the rescue team, it fell to Ashe to work through the ramifications of this new wrinkle with the team, to make sure everyone was on the same page.

"The brother, henceforth to be referred to simply as Max, may be one of the kidnappers—or he may be a hostage himself. I will have to make that call on the fly. If I deem him hostile, you are green-lighted to neutralize him as necessary. Same rules of engagement as the other hostiles."

He hated saying those words. Hank would never forgive him if she found out he'd given his team permission to kill her brother, if required. But if Max was indeed part of the gang of mobsters, he would have to suffer the same fate as the others.

"If I deem Max to be a hostage or nonhostile, we will extract him simultaneously with Hank."

The various members of the team acknowledged the update by quietly muttering, "Copy," or by clicking their throat mikes twice.

When everyone had checked in, Ashe asked grimly, "Say physical status of Hank and Max. Do we have two healthy and ambulatory hostages?"

"They're hugging," Trina replied drily. "Affirmative on ambulatory for both targets."

For now. Assuming neither of them got shot up before the night was over. And he got the feeling that was a mighty big assumption.

Hank gulped as Max set her away from him, murmuring, "Ready for this, sis?"

"No. But it's not like we have any choice." She hadn't been exactly ready to work in the Who Do Voodoo, or to get romantically entangled with a Special Forces operative, or to be an unwitting hostage in an illegal arms deal. But here she was anyway.

Max nodded tersely and turned away from her. "Stay out here until I call you in. This first meeting has nothing to do with you."

Hank stepped back into the shadow of the yacht's bridge as a group of men moved into the brightly lit salon. She gasped as she recognized Vitaly among the half dozen men. He looked tenser than she'd ever seen him. She also spotted the bouncer who usually stood guard at the entrance to the lap dance lounge. Had Vitaly brought the guy along to act as muscle to protect him, or just for show? She wouldn't put it past the creep to bring along his own bodyguards to make himself look more important.

Surely this meeting between Vitaly and his bosses was

some sort of reckoning over the stolen money from his club. Given that she'd emptied all the money out of his safe, she had to believe he hadn't passed his weekly quota of cash up the chain of command. She looked on with interest, curious to see how pissed off his bosses were about it.

Hank couldn't hear the meeting for the most part, but she didn't have to. Remi was angry and did a lot of gesturing with his hands. Vitaly talked at length and did a lot of hand gesturing back. Except his hands were moving placatingly, pleadingly even, while Remi's hand gestures grew increasingly agitated. A few of the loudest words floated out to her on the deck: phrases expressing fury and worry over a security breach. From what she could ascertain, Remi was a lot more concerned about covers being blown than money.

Covers? Why would a mob outfit be panicked about those? Wouldn't a mobster be most concerned about the cash? Or maybe about looking weak to his enemies?

The silver-haired Russian got progressively redder in the face, and Vitaly grew progressively paler. Yikes. If even Vitaly was scared of this Remi guy, then he must be as psychopathic as her brother said.

Eventually, Max stepped between the two men and appeared to play peacemaker. Vitaly took advantage of the interference to ease backward several feet. From her vantage point, Hank was able to see Vitaly surreptitiously unbutton his sports jacket, as well. He must have a gun under his coat and want quick access to it. Not reassuring.

Remi looked surly at her brother's interruption, but gradually looked more willing to be talked down off the emotional ledge. As Remi unwound, the men standing around the edges of the room relaxed, also. They clearly took their orders from the silver-haired Russian. He was the top dog around here, then.

Funny how she'd spent so many months searching for Vitaly's secretive boss, and now that she finally knew who he was, it didn't matter. She'd already found her brother without uncovering Remi's identity. That was how life always seemed to go. When she finally got something she wanted worse than anything, it didn't really mean anything by the time she got it.

Although Ashe had been a notable exception to that rule. She hadn't known how much she wanted him until she'd run away from him. Hadn't realized how much she trusted him until he wasn't there to look out for her. Hadn't understood just how deeply she felt about him until she'd tried to rip him out of her heart and found him firmly lodged there. No doubt about it. She loved him. It wasn't that she loved her brother more than Ashe. It was...different. Her brother was family. Ashe was...

She didn't know how to finish that thought. He was the breath in her lungs? The fire in her belly? The laughter in her heart? All of the above?

It had been foolish to come out here without telling him where she was going. He would have vetoed her coming, of course. But now that she was trapped aboard a yacht full of armed, violent men, this caution sounded pretty darned good.

Hank sighed as her brother continued talking to Remi inside. She *really* wished she'd thought all this through first. But then, her impulsiveness always had gotten her into trouble. This pickle was worse than most, however. She might actually die this time around. If she made it out of this mess alive, she really ought to settle down and live a nice, quiet, boring life restoring old, ugly paintings. Maybe she would get a cat. Take up knitting. Yup, the quieter the life, the better. Except Ashe would never stand for boring. He was Mr. Action-and-Action. She wasn't in his league no matter how hard she tried.

Max stepped back from Remi, a momentary look of relief flashing across his face. Her brother moved over to the bar and poured himself something amber-colored and alcoholic. The tension in the room drained as quickly as it had flared up before.

So fast Max didn't even have time to set the glass down before Remi whipped out his Makarov pistol from under his coat and shot Vitaly's bouncer in the face at point-blank range.

Hank lurched backward against the bulkhead in horror. That man had just been *shot*! She couldn't see the bouncer's body on the floor, but she could see Remi take two quick strides forward and point his pistol downward toward the floor. The man pulled the trigger again.

Vitaly stared down at his man in a combination of horror and terror. He had to be thinking he was next. God knew she did. What kind of monster was this Remi guy? And why in the world was Max working with him? Panicked so much she couldn't breathe, let alone move, she looked up at her brother.

And got yet another shock, almost as bad as seeing Remi shoot Vitaly's man. Max looked *bored*. Utterly and completely bored. He'd just witnessed a man's murder, and he looked about as interested as if he'd been casually cleaning his fingernails.

Stunned, she stared more closely at Max's face. There might be a miniscule hint of tension around the corners of his eyes, but a person would have to know him very well and look very closely to see it. Since when had her brother become such a cool customer and so completely unimpressed by bloody violence?

An abrupt sense of not knowing Max at all coursed through her.

She'd seen Ashe shoot a man in the backyard of his parents' house, and it hadn't fazed her. That had been a kill-or-be-killed situation in which the other guy shot first, and she'd been delighted to live, thank you very much. Was Max more like Ashe than she'd realized?

When in the hell had *that* happened? Two of Remi's men dragged the body outside onto the deck, and she backed away from them in horror, retreating to the farthest corner of the deck from the trail of blood leaking out of the towel wrapped around the guy's head.

The men rolled the body overboard, and a big splash announced the end of that poor man's life. She'd barely known him, and he'd always been gruff with her and the other waitresses, but he'd been a human being, for crying out loud.

Max stuck his head outside, sparing her only the briefest of glances before he spoke to Remi's men. "You know you're going to have to fish that corpse out of the water, right? We can't leave it here for anyone to find. In the morning, you'll need to collect the body, take it into the cypress swamps and dump it."

"Yeah, fine. But in the meantime, it won't bleed all over and make a huge mess for us to clean up."

Max shrugged. "I hear ya. Good thinking. Remi wants you guys to head down to the aft deck. The American arms dealer should be here soon, and you guys need to frisk him. Check him for weapons and wires."

"Sure thing, sir."

Sir? They'd called her brother "sir"? They took orders from Max? What the heck?

Ashe rounded a point of land and spotted the marina up ahead. It looked just like the satellite pictures he'd seen of it this afternoon, except lit only by scant moonlight now.

Not that the low light conditions posed a problem for him. He preferred operating in the dark.

"Oy!" A sailor aboard the yacht shouted to him as he maneuvered close to the large vessel. "Tie up here!"

Tie up to the yacht itself? Not a chance. He waved off the man and pulled up two slips away from the yacht. He jumped ashore quickly before the guy could stop him and slip-tied his own craft. The knot would release with a single tug of a rope if he had to get out of here in a hurry.

"You are clear to proceed, Hollywood," Perriman murmured in his ear.

Ashe strode down the dock to the looming yacht. He had memorized the floor plan earlier in the day and knew the gangplank would be located on the far side of the ship.

The guy whose instructions he'd ignored met him at the entry point, looking annoyed. Ashe lifted his arms without having to be asked, pasted on a patient expression, and waited for the guy to frisk him. He wasn't worried about this thug finding any of his hidden gear. The SEALs' reputation as the most feared and best-equipped Special Forces outfit on earth wasn't earned for nothing.

"This way. They're waiting for you," his escort growled.

He'd bet they were. If he was legit and this arms deal went through, the Russian mob in that part of the country would be better equipped than most of the law enforcement agencies in the region, let alone the other criminal elements.

Ashe stepped up into the crowded salon. Vitaly Parenko was seated off to one side. The guy looked shaken. Probably had something to do with the shooting Trina had reported over the radio about thirty minutes ago. Ashe identified the shooter standing at the far end of the triangular space, a white-haired man who looked about fifty years old. Max had apparently called him by the name Remi.

He'd been tentatively identified by the support team as Vitaly's boss and the man giving the orders around here. Ashe observed Remi closely. For a man who'd just shot and killed someone, he was shockingly calm. He didn't show even the slightest hint of stress. Interesting.

Vitaly moved as if he were going to stand up, but Ashe wanted to cut him out of the power equation in the room as soon as possible. He strode past Hank's boss, went directly to Remi and held out his hand. He said in Russian, "Asher Konig. Pleased to meet you."

Remi blinked owlishly. Apparently no one had told him Ashe could speak Russian. *"Ochyen priyatnuh."* Very pleased. "You may call me Remi."

No last name, huh? Remi was probably an alias, then. That was okay. Jennie would already have a picture of the guy from Ford and Trina and be running his face through every database, legal and otherwise, in existence.

"Drink?" Remi offered.

Vitaly piped up, "He likes expensive vodka." Hank's boss was trying to regain some status by reminding the big boss that he was the one who'd brought Ashe to this meeting.

Ashe threw Vitaly a disparaging look. "I never mix alcohol and business. A club soda with a twist of lemon will do just fine."

Remi nodded slightly, not necessarily in approval at Ashe, but more as if he were checking off a demonstration of credibility. "Tell me about yourself," the Russian demanded.

Ashe perched a hip on a tall barstool and arched an eyebrow reproachfully at the guy. "How offended would you be if I asked the same of you?"

Remi held out his hands and said expansively, "I am an open book. Ask me anything you wish to know."

Ashe shrugged. "I don't need to know anything except the color of your money."

Another miniscule nod from Remi. Then, "You do not wish to establish trust with me before we do business, Mr. Konig?"

"Call me Ashe. And no. I trust nobody. If you double-cross me, I'll kill you. And I expect the same of you in return."

Remi's hands moved from collar to pants pocket to a button on his sports coat. The guy's shoulder holster was clearly visible as a bulge under his left arm. He didn't like that answer from Ashe. Which was fine with him. He'd just as soon keep this criminal mentally off balance.

"Vitaly tells me you are in the import-export business."

Since there was no question in that statement, Ashe merely sipped his club soda, forcing the Russian to carry the conversation. It was amazing the things people would reveal in their discomfort over awkward lulls in conversations.

"I am in the same business. Although I mostly import sin to America." He seemed to think that statement was hilarious and laughed at his own joke. Ashe did not join in.

Abruptly Remi's cackling cut off. "I do not like you, Mr. Konig. You do not accept my hospitality and drink my vodka nor do you laugh at my jokes."

Ashe shrugged. "I have no vested interest in doing business with you. If my weapons are not appealing to you, I'm happy to sell them elsewhere." He set down his drink and stood up.

"Not so fast, my friend."

Ahh. So now he was Remi's friend, huh? Ashe sank back onto the stool and took another sip of his club soda.

"Did you bring a sample of what my man, Vitaly, discussed with you?"

"Would I be here if I didn't?" Ashe replied drily.

"Show me these weapons of yours, then."

"Show me the girl."

Chapter 19

Ashe stared icily at the Russian psychopath as Remi asked innocently, "What girl?"

Mission or no mission, he was done playing games with this ass. He was collecting Hank and getting out of here, now.

Ashe stood up. "I am a businessman. You took the girl as insurance that I would come and that I would bring you weapons. I have done both, and my patience is growing short."

"You like the waitress, then? She's good in the sack, yes?"

Ashe merely gazed at Remi, his stare flat and cold. He let all his years of lethal training and every bit of his dark experience with violence seep into his eyes.

"All right, all right. We have the girl. Bring her in."

If Hank was working with the Russians, they were either willing to give her up to him permanently at this point, or else they wanted her to stay undercover with him and burrow deeper inside his business.

The thing was, she hadn't shown any interest whatsoever in the weapons that he and Bastien and Perriman had chosen to dangle as bait in front of the Russian mobsters. The guns had never come up once in conversation with her. If she were a plant by the mob, surely they would have wanted her to find out how many guns he had access to, where they were, and who else he was prepared to sell them to.

The sliding door to the foredeck opened and Hank stepped inside, squinting in the bright light. She looked as beautiful as ever. Unharmed, if apprehensive as she glanced in the direction of his shoes. A rush of relief washed over him so hard it threatened to throw him entirely off his game.

"Come here, Hank," he bit out, his throat tight. He held out his left arm and she rushed over to him, burrowing herself against his side. "These gentlemen treat you all right?"

"Umm, yes. Fine."

Either that was real fear in her voice or she was the best freaking actress in the universe. If she *was* working with these guys, she obviously was convinced her usefulness to them had ended and that she was expendable. No way did Perriman have it right. She wasn't in cahoots with these Russians.

"I have a little business to conclude, and then I'll take you home. Why don't you go wait outside?"

"No," Remi barked. "She stays in here."

Ashe's back molars ground together. Dammit. He'd wanted to get her away from Mr. Trigger Happy. "Fine. Whatever," he conceded. "There's a wooden crate in my boat. If you'll have a couple of your guys carry it over here, you may inspect the merchandise."

While Remi's men fetched the crate of rifles, Ashe allowed himself to make eye contact with Hank. She looked scared out of her mind. But he also saw a core of determination not to give in to that fear. He let a hint of encouragement creep into his expression.

He caught sight of Max studying him intently and perhaps a bit hostilely. Maybe if the guy had stuck around to look out for his sister, she wouldn't be huddling against some arms dealer's side instead. Not that Ashe was complaining. She felt like a little slice of heaven next to him. He would get her out of here safely if it was the last thing he did.

Ashe asked huskily, "You hungry, kitten? Thirsty?"

"No, thank you. I ate a little while ago."

She was trembling against his side, and it damn near destroyed him that there wasn't much he could do about that. "This shouldn't take long," he murmured to her. "Just be a good girl, okay?"

She looked at him quizzically for a second and then obviously caught his meaning: to do what he told her to without questioning him. "Okay," she replied, relaxing fractionally and giving him a tiny, secret smile.

Thank God. Both of them might just make it out of here alive if she would work with him and not against him.

Two sailors horsed the heavy crate up the steps into the salon and dropped it onto the floor with a thud. Hank's brother snapped something about watching the carpet. Was this his yacht, then? Interesting. Where did a young antiques dealer get this kind of cash? This yacht had to be worth a cool couple of million dollars.

The lid was lifted, and Remi stepped forward eagerly. "Nice," the Russian purred.

He ought to be pleased. These were state-of-the-art assault weapons with the very latest in metal alloys, weight balancing and sighting technology. They weren't available on the commercial market yet and were being sold to only a handful of governments.

Remi picked up one of the guns and crowed, impressed, as he lifted it to his shoulder. Ashe's jaw clenched as the guy sighted down its length at Hank. She stiffened, as well.

"If you plan to shoot that, let's take it outside," Ashe barked. He released Hank, scooped up one of the guns and a pair of clips and strode out the door. The Russian followed. He moved around to the aft deck and took up a shooting stance, pointing out into the moon-touched black surface of the open bayou.

He gave a quick demonstration of handling and loading the weapon to Remi and then let rip with a controlled burst of fire. The weapon really was sweet. It was light and responsive and handled like a charm.

The Russian clicked his weapon over to full automatic and unleashed a long burst from beside him. Damn. He'd just burned through about half the firing life of that tampered-with firing pin.

Remi turned fast, aiming the weapon at Ashe's chest from a range of about six feet. "You are a man of your word, Mr. Konig. Thank you for giving me these excellent guns."

"I'm not exactly giving them to you. They do not come cheaply, given their newness and difficulty of procurement."

"Ahh, but you see, I am not going to pay you for them. You are going to hand them over to me free of charge."

Ashe mentally cursed. Here came the attempted double cross. Which was unfortunate. He'd really hoped to get out of this meeting without bloodshed. "And why am I going to do that, my friend?"

"Because I will kill you and your little whore if you do not."

Dammit. All hell was going to break loose any second, and he still had not determined whether or not Hank's brother was a kill or no-kill target. Ashe whipped to his right to face Max and bit out fast and low in English, "Are you willing to die beside this scumbag, or do you want to live?"

Ashe wasn't so interested in how Max answered. He needed to look into the man's eyes as he gave his answer. To see the truth or lie in his words.

Max's stare never left his. "Of course I am willing to die beside my family."

Family. Hank. He was declaring himself to be on Ashe and Hank's side, not Remi's.

"I stand beside my friends, always," Max added defiantly in Russian. Posture too stiff, delivery working too hard to be convincing. The guy was lying about standing beside his Russian friends.

"Message received, loud and clear," Ashe replied grimly, meeting Max's intent stare with one of his own. Without breaking eye contact, he tossed his automatic weapon to Hank's brother and jumped at one of Remi's thugs. He dived behind the guy just as a burst of gunfire erupted behind him. The big bodyguard slammed backward into Ashe, almost knocking him over the railing. The thug sagged, his legs slowly collapsing. Ashe grabbed him under the armpits and heaved him up and forward into the other bodyguard on deck.

As the shot man fell forward, Ashe spotted the holster tucked in the back of the guy's belt and snatched out the handgun there.

Recognizing the shape of a Makarov pistol, he flipped off the safety with his thumb, turned and dropped to one knee and double-tapped two shots into Remi's torso. The Russian grunted but smiled wolfishly.

Dammit. Remi was wearing a bullet-resistant vest.

He dived and rolled as Remi fired back. Fiberglass shattered over Ashe's head as he spotted something big and dark leaping toward him. Vitaly landed on him in a tackle a professional football lineman would be proud of. Ashe's breath was knocked out of him as Vitaly's hands closed around his neck.

"Run, Hank!" he forced out with the last air in his lungs as Vitaly's fingers clamped down on his larynx and made further speech impossible.

Although Vitaly had no doubt intended to play the hero by immobilizing Ashe, the man effectively was acting as a human shield, and thankfully, Remi didn't seem prepared to shoot Vitaly full of lead. Ashe got his hands up in between Vitaly's forearms and commenced prying at them. Vitaly's death grip eased enough for Ashe to drag a tiny bit of oxygen into his lungs, but he was far from out of the woods.

They rolled over and over across the deck as they wrestled. Past Vitaly's shoulder, Ashe spied Max grimly pointing the automatic rifle at the two of them. He could only pray the guy was as good a shot as his little sister.

Ashe heard Perriman call tersely in his ear, "Operative down. Two hostages to extract. Green light. Go, go, go!"

A cluster of Remi's thugs surged out onto the deck, no doubt in response to the gunshots and shouting. They only added to the chaos, further robbing Remi and Max of clean shots.

Vitaly heaved, flipping Ashe onto his side. The bastard was obviously a trained wrestler, and the slick move was irresistible. Vitaly shifted his grip, wrapping his forearm across Ashe's throat with shocking strength. The good news was that Ashe knew how to twist to the side and free up his airway and blood vessels to his brain within that grip.

From his awkward position with his face smashed against the bottom rail of the deck, Ashe saw a dozen dark, wet-suited shapes rise up silently out of the black water around the yacht. They were arguably the prettiest sight he'd ever seen. Rubber-coated grappling hooks hit the edges of the deck with quiet thuds, and the SEAL assault team shimmied up the sides of the yacht with acrobatic dexterity.

Max was shouting conflicting orders behind him in a mixture of Russian and English that added exponentially to the confusion. Dammit, Ashe needed Max to get Hank out of here before a stray bullet hit her!

Ashe managed to tear Vitaly's arm away and shouted, "Go, Max!"

He jabbed backward over his shoulder toward where Vitaly's eyes should be.

The first SEAL rolled aboard the deck, firing as he came. Vitaly swore in his ear and jumped up, abruptly freeing Ashe.

He leaped to his feet, looking around frantically while he gasped for air. Where the hell was Hank?

Chapter 20

Hank slapped a hand over her mouth as Vitaly and Ashe fought furiously with one another, evenly matched, both big, strong men and both lethally trained. Remi and Max both shouted, darting around the deck in an effort to get a clean shot at the grappling men.

Remi made a sound of satisfaction as he moved past her, raising his weapon to his shoulder like he had the shot he was looking for. Vitaly had Ashe pinned up against the railing, and Remi would safely be able to shoot Ashe in Vitaly's arms.

She lurched forward, slamming her shoulder into Remi's back, knocking him off balance. A spray of bullets shot skyward from his gun. The Russian swore violently and half turned toward her.

But Max grabbed her arm and yanked her behind him, shouting at Remi to keep his attention on the real target.

Remi turned back toward Vitaly and Ashe just as Vitaly let go and rolled to his feet all in one fast move. For just a second, Vitaly blocked Ashe from Remi's view, and in that instant, Ashe also gained his feet.

She screamed as a dark shadow materialized beside her. Man-sized, it looked like the Creature from the Black Lagoon: slick, wet, black, and with eyes that bugged out abnormally far.

She'd just registered the shape as a human wearing some sort of goggles when Max all but pulled her arm out of its socket. "C'mon, sis," he yelled at her over a deafening fusillade of bullets.

"Stay down and run!" Max shouted.

"No! I'm not leaving Ashe!"

"You'll both die!"

A moment of clarity washed over her. It was as if for that instant, time stopped while her mind turned over Max's words. Absorbed them, accepted them, and become one with them. If Ashe died, she would die, too. And that was how it was supposed to be. She didn't want to live without him, and she definitely couldn't live with his blood on her hands. The two of them were an all-or-nothing proposition.

"So be it!" she shouted back with calm that stunned her.

Max swore and turned around, searching the chaotic melee of wet-suit-clad invaders and Remi's thugs. She looked desperately for Ashe's beloved familiar face, his silhouette, anything to spot him.

Remi's men were figuring out that they'd been attacked by a vastly superior force and were starting to scatter. Some dived overboard. Others ran for the salon. Some jumped over the railing to the walkway on the lower deck.

"There!" Hank yelled, pointing at two men tearing down the dock toward shore at a dead run. Ashe was chasing someone. Relief that he was alive and unhurt roared through her.

One of the wet-suited men came up beside her and Max. "Come with me, now."

"Who are you?" she demanded. The last thing she wanted to do was jump out of the pan, into the fire. Who were these new attackers? Friends of Ashe's? Enemies of Remi's?

"Ashe sends his regards to both of you. Move out."

His tone of command left no room for discussion. Was that Ashe's boss, Commander Perriman? It was impossible to tell in the dark and chaos. Two more men joined him, and they hustled Max and Hank down the side of the yacht by way of a ladder that dropped them onto the pier.

Their wet-suited rescuers took off running, dragging both of them down the dock.

A boat motor roared a half dozen slips away, startling Hank badly. All three men spun and brandished weapons slung from wide webbing straps over their shoulders. Interestingly enough, Max did the same by reflex, as well.

A man wearing civilian clothes peeled away from the shadows ahead of them and sprinted back toward them. All four guns came to bear on him with lethal intent. One of the rescuers bit out, "Stand down. It's Hollywood."

"Don't shoot him, Max!" she cried out. Her brother wouldn't know Ashe's Special Forces nickname. Obviously, these men who called him by the moniker worked with Ashe.

Max's rifle tip swung up sharply toward the black sky.

Hank flung herself forward, not stopping until she slammed into Ashe and wrapped her arms around him like she was never going to let go.

"Ship secure?" Ashe bit out over her shoulder at someone.

"Contained. Still clearing the vessel," the leader of the rescuers retorted. "Report."

"Vitaly's in the boat that just took off."

"Go get him, Hollywood."

"Yes, sir," Ashe declared eagerly, violence vibrating in his voice.

"I have to go back," Max declared without warning.

Everyone turned to stare at him.

"Come again?" Ashe asked tersely.

"My name is Max Kuznetsov. I'm CIA. I'm undercover infiltrating a Russian mob outfit that I believe to be a front for an espionage operation. I have to go back in there. Arrest me. Throw me in jail. But don't blow my cover. I've been building it for *years*."

Hank's brain froze, turning into a mental blue screen of blank doom. CIA? Espionage? Her brother was an undercover operative? For the United States? *What. The. Hell?*

"You catch that, Jennie?" Ashe demanded. "Confirm immediately."

The scenario dragged out for what was probably only a few seconds but felt like a lifetime to Hank. Finally, the three wet-suited men and Ashe all nodded in unison, as if they'd all heard something together.

Ashe spoke to her. "Your brother's identity is confirmed." To Max he murmured, "You're sure about this? It's going to be dangerous as hell around that Remi guy for a while. He's a nutball."

"Tell me about it," her brother grumbled.

The leader of the trio from the water piped up. "You ever need backup, you give us a call. We owe you one for helping get our guy and his lady out."

Ashe's lady? Cool.

Max stepped forward and wrapped her in a quick, hard hug.

"I may not see you again for a while, so tell me one thing. Were mom and dad spies, too?"

"Yeah. For the other side, though."

She was startled to realize that his answer didn't surprise her at all. Apparently, she'd known it for a long time and just been unwilling to consciously acknowledge what had been staring her in the face all along. Her family had been Russian spies.

"You're not a double agent are you?" she blurted in sudden horror.

"No." He laughed. "I swear, I'm mom-and-apple-pie American through and through. I'm one of the good guys."

She hugged him tightly and he hugged her back.

"Love you, sis. You chose a good man. Take care of him." Over her head he growled at Ashe, "And you take care of her, or you'll have me to answer to."

Ashe answered grimly, "She's not going anywhere without me plastered to her side for a good long time. I'll protect her with my life, man."

Max's arms loosened. He started to step away from her. Panic erupted in Hank's chest. She could lose him again. This might be the last time she ever saw him. "Call me, you idiot. If you go incommunicado on me again, I'm going to hunt you down and have Ashe kick your butt."

"You got it, kid."

And then he was gone. Two of the wet-suited guys slapped him in plastic zip cuffs and marched him, albeit gently, back toward the yacht.

The remaining wet-suited man, who she was convinced was Commander Perriman, spoke tersely to Ashe. "Report."

"I've got two loose ends to wrap up, sir. I'll meet you back at the naval air station. Take Hank and keep her there this time—"

"No way," she declared forcefully. "I'm not leaving your side."

Ashe and his boss, the second man, traded a long look that spoke volumes. Perriman finally nodded and said, "Go."

Ashe grabbed her hand and took off running, with Hank following along as best she could. "Where are we going?" she gasped as he raced toward a gigantic cigarette boat.

"Strap in."

She did as Ashe ordered while he powered up the twin engines and backed the boat out of the slip. He cleared the dock and opened up the throttles. To say the boat took off like a bullet didn't begin to describe the speed and power of the vessel. She actually had trouble drawing breath, the wind was whipping past her so fast.

They hit the open water of the bayou and then the boat really flew.

"So! You wanna tell me why you took off like that?" Ashe shouted at her.

"You seriously want to have this conversation now?" she shouted back.

"The conversation I really want to have is the one where you tell me why you lied to me about your past and your family and kept so much from me!"

"I didn't know they were spies. Not until just now when Max confirmed it!"

"But you knew they weren't a normal family. You knew they had secrets! Why didn't you trust me enough to tell me?"

She couldn't believe they were shouting back and forth like this about something so important. Although, honestly, it felt good to shout about it. "I was taught my whole life to be private and not to trust strangers! Why can't you understand that I was terrified for my brother and not sure who you were?"

"After I told you exactly who I was, you still didn't

come clean with me! Were you just using me to get to your brother?"

She winced. She could see where he might think that. "No!" she shouted. "I love you, dammit!"

"You sure about that?" he yelled back.

"Yes!"

He fell silent. The roar of the engines became so deafening she couldn't stand it anymore.

At the top of her lungs, she shouted, "Look, Ashe. I'm sorry. I should have told you everything sooner. I knew you'd be mad when you found out I lied to you and withheld information from you. And I don't blame you. But please understand that it had nothing to do with you or with me not trusting you. It was my problem. I couldn't trust an outsider. And by the time I thought of you as family, it was too late. I'd already hidden a bunch of stuff and couldn't go back and change it."

In response to her very loud apology, he merely glanced over at her grimly and then turned his attention back to steering the boat. He had to believe her! She was—admittedly belatedly—being completely honest with him.

She started to reach over to him, but another boat came into sight ahead of them, also moving fast.

Ashe picked up the boat's radio transmitter and called into it, "Target acquired."

Frowning, she squinted into the darkness ahead. A lone man was hunched over the controls of a powerboat in front of them.

"Take the wheel!" Ashe shouted to her.

Her? Drive this beast? Was he crazy?

Ashe gestured to her to take his place. He stood up and moved behind the pilot's seat, keeping his hands on the steering wheel. She slipped under his arms and put her hands on the wheel below his.

His lips brushed her ear as he yelled to be heard, and she jumped about a foot out of the seat in her nervousness. "Keep the boat steady and straight. Stay inside his wake and run right up his tail."

"What are you going to be doing?"

"Killing your boss."

She started to look at Ashe, but he snapped, "Keep your eyes on that boat. I'll be back."

His arms fell away from her. Oh, God. She was driving a boat at one hundred ten miles per hour, if the speedometer in the instrument panel was to be believed.

In a few seconds, Ashe was back. She saw him out of the corner of her eye, and he was indeed carrying a snazzy rifle of some kind. It was blunt and dangerous-looking in his arms, but he handled it like a pro. Sometimes she forgot how accomplished a warrior he was.

Feet braced wide, he took up a shooter's stance beside her.

"Pull up as close as you can!" he shouted.

She reached for the throttles and was alarmed to discover that they went even a little further forward from their current position. She nudged the last bit of power out of the boat's incredible engines, and the gap between the boats closed even more.

The bad news was that, this close to Vitaly's boat, the V of his wake was very narrow and took intense concentration to steer within.

Ashe raised the rifle to his shoulder. Sighted down it. And took the shot.

It was two shots, actually. Vitaly slumped, falling over the steering wheel. His boat swerved to one side violently and flipped up in the air, turning over and over in a high-speed rolling flight.

Her own boat went airborne, launched by crossing the

wake of Vitaly's boat. In a slow-motion movement as they sailed through space, Ashe dived for the steering wheel, grabbing it above her hands just as their boat crashed back down into the water.

It tried to swerve, but with both of them hanging onto the steering wheel with all their strength, they were able to muscle it forward.

A huge crash to their right and behind them announced that Vitaly's boat had hit the water.

Ashe slammed the throttle back, and their boat slowed rapidly. She slipped out of the pilot's seat, breathing hard, and Ashe took her place. He turned the boat in a wide sweep, heading back toward the burning debris field in the bayou that had once been Vitaly's boat.

"What are you doing?" she asked him, confused.

"Take the wheel again. Keep it slow, and stay down low behind the windshield. I'm going to confirm the kill. Your boss is not getting out of this night alive to threaten you ever again."

They cruised slowly toward the debris field with Ashe scanning the water through the sight on his weapon. The hull of their powerboat scraped against random pieces of Vitaly's boat as they eased close to the point of impact.

"Over there," Ashe called low. "Turn left."

She did as he ordered, and as the cigarette came about, she spotted what Ashe had seen. A human body floated in the water, facedown.

She pulled up beside the corpse, and Ashe used a grappling hook from the fishing equipment locker to snag the body. She moved away from the edge of the vessel, not eager to look at a corpse.

Leaning far over the edge, Ash grunted with effort as he obviously attempted to roll the body face-up. "Come over here, Hank. I want you to see this."

Reluctantly, she moved to Ashe's side and forced her gaze over the side of the boat. It was Vitaly. And Ashe's shots had obviously penetrated the back of her boss's head and emerged from the front of his skull, tearing away the right side of his face.

She looked away quickly from the destroyed remains of Vitaly's face, horrified. Although the sight was gory and awful, something settled in her stomach. She actually felt the pervasive fear she'd lived with for all these months lifting away from her. Vitaly was dead. He would never threaten her again.

She understood all of a sudden why Ashe had wanted her to look at Vitaly's body. It gave her closure.

"Help me drag him aboard," Ashe murmured. "Our people are going to want to make a positive ID on him before we contact the Russians to make a trade for him."

"But he's dead."

"They hang on to the bodies of our fallen operatives. Vitaly's remains will be put in cold storage until such time as a trade is necessary."

Eeyew. For the sake of America's undercover operatives abroad, she hoped such a trade didn't occur for a very long time.

Laboriously, they dragged the Russian's body aboard the vessel. Ashe took the wheel once more and continued back toward New Orleans at a more moderate pace. At the north end of the giant bayou, Ashe steered the craft into a canal and followed it all the way to the Mississippi River. He talked on the boat's radio and got permission to enter the mighty river, and from there, it was a short ride to what turned out to be a navy dock.

Ashe helped her ashore and then had a fairly lengthy conversation about what to do with the dead man in the back of his boat with a bevy of official people who showed up to meet them.

But eventually, Ashe escorted her off the pier and into a police car. It drove them across the base to what she recognized as the ready room for the security team that she'd escaped from before.

He had yet to acknowledge her apology. Or maybe he wasn't planning to. Maybe she'd made it too late. Maybe she had already lost him. Goodness knew, he'd made it perfectly clear from the outset that honesty was of utmost importance to him. She'd just hoped he could find room in his heart to forgive her.

Her own heart breaking, she let him hand her out of the backseat of the police car. He didn't make eye contact with her. Oh, God. He really wasn't going to forgive her. Despair washed over her, cold and dark, and blotting out all hope. How was she ever going to survive without him?

Instead of taking her inside, though, Ashe led her to a bench underneath the spreading branches of a giant live oak tree in front of the building. He sat down and gestured curtly for her to join him.

She perched on the edge of the bench, too tense and in too much pain to do anything else.

At least Ashe was safe, and Vitaly was dead.

She lurched all of a sudden. "What about the girls back at the club? Are they okay?"

"Raid on the Who Do Voodoo went off about a half hour before I boarded the yacht. A whole bunch of girls were rounded up and taken into protective custody at a hospital. They'll be treated for their addictions, debriefed and repatriated to their homes and families. Or, if they want, they can stay in America and make a new start here."

She took a deep breath and gave voice to the burning question hanging between them. "And what about us? Is there any chance we can make a new start? I'm so sorry, Ashe. Really—"

He held out his arms to her silently, and she dived into them, burrowing against his chest hungrily. At least until it dawned on her that he still hadn't said anything to indicate that he forgave her.

She pushed away from his warmth to look up at him. "You still haven't answered my question. Are we okay?"

He stared down at her for a long time, searching her face and her eyes for something she desperately hoped he found. Then, at long last, he answered gruffly, "We're good."

She sank back against his chest, afraid to push for any more than that. It was enough for now. As long as he gave her a chance, she would earn back his trust, no matter how long it took.

Gradually, she relaxed against Ashe's big, comforting chest, replaying events of the evening through her mind. But then she lifted her head sharply as something occurred to her.

"What's up?" he asked.

"You said you had two loose ends to clear up. Vitaly was only one of those, right?"

"Correct." Ashe suddenly sounded cautious. Alert.

"What was the other one?"

He sat up straight beside her, towering over her in the shadows. Lord, he was a big, powerful man. If she hadn't known how good a heart he had, he would have been awfully intimidating.

"You. You're the other loose end."

"I—I'm a loose end?" she repeated in a small, quavering voice. Her heart dropped out of her chest and thudded to the ground somewhere in the vicinity of her shoes. Was he going to leave her after all? Just like Max. Was he going to disappear into his shadow world and never contact her again?

Her heart cracked right down the middle and split in two inside her chest. It hurt so badly she couldn't draw her next breath. She had to find a way to let him go. But how on earth was she going to survive losing him, too?

First Max, and now him. Both of the men she loved were lost to a world of darkness and danger that she knew now she did not belong in. She wasn't remotely equipped to handle their way of life.

But she also knew now exactly how dangerous a place they inhabited.

Ashe slid off the bench to face her, kneeling on one knee. "I know I'm not a forgiving person and that I set ridiculously high standards for the people around me. Although to your credit, you've pretty much risen to those standards. I get why you weren't square with me from the beginning. And I think you won't make that mistake again. Am I correct?"

She nodded, unsure of where he was going with this soliloquy.

"I saw how bad it freaked you out when your brother went dark on you, and my work has been known to require me to do the same thing from time to time. I can't promise to be home for holidays or anniversaries, or even to be able to call you on the important occasions. I would suck as a boyfriend, and I would probably suck ten times worse as a husband. But is there any way at all you would consider trying to make it work for me?"

"What?" That mental blue screen of doom thing was back. "What are you saying?"

"I'm saying that I love you, Hank. When I saw those bastards pointing guns at you, the only thing I could think of was throwing myself in front of you and taking every bullet myself. The idea of you coming to harm was more than I could bear."

"I felt the same way when that Remi guy tried to shoot you. But Max jumped in front of me before I could dive on you to protect you."

"Remind me to thank Max for stopping you."

She nodded, and Ashe looked up again, his gaze more intense than she'd ever seen it. He continued, "When Vitaly was choking me, I promised myself that if you and I both made it off that yacht alive, I was going to marry you, settle down somewhere quiet with you and have a bunch of kids."

She blinked at him, stunned. He'd actually uttered the *M*-word aloud? And his head hadn't exploded and disintegrated into a pile of dust?

"What about it, Hank? Will you marry me?"

She could only stare at him in shock. Her mouth opened and closed several times before she managed to form words. "I would love nothing more. However, you don't have to do this. You don't owe me anything—"

"I owe you everything! You showed me that there's more to life than the job. You helped me face my issues with my father and accept that, for all his flaws, he helped make me the man I am. And if you love that man, then I'm good with everything he did—and didn't—do. Hell, you taught me that I'm capable of loving another person: genuine, messy, all-in, true love."

"Maybe after you retire…when you get off the teams… I don't think I could sit at home, knowing what I do now about the nature of your work…" she stammered.

"I already told Commander Perriman that this would be my last combat mission. I'm done. I finally found something I want to live for more than I want to risk dying on the teams. Or more precisely, *someone*. You, Hank."

"You'd give up your job for me?"

"It's a done deal, baby. Cole Perriman has already offered me a job in the ops center supporting teams in the field. The rest of the time, I'm going to stalk you until you accept my marriage proposal."

It was all there, right in front of her. Everything she'd ever dreamed of. A man who would never leave her. A home. Family. Safety. And most of all, love. Real, no-kidding, over-the-moon love. And all because a warrior in pain had wandered into a bar looking for oblivion. But instead, they'd found each other.

What were the odds?

No odds at all. It hadn't been an act of chance. It had clearly been an act of fate that they'd been brought together. She sent out a silent thanks to whatever force in the universe had crossed their paths and uncrossed their stars.

"You won't have to stalk me, Ashe," she replied, a slow smile unfolding across her face and spreading to encompass her heart. "If you'll have me, I'm all yours."

He swept her up in his arms and rose to his feet, kissing her exultantly and spinning her around in the shadows that had been his home for so long. The night wrapped around them in a soft blanket of joy, the moonlight finding its way through the leaves mirroring the love bubbling over in her heart and spilling out of her to encompass Ashe.

And for the first time in a long time, she wasn't afraid of the dark at all.

* * * * *

*If you love Cindy Dees, be sure to
pick up her other stories:*

*HIGH-STAKES PLAYBOY
HIGH-STAKES BACHELOR
A BILLIONAIRE'S REDEMPTION
DEADLY SIGHT*

Available now from Harlequin Romantic Suspense!

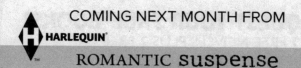

REQUEST YOUR FREE BOOKS!
2 FREE NOVELS PLUS 2 FREE GIFTS!

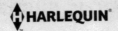

ROMANTIC suspense

Sparked by danger, fueled by passion

YES! Please send me 2 FREE Harlequin® Romantic Suspense novels and my 2 FREE gifts (gifts are worth about $10). After receiving them, if I don't wish to receive any more books, I can return the shipping statement marked "cancel." If I don't cancel, I will receive 4 brand-new novels every month and be billed just $4.74 per book in the U.S. or $5.49 per book in Canada. That's a savings of at least 12% off the cover price! It's quite a bargain! Shipping and handling is just 50¢ per book in the U.S. and 75¢ per book in Canada.* I understand that accepting the 2 free books and gifts places me under no obligation to buy anything. I can always return a shipment and cancel at any time. Even if I never buy another book, the two free books and gifts are mine to keep forever.

240/340 HDN GH3P

Name	(PLEASE PRINT)	
Address		Apt. #
City	State/Prov.	Zip/Postal Code

Signature (if under 18, a parent or guardian must sign)

Mail to the **Reader Service:**
IN U.S.A.: P.O. Box 1867, Buffalo, NY 14240-1867
IN CANADA: P.O. Box 609, Fort Erie, Ontario L2A 5X3

Want to try two free books from another line?
Call 1-800-873-8635 or visit www.ReaderService.com.

* Terms and prices subject to change without notice. Prices do not include applicable taxes. Sales tax applicable in N.Y. Canadian residents will be charged applicable taxes. Offer not valid in Quebec. This offer is limited to one order per household. Not valid for current subscribers to Harlequin Romantic Suspense books. All orders subject to credit approval. Credit or debit balances in a customer's account(s) may be offset by any other outstanding balance owed by or to the customer. Please allow 4 to 6 weeks for delivery. Offer available while quantities last.

Your Privacy—The Reader Service is committed to protecting your privacy. Our Privacy Policy is available online at www.ReaderService.com or upon request from the Reader Service.

We make a portion of our mailing list available to reputable third parties that offer products we believe may interest you. If you prefer that we not exchange your name with third parties, or if you wish to clarify or modify your communication preferences, please visit us at www.ReaderService.com/consumerchoice or write to us at Reader Service Preference Service, P.O. Box 9062, Buffalo, NY 14240-9062. Include your complete name and address.

HRS15

SPECIAL EXCERPT FROM

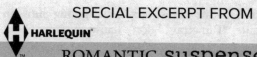
HARLEQUIN®

ROMANTIC suspense

*When a beautiful stranger is run down by a car right
in front of him, surgeon Eric Colton rushes to help.
Miraculously, she isn't badly hurt—except she has
amnesia. Can he keep her safe long enough for her to
regain her memory?*

Read on for a sneak peek at
THE TEMPTATION OF DR. COLTON
by **Karen Whiddon***,*
the latest in Harlequin® Romantic Suspense's
THE COLTONS OF OKLAHOMA *series.*

Flipping through the chart, Eric Colton barely noticed
when the nurse bustled off. Unbelievably, all Jane Doe
appeared to have suffered was a concussion and some
bruised ribs. No broken bones or internal injuries. Wow.
As far as he could tell, she was the luckiest woman in
Tulsa.

He might as well take a look at her while he was here.
Chart in hand, he hurried down the hall toward her room.

After tapping briskly twice, Eric pushed open the door
and called out a quiet "Good morning." Apparently, he'd
woken her. She blinked groggily up at him, her amazing
pale blue eyes slow to focus on him. He couldn't help but
notice her long and thick lashes.

"Doctor?" Pushing herself up on her elbows, she
shoved her light brown curls away from her face. "You
look so familiar."

"That's because I rode with you in the ambulance last
night."

"Ambulance?" She tilted her head, giving him an uncertain smile. "I'm afraid I don't know anything about that."

Amnesia? He frowned. "How much do you remember?" he asked.

"Nothing." Her husky voice broke and her full lips quivered, just the slightest bit. "Not even my name or what happened to me."

He took a seat in the chair next to the bed, suppressing the urge to take her hand. "Give it time. You've suffered a traumatic accident. I'm quite confident you'll start to remember bits and pieces as time goes on."

"I hope so." Her sleepy smile transformed her face, lighting her up, changing from pretty to absolutely gorgeous.

Unbelievably, he felt his body stir in response. Shocked, he nearly pushed to his feet.

This kind of thing had never happened to him.

Ever.

Don't miss THE TEMPTATION OF DR. COLTON
by Karen Whiddon,
Available August 2015,

www.Harlequin.com